Past Ghosts

A Detective Toby Mystery

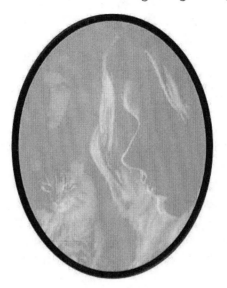

To Jeannette

All ghosts are not in the attic!

By Mary M. Cushnie-Mansour

Mary M. Cushnie-Mansour

CAVERN
OF DREAMS
PUBLISHING

Past Ghosts

Ordering Information:
Books may be ordered through Amazon or directly from the author's website: http://www.writerontherun.ca For volume order discounts, contact the author via email, mary@writerontherun.ca

Cover Art by Jennifer Bettio

Published by
CAVERN OF DREAMS PUBLISHING
Brantford, ON, Canada

Printed and bound in Canada by
BRANT SERVICE PRESS
Brantford, ON, Canada

ISBN 978-1-989027-13-4

What Readers Are Saying About "Past Ghosts"

"Past Ghosts" grabs you right from the beginning and holds you in suspense until the very last word. It keeps you wanting more. A delightful and exciting read! Well Done! Mary Cushnie-Mansour is a very gifted writer!

…Mary Sass

I couldn't put this book down. Very intriguing and full of surprises. I enjoyed *"Past Ghosts"* thoroughly and look forward to the sequel.   *…Isobel Dobbin*

"Past Ghosts" was a gripping, fast-paced book with suspense, detail, and drama. I could not put it down. Masterfully written. Toby, the cat, was quite an insightful detective. I look forward to seeing where Toby leads us in the future.   *…Barb*

Past Ghosts: an original concept having a cat as a detective. A fun read, which was hard to put down. It keeps you wondering what will happen next.   *…Steve Hasper*

Cushnie-Mansour definitely keeps the reader's attention. I was intrigued enough to keep reading, while internally trying to guess which direction the characters would take us. With the surprising twists and turns of Emma's escapades and her clearly defined guilt, it left me unsure of my feelings towards her. I also found her conspiring ways and lies, especially to Jack and Toby—her only true friends—disturbing. The author definitely leaves the reader wanting more and sets up a good precedent for a sequel. *"Past Ghosts"* was a quick read that flowed at a good pace and kept me turning pages to see what would happen next!

…Janna Maranda

Books by Mary M. Cushnie-Mansour

Night's Vampire Series
Night's Gift
Night's Children
Night's Return
Night's Temptress
Night's Betrayals
Night's Revelations

Detective Toby Series
Are You Listening to Me
Running Away From Loneliness
Past Ghosts

Short Stories
From the Heart
Mysteries From the Keys

Poetry
picking up the pieces
Life's Roller Coaster
Devastations of Mankind
Shattered
Memories

Biographies
A 20th Century Portia

Youth Novels
A Story of Day & Night   The Silver Tree

Bilingual Picture Books
The Day Bo Found His Bark/Le jour où Bo trouva sa voix
Charlie Seal Meets a Fairy Seal/Charlie le phoque rencontre une fée
Charlie and the Elves/Charlie et les lutins
Jesse's Secret/Le Secret de Jesse
Teensy Weensy Spider/L'araignée Riquiqui
The Temper Tantrum/La crise de colère
Alexandra's Christmas Surprise/La surprise de Noël d'Alexandra
Curtis The Crock/Curtis le crocodile
Freddy Frog's Frolic/La gambade de Freddy la grenouille

Picture Books
The Official Tickler
The Seahorse and the Little Girl With Big Blue Eyes
Curtis the Crock
The Old Woman of the Mountain

Dragon Disarray

Acknowledgments

I would like to thank all the fans of the "Detective Toby Series," who, after reading the first book, asked for more 'Toby.' Muses come from many sources, and the initial inspiration for this series came from an old orange tabby cat sitting on a windowsill in a house in Hamilton, Ontario. As my mom and I walked past the house, there he was, staring at us. I turned to my mom and said: "I wonder what the old fellow has witnessed looking out his window?" From there, I wrote the first story about Toby—The Witness—which was a three-part short story for the *Brantford Expositor*. "Past Ghosts" is the third novel in this series now.

My love and understanding of cats, something I believe I inherited from my mom, and her mother before her is echoed loud and clear in Toby's voice. Thanks, Mom … and Grandma Small.

Again, as always, I would like to thank my editor, Bethany Jamieson, for her edit on the final manuscript, and Cavern of Dreams Publishing for publishing yet another of my books.

Thanks go to Jennifer Bettio for the cover art. She managed to capture exactly what I wanted. Adding the finishing touches to my cover, as always, is Terry Davis from Ball Media. Collaborating with Terry to finalize the details is always a creative pleasure. And, never to be forgotten, Randy Nickman from Brant Service Press, for the superb printing job.

As always, last, but never least, thanks to my husband and family for their continued faith in my dream.

Dedicated to "Survivors"

"Terror made me cruel." ...*Emily Brontë* ... 1847

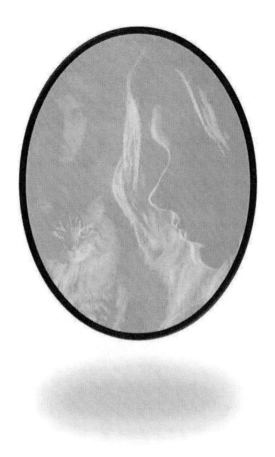

"There is an idea of a Patrick Bateman, some kind of abstraction, but there is no real me, only an entity, something illusory, and though I can hide my cold gaze and you can shake my hand and feel flesh gripping yours, and maybe you can even sense our lifestyles are probably comparable: I simply am not there."

...*Bret Easton Ellis* ... 1991

Prologue

Emma had taken to jogging around town regularly, Duke, her dog, always accompanying her. Usually, her route would take her through downtown Brantford, and many times, she would veer off the sidewalks and hit the trails, especially the ones running along the Grand River. She'd also taken to hanging out at various parks in the central part of the city. Some of the incidents she witnessed were appalling.

With each unsavoury incident Emma witnessed, the rage inside her escalated. The need to do something about it became more urgent. Within the past two weeks, Emma had observed four abusive situations where a guy was pushing his girlfriend around aggressively or screaming verbal abuse at them. Red lights flashed before Emma's eyes each time until her wrath was so deep-seated that she knew she had to do something to stop the onslaught of abuses.

Life wasn't the same without her brother, Camden, who was serving a life sentence for murdering several people. At times, Emma felt life was better, though. She could be herself. She didn't have to act the fragile female—well, not within the confines of her four walls, that is. To the outside world, to her friends, Jack and Toby, she still needed to keep up the façade of the weak female.

There was nothing weak about Emma. She'd been training for a long time, building her strength and her fighting skills. Even Camden hadn't known the extent of what she was doing. After he was incarcerated, Emma purchased a punching

1

bag and set it up in the basement, escalating her training. She felt ready now—as prepared as she was ever going to be.

Emma began researching online drugs she could procure to help with the mission she was about to embark on. Not medications for herself, but ones to administrate to the vile creatures that deemed it their privilege to abuse women.

Emma came across the drug, Rohypnol. It was a tranquillizer said to be ten times more potent than valium and said to impair the memory. Reading on, she discovered it caused loss of muscle control, confusion, and made a person drowsy. Emma smiled when she read the line about Rohypnol's street name being *roofie* and that it was used as a date rape drug. So perfect for her upcoming mission.

Emma read several accounts of female victims having been sexually assaulted at parties after having had a drink. Many of them described their inability to move and stop what was being done to them, and later, when the drug wore off, their memories were impaired and they could not recall what had happened to them.

"This sounds like just what I need to teach abusive men a lesson," Emma mumbled as she searched Google how to obtain the drug. "I know you're illegal in Canada and the United States, but guys must be getting it from somewhere..."

Several sources showed up in the feed. "Well, well..." The grin on her face was broad as she sat forward and clicked the link to a source in Mexico.

"Expensive," Emma grumbled as she got up and went to her dresser to get a credit card from her wallet. "But going to be oh so worth it! Using this stuff, I'll be able to teach these guys a lesson, let them go, and they won't remember what happened to them—or who did it to them!"

Emma turned her computer off and walked downstairs for some breakfast. Duke stood to attention when she entered the kitchen, his tail wagging a greeting.

"Need to go out for a few minutes, boy?" Emma pushed the sliding door to the three-season room across and proceeded to the outer door, Duke close on her heels. "There you go, Duke," she said, letting him out into the yard.

As Emma prepared a protein drink for her breakfast, she felt the blood palpitating through her veins, the heat of it flushing her usually pale skin. Emma sipped her drink, thinking what her next move was to be. Before she did anything concrete, she'd have to wait for the Rohypnol to arrive.

Finishing her drink, Emma rinsed her cup and left it in the sink. She gazed out to the yard; Duke was laying in the shade under a big maple. She smiled, comforted by the sight of her faithful companion.

"Time for a workout," Emma said, checking her watch. "Then, Duke and I will go hunting."

One

Emma paced in her kitchen, her blood boiling from what she'd witnessed at the park while out for an early evening walk. Duke sat in the doorway between the kitchen and the living room, a worried dog-look in his eyes.

Stopping for a moment in front of her companion, Emma pursed her lips. "How dare that guy shout at the innocent young woman like he did, Duke!"

Emma resumed pacing, but this time, she was not silent. Her thoughts echoed off the walls as the hatred for what she'd witnessed was relived!

"He was screaming at her ... calling her a bitch ... a whore ... he was pressing her up against the slide ... shouting in her face ... I could see the spit in his words! ... She cowered ... defenceless to fight back ... afraid to ... I saw her open her mouth at one point ... his fist raised to her ... she cowered again ... then, he yanked her by the arm and dragged her from the park ... shoved her into a beat-up old truck and slammed the door ... she was crying ... the licence on the truck was A4784900..."

Emma stopped and leaned over the sink. Her breath came in exaggerated gasps.

"I need to find out who this guy is and save the girl before it's too late!"

Two

Toby was bored. Jack was out for the evening, on a date with Tessa. Jack and Tessa had been dating regulary since they'd returned from their trip to Kingston, where Toby had saved a woman named Violet from a horrible death, and Jack as well when he'd been shot by a renegade prison guard. Toby found he was spending more and more time alone.

I think I'll take a jaunt over to see Emma ... been a few days ... she's not been home much lately ... always out jogging with that overgrown mutt of hers!

Standing up, stretching, and giving a wide yawn, Toby finally jumped off the couch and out the back door. He didn't bother stopping at his dish because Emma always had treats for him, and his girth had an extra inch or two around it at the moment.

As Toby drew near to Emma's back door, he was shocked to hear her shouting in the kitchen. *She must have company...* Toby paused, not wanting to intrude. *I wonder who it could be ... I don't know anyone she would have met ... a guy maybe ... is he hurting her ... she is yelling!*

Toby started to panic as his mind raced with all the possible scenarios. He moved quickly to the side of the house and sat down on the walkway, looking up at the kitchen windowsill, trying to figure out how he was going to get up there.

Too damn old to make that jump!

Looking around and seeing nothing he could hop on to get closer, Toby decided to wait until there was a break in the shouting. He proceeded to the front veranda, where there was a living room windowsill he'd be able to jump on. From there, he hoped to get her attention by pawing at the glass and meowing. If not Emma's attention, then for sure Duke would sense him and charge at the front door, thus alerting Emma.

A few minutes later, silence filled the house, and Toby rushed to his well-thought-out destination and put his plans into action. Within seconds of jumping up on the sill, Duke, as expected, charged at the front door, barking furiously.

Toby waited patiently, knowing there was a wall between him and the dog. Finally, the door cracked open, and Emma stuck her head out. A look of surprise spread across her face when she saw Toby. Hastily, she grabbed hold of Duke's collar and led him through the house to the backyard, leaving the front door open for Toby to enter. Seconds later, Emma returned to find Toby in the living room. She sat down on the couch and patted the cushion beside her.

"What a pleasant surprise, Toby," Emma said.

Toby purred and rubbed his head against her arm. He looked up into Emma's eyes and noticed, despite her joy at seeing him, a vacant look. Emma's fingers dug into Toby's shoulders, much harder than usual.

What's up, my friend? What's going on with you? Why were you yelling? Who were you yelling at? Doesn't seem like anyone is even here, unless they slipped out the back door when you let the dog out.

Toby continued staring at Emma as he tried to figure out what was wrong with his friend.

Suddenly, Emma heaved a shuddering sigh, and her fingers relaxed, becoming gentler on Toby's neck. He began to purr.

"Oh, Toby ... the world is just so cruel sometimes. The world was cruel to my brother, and he's being punished for retaliating. Don't take me wrong, Toby ... Camden should never have killed all those innocent people ... they weren't the ones who really hurt us … those people have gone unpunished! Unpunished!"

Emma's fingers stroked Toby, as though she was in a trance, and she continued to ramble. "Why should such people go unpunished for what they did to us … our parents, who abandoned us … the foster parents who treated us so horribly … beatings … starvation … and … and … the one where it ended … the one we ran from … who was the reason for my dear Camden to tip over the edge, to commit the horrible crimes! But he wasn't the first … there were many before him. Where's the justice? Why are those men, who were the planks breaking my brother's back—his spirit—why are they still walking around? And my poor brother, he only knew of the one—there were so many before him! I couldn't tell him … they would have killed him … they told me so."

Tears broke free from Emma's eyes, dropping on Toby's fur. He lay still and allowed his friend to pour her grief onto him. The two pals sat in silence for several more minutes before, finally, Emma stood, and scooping Toby into her arms, she made her way to the kitchen.

Treat time. Poor girl … what pain she's been through in her short life. Despite what a cad Camden is, he suffered too … maybe all he was trying to do was protect his sister … just cracked and took matters into his own hands! Now, sweet Emma is suffering... Thoughts rolled through Toby's mind.

Emma went straight for the cupboard where she kept Toby's treats, and his heart burst with love. Duke was whining at the kitchen door, having had enough of being locked in the sunroom, especially while the cat received all his mistress' attention.

After setting Toby down, and handing him a couple treats, Emma began to clear away the dishes from her table, placing them neatly in the sink. "I'll wash these later," she informed Toby.

Toby flipped his tail in acknowledgement—not that he cared when Emma did her dishes—then finished his second treat. He glared at Duke, who was still causing a ruckus at the door.

Well, guess I've stayed long enough ... Jack should be home soon ... he'll be wondering where I am ... time to leave.

Circling around Emma's legs, Toby let out a couple of soft meows before strolling out of the kitchen toward the front door. Emma smiled and followed.

"Time to go, Toby? Okay, sorry for my outbursts. I'm just so lonely without my brother—despite what he did. He's family, and the only one I have." Emma opened the door.

Toby paused in the doorway, and, looking back at Emma, meowed softly. *You have me, Emma ... and Jack ... and Tessa.*

As though Emma understood what Toby was thinking, "Thank you, Toby; you're a true friend."

The door shut and Toby wandered home, his head filled with thoughts, trying to figure out how he could help his friend.

Three

Jack and Tessa were sitting in the living room watching the news when Toby arrived home. They were cuddled close, the old cat noticed, so he decided to check out his dish and see if Jack had remembered to fill it with kibble. No such luck!

Come on, Jack ... I mean, I like Tessa and all, but you need to get your priorities straight. I was here first ... we're partners ... supposed to be. She's pretty awesome, but I need to be fed ... never know when our next big case will come up and I have to be well-nourished to fight the evil deeds of crime!

Toby made his way into the living room and jumped up on the back of the couch, directly behind Jack's head, and meowed, making sure it was one of his more annoying meows—harsh and gritty from the depths of his throat.

Jack started to laugh as he pushed himself up from the couch. "Busted, eh, old man? Dish empty?" Turning to Tessa, still chuckling, "Need to feed the king of the house."

You bet you do, buddy! Toby jumped down and followed Jack to the kitchen and sat impatiently by his dish, swishing his tail in frustration.

"There you go, old man," Jack said, filling the dish. He patted Toby on the head.

I really wish you'd quit 'old-manning' me ... I'm the one who keeps saving your ass!

Toby dug into his meal.

Emma looked around her kitchen after Toby left. She usually didn't allow things to become so cluttered and messy, but tomorrow was another day. Tonight, she just didn't have the energy to clean up. Emma sat in a chair at her table, a troubled look on her face. Duke slunk up to her and shoved his nose under his mistress' arm, knowing something wasn't quite right with her.

Aimlessly, as she had with Toby, Emma stroked her companion's head. "It's going to be okay, Duke. I'm going to fix it."

Gently she pushed Duke away, stood, and took the stairs up to her room. As she passed Camden's room, a shudder rolled down her spine. A peculiar smile crossed her lips as she paused in front of her bedroom door before entering.

Four

Mike Sanderson crawled off his couch and staggered to the kitchen to make a cup of strong coffee. His head was pounding from all the alcohol and drugs he'd consumed the night before. As he passed by the bathroom door, he heard the shower running.

"What the hell..." Mike mumbled, running his hand through his sticky hair. Then, a light bulb went on in his head as he remembered what had happened the day before—at least some of the events. Some of what had taken place was still foggy, but one thing wasn't.

Mike's girlfriend, Janine, had called and told him she needed a break from the relationship, and she'd asked him to meet her at the park so they could talk. Mike faintly recalled that their meeting hadn't gone as he'd hoped; he'd had a few shots of rye—liquid courage—before going to meet her. Mike had sensed Janine pulling away from him over the past few weeks but he hadn't believed she would ever leave him.

However, that was what she said she was going to do—leave him. He faintly remembered being upset, and then angry when she wouldn't listen to his pleading.

The shower shut off, so he continued to the kitchen and his liquid salvation. Mike smiled as he noticed a full pot of coffee already made.

Maybe she changed her mind ... must have, or she wouldn't be here ... showering ... making me coffee.

Mike poured a cup of coffee and sat down at the table, stretching his legs full length as he leaned back in the chair and waited for his beverage to cool. Black was best for hangover relief. His mind wandered to when he'd first met Janine.

It had been at a Buck and Doe party for one of his friends, and Janine was there with some girlfriends who knew the bride-to-be. Mike was fresh off another failed relationship, but being alone was the one thing he hated the most.

He and Janine hadn't connected until the end of the night when a few party-goers had stayed back to assist with clean-up. They'd exchanged numbers after sharing a cab home and discovering they didn't live too far from each other. They also realized they had quite a few common interests.

To be truthful, Mike had picked up on her interests and had just said he liked those things too. What he really was partial to was how Janine looked; she was his type of woman, petite and cute.

The bathroom door opened and Janine stepped out, fully dressed. She walked with a limp into the kitchen but hesitated when she saw Mike sitting there, her face turning white. Mike swallowed hard, shocked when he saw the condition Janine was in, noticing that where her skin wasn't pale, it was mottled with cuts and bruises. He began to get up from the table, but Janine raised her hand warningly.

"Don't!" she spoke, her tone hoarse. "Don't come near me."

"Janine," Mike's hands were open as he stepped closer to her, ignoring her warning.

"I said don't, Mike, and I mean it. Stay away from me—far away!" Janine was backing up.

"Can we talk?" Mike implored.

"You talked enough with your fists and your boots last night!" Janine hissed.

Mike's heart hardened slightly. "Why are you still here if you don't want to talk?"

Janine laughed, although it wasn't a pleasant sound. "You dare to ask me that? You dragged me back here, from the park, and continued your beating on me. I couldn't move, I was in such pain. I believe I blacked out before you finally stopped." She paused, and despite the pain still stinging her body, her voice was steady. "Just stay back; stay where you are. I'm going to gather a few things and leave. I'll return another day, with a police officer, to get the rest of my belongings."

Janine's words were beginning to strike Mike hard, right to his core. She was really leaving him! He couldn't believe she was following through with this. He attempted to approach her again; and once again, her hand rose in a warning.

"Mike, I'm cautioning you. At the moment, I'm not going to the police for what you did to me yesterday, even though I should. You would end up in jail if the authorities saw the condition I'm in—and not just my face!"

Mike went pale with fear. None of the girls he'd ever been with had been this angry—they'd just left, most without a word. Some had left a note telling him they wished they'd never met him. One of the women even said she hoped he rotted in hell; it had been the worst three months of her life!

Janine walked down the hall to the bedroom, where Mike assumed, she was going to gather some of her things. Despite her previous warnings, he strode after her and planted himself in the doorway.

"Please, Janine," Mike begged. Janine had lasted the longest of all his girlfriends—almost a year—and he wasn't ready to give up yet. In his mind, she was The One, and he couldn't believe how stupid he was to have done what he did.

Janine was busy throwing clothes into a suitcase. Her muscles tensed when she realized Mike was blocking her way out of the room. She felt the sweat gathering on her skin and panic crawling into her stomach. Closing her suitcase, Janine turned

13

slowly and faced the man who had beaten her within an inch of her life the night before.

"Please, Mike … just let me go. Don't make this more difficult for me than it already is." She paused, trying to think of something—a tidbit—that would give him enough hope to have him step aside and allow her to leave. "We can talk later," Janine finally promised, even though she knew it was a lie. She never wanted to see or talk to him again, only when she came, escorted, to retrieve the rest of her belongings. Janine prayed Mike couldn't see the lie in her eyes.

To her surprise, he stepped aside, his shoulders slumped, a hint of tears in his eyes. Mike realized if there was going to be any hope to save his relationship, he was going to have to give Janine her space for now.

"Call me," Mike mumbled as Janine swept past him, hurrying toward the front door. At the door, she grabbed her car keys and, finally, taking one last look at Mike, she left.

Mike gazed at the closed door and around at the emptiness before shuffling to the bathroom. Maybe a shower would wash away some of his pain.

Five

Emma woke early in the morning and turned on her computer. After a few minutes of typing, seeking information on how to access owners of license plates, she leaned back in her chair and scowled. Only law enforcement had access to such information.

"Damn!" Emma cursed, shutting the computer off before heading downstairs for some breakfast.

After eating, Emma cleaned the kitchen, then, decided to go for a run to the park. Maybe she'd see the guy again and be able to follow him to his residence somehow. It was fortunate she was in good shape and could jog quite a distance. Duke would be with her, so there was no fear of the man confronting her.

On her way out the door, Emma checked her mailbox, hoping the package of Rohypnol she'd ordered would be there. Luck was with her. Smiling, she removed the bubble wrap envelope and took it into the house. Duke whined at the delay, anxious to be off for their run.

"Settle down, Duke. This is important stuff here. I need to make sure no one sees I have this." Emma opened a cupboard and, leaping nimbly onto the counter, placed the envelope behind some empty canisters on the top shelf.

Jumping down to the floor, Emma swiped her hands together. "That should do for now," she said. Taking hold of Duke's leash, "Let's go, boy. Time for a good run."

Six

Mike forced a couple pieces of plain toast down, then decided a walk—an unusual exercise for him—in the fresh air might help clear his head. He made his way out of the house and turned in the direction of the park where he and Janine had the fight. Despite it being quite a few blocks away, Mike felt he needed to go there.

"Maybe Janine will be there and will have had a change of mind," he mumbled hopefully.

Tripping over a bump in the sidewalk, Mike almost lost his balance, being saved only by a fire hydrant. "Damn!"

Collecting himself, Mike took a deep breath and continued on his way.

Seven

As Emma approached the park, she couldn't believe her luck. There he was—sitting at one of the picnic tables, his head buried in his hands. She slowed her pace as she entered the park and sat down at a table close to Mike. Emma stared at the guy, wondering where the girl was, hoping she was okay.

Suddenly, as though he sensed someone was watching him, Mike raised his head and looked over at Emma. "You want something, lady?" he asked, a sharp hint of tension in his voice.

Emma swallowed hard. Duke growled softly. *Think, girl! Think!* "Sorry," she finally began. "It's just that you look like you need a friend to talk to. You okay?" Emma hoped the guy wouldn't detect the nervousness in her tone. "My name is Sally," she lied.

Mike cleared his throat. *Last thing I need is another woman poking into my life...* His eyes raked over Emma from head to toe. *Even if she is my type—body-wise, anyway.* Mike shook his head: "Well—Sally—I just want to be left alone ... if you don't mind, that is," he added with a sneer.

Emma coughed uneasily. *What am I doing here ... what is my goal ... what am I trying to prove?* "Sorry," she said for the second time, "I didn't mean to bother you. Just thought you might need a friend." Emma stood, and taking hold of Duke's leash, "Come on," she said, giving his leash a jerk.

Mike observed Emma walk down the sidewalk and turn the corner. What he didn't see, because of all the trees, was Emma stop behind a large maple. Nor did he see the dog sitting patiently beside his mistress.

Half an hour later, Mike left the park and made his way home, totally unaware of the shadows following him.

Eight

Emma filled Duke's dish with kibble and topped up his water bowl before plugging the kettle in to make herself a cup of tea. It had been a long day. Now that she knew where the guy lived, Emma began to formulate a plan. She was happy to see— or not see—the girl. Hopefully, that meant she was out of danger—for now.

"One of two things, Duke … either that guy has the girl confined in his place, or she's managed to escape him," Emma stated. "But what to do about him, so she doesn't get hurt again or so he doesn't hurt some other defenceless woman? His kind never change their colours!"

Emma finished her tea, then headed to the basement to confirm everything was in place. She needed to ensure she was ready to take on this task she'd set out for herself. It had taken a couple weeks to clean the basement in the old house once she'd decided what her mission in life was to be. It still smelled a hint of dust and moisture, but it was ready enough for what was to come. Mike was not the first man she'd observed abusing a woman; however, he was going to be the first one to taste the wrath of her interrogation!

Stripping down to panties and bra, Emma gazed in the mirror on the wall behind the punching bag. She smiled as her eyes traced her lean, well-muscled shape—something she kept hidden from the world. Not even her brother had been aware of how fit his sister was. It was best that people—even Camden— considered her to be fragile and weak.

Emma turned the CD player on and music filled the room—her favourite song from *Queen*, "Bohemian Rhapsody."

She began dancing around the room, warming her body up. She moved like a jungle cat, soft and graceful. As droplets of sweat started trickling over her skin, Emma paused. Then, with a deep breath, she set to work on the punching bag, violating it with years of pent-up fury and pain!

With each hit on the bag, Emma envisioned his face. The features of the man—the foster father—the first one who had raped her. She envisioned, with each strike, his face bloodied, his eyes begging for mercy—as her eyes had pleaded that first time, and so many times afterward. She envisioned the others, too, but the first face suffered the brunt of her anger!

What Camden didn't know was that there were numerous rapes before he'd discovered what was happening to his sister. Emma never told him all the sordid details because she feared for his life. Even at such a young age, Emma knew Camden was too fragile to handle such things, despite how he tried to protect his sister in so many other ways!

Emma finally stopped and stepped back from the punching bag. She stood on the mat, like a wild warrior, her hair dishevelled, her body flexed, her legs firmly apart, her fists curled. Her knuckles hurt. She glanced at them and saw her skin was bleeding. Emma bowed to the bag, then stood tall, squaring her shoulders. Her eyes, staring back at her from the mirror, were flaming with anger.

"You were weak, Camden. I am sorry I allowed you to kill all those people—innocent people—but I wasn't ready yet to exact my revenge. I want you to know, brother, mine is going to be so sweet because my retribution will be on the guilty parties— on the ones I know don't deserve to live!"

Turning, Emma studied her preparations. *Yes, it's time ... the room is ready ... I am ready ... the apocalypse of justice is about to begin!*

Nine

Mike poured himself a generous glass of whiskey before heading into the living room. He was both angry and sad. Annoyed at himself for what he'd done to Janine—more times than once. Sorry for his loss, because once again, he was alone.

The first whiskey went down slowly, the second slightly quicker, the next few quenching his thirst for revenge.

"You'll be sorry you left me, Janine," Mike slurred to the empty walls, the liquor changing his attitude from remorse to anger. He lifted the whiskey bottle and checked, through blurry eyes, how much was left. Just a few drops. Tipping it to his lips, he downed the last of his liquid courage, then threw the bottle across the room.

Mike attempted to stand, but his body wasn't co-operating. Finally, giving up, he flopped back on the couch and closed his eyes. "Fuck you, Janine!" he mumbled before letting the liquor take him into a world of fitful dreams.

The dreams came swiftly ... always the same ones. Tonight they were more intense than usual—more violent. Both his parents were there, standing over him, faces sour with disgust as their words struck him over and over again until his tears flowed in a torrent of pain. And when the tears began, so did the beatings.

Mike's father held a leather strap in his hand, the one he used to sharpen his shaving blade; his mother clasped the stainless steel BBQ flipper, three times the size of the small kitchen one she used for everyday cooking. Smiles spread across his parents' faces. Then laughter—hideous to the ears of the young boy—as they advanced.

21

Mike's screams filled the room. He'd promised himself, after each episode, he wouldn't give his parents the satisfaction of allowing them to hear him scream. But the pain was always too severe. The humiliation too great. His worth as a human being was not enough ... to him ... to them.

As the blows rained down on him, night after night, Mike planned for the day he would escape. It was the only hope he had that kept him alive through those turbulent years!

Mike finally woke out of his dream world. Staring into the emptiness of his room, he thought back to what happened after he finally walked out the door of his childhood home, at the age of fourteen. Mike never looked back. He lived on the streets, scavenging food from garbage cans, sleeping in alleys, smoking discarded cigarette butts, wrestling bums for drops from their whiskey bottles.

At the age of eighteen, a local pastor found Mike sleeping on a rock down by the Grand River and had taken him home and fed him a hot meal. The pastor had given him a warm bed to sleep in that night. The next morning, he'd talked to Mike over a breakfast of bacon, eggs, and toast. He told Mike that there could be a bright future ahead for him if he wanted to walk a different path than he was on now. The pastor talked to Mike of a loving God and a wonderful Saviour, both who could help him heal from his pain.

Mike stayed with Pastor Dale for a month, listening and healing. Dale got in contact with social services, and they arranged for Mike to live in a room at the St. Leonard's Society, as long as he went to school to get his grade 12 diploma, and worked part-time to help out toward his keep.

Pastor Dale kept in touch with Mike weekly, and within two years, he was pleased to attend Mike's high school graduation. From there, Dale put Mike in contact with a machine shop owner who was looking for an apprentice and who had a soft spot for helping out those with troubled pasts.

Life was good. Mike's demons were buried. However, all too soon, as life's realities crowded in, the demons began to gnaw at the door, splintering the peace in Mike's mind. The things he swore he'd never do again began to creep into his life, more pronounced with each failed relationship, and Mike dropped deeper into his old world, despite swearing it would never happen again.

Having come out of a toxic relationship, this time without falling into a depression where demons could take hold of him, Mike met Janine.

Life was good for the first few months. He was happy. Janine was happy. They moved in together, not being able to have enough of each other. They enjoyed their life, both working hard toward a common goal. They talked about the dreams of owning a house and having a family. Janine kept Mike grounded. She wasn't like any of the other girls he'd been with. She didn't nag him for more than he was able to give. So the demons stayed away.

However, as fate always seemed to decree for Mike, his life spiralled out of control the day he was laid off—the same day Janine told him she was pregnant. As the first few weeks passed without any promise of returning to work, Mike's demons returned, tempting him back to their world—one that was too familiar and too easy to embrace. He began drinking heavily, and when Janine came home from work, Mike was in a constant state of drunkenness.

At first, Janine tried to be understanding, but then the verbal abuse started. Defending her position, and the life she'd thought she was going to have with Mike, Janine eventually fought back verbally, which only made matters worse. The hitting began. Slaps at first. Then fists. Always begging

23

forgiveness afterward. Always promises to never strike her again. Broken time after time—constantly!

The only reason Janine gave for staying as long as she did was the baby inside her, and because she knew the kind of man Mike used to be and could be again if he wanted to—if he would just stop drinking and doing the drugs she suspected he was taking. She'd tried to reach out to Pastor Dale, but he'd transferred out of the city to a different church. Janine called his new number several times but kept getting an answering machine. She never left a message, fearing someone besides the pastor might pick it up; she didn't want the whole world knowing about her problems, or Mike's.

Finally, Janine had enough. Mike sensed it when she said she wanted to meet him in the park so they could talk. In his few and far between sober moments, he knew she was afraid to be alone with him. Mike drove to the meeting place instead of walking, despite having downed a couple generous shots of rye to chase the three beers he'd already consumed. It was only ten o'clock in the morning.

When Janine told him she was leaving, his world tumbled. The demons, drunk with their renewed power, took over. Now, Mike was alone again because, once their job was completed, they too deserted him to play havoc on other victims.

Ten

Janine left the house and walked the few blocks to the park to get her car. She felt the painful turmoil in the pit of her stomach and had a sinking feeling she was going to lose her baby. She drove around until she could no longer drive, the pain in her gut overwhelming her. Janine found herself back at the park where the finality of her decision to leave Mike had been sealed.

Getting out of her car, Janine staggered to the swings. The park was empty at this time of the morning, children most likely still tucked in their beds or glued in front of a television show or video game. Janine's hand reached to the epicentre of her pain. *Will I ever get to tuck you into bed?* Janine scrunched over as another pain ricocheted through her stomach. A groan escaped her pursed lips. When she looked up, there was a woman with a large dog standing in front of her, a worried look on her face.

"Do you need help?" Emma asked, not believing her luck at having found the girl so quickly. She also noticed the fresh cuts and bruises on her face. *Bastard!*

Janine, despite not wanting to depend on a perfect stranger, nodded her head. "Can you call 911 for me; I think I'm losing my baby."

Quickly, Emma reached into her fanny pack, pulled out her cell phone, and dialled 911. Within seconds an operator answered. Emma relayed details of what was happening and the location. She hung up and returned her attention to the young woman. Duke sat obediently beside her, a worried dog-look in his eyes.

"Here, let me help you off the swing," Emma said, taking Janine's arm. "You'll be more comfortable if you lay down over here in this grassy area," she added.

Janine groaned in pain and followed Emma's directions, curling into a ball on the thick grass, feeling her stomach about to explode.

Emma sat down and placed Janine's head in her lap. She stroked Janine's hair away from her face and rubbed her back. "What's your name?" she finally asked.

"Janine."

"My name's Emma," she informed. "Lucky for you, I came along when I did," she added.

Janine groaned and clutched her stomach. "Will you stay with me until the ambulance gets here?" Janine paused for a breath. "My keys are in my back pocket; if you'd be..." a gasp ... "so kind as to get my purse from the car. I'll need my..." another gasp... "health card..."

Janine's voice was cut off by the wail of the approaching ambulance. Emma reached into the back pocket of the young woman's jeans and found the keys, ran to the car, and quickly returned with Janine's purse.

The ambulance pulled to a screeching stop and two paramedics jumped out and raced across the field to Emma and Janine.

"What do we have here?" one of the paramedics questioned.

Emma jumped to her feet again. "The girl says she believes she's miscarrying," she informed.

"And you are?"

"Just a passer-by who saw someone who needed help."

"Good of you to stop," the paramedic said before turning her attention to Janine.

Emma stepped aside and watched as Janine was worked on and finally lifted onto the gurney. Before being pushed across the grass to the waiting ambulance, Janine managed to motion to Emma and mouthed *"Thank you."* Emma nodded, turned and picked up Duke's leash, and walked out of the park. There were things to do, to finish, especially after what she'd just witnessed. She was sure now that she had chosen wisely the first perpetrator to teach a lesson to.

How far that lesson went would depend on how quick a learner he was … and if he was truly repentant for what he had done!

Eleven

Toby was surprised to see Emma leave the house for so many runs with the dog. *What's going on? Emma never goes out this much.*

Heading for the cat door that Jack had installed for him after the first case Toby solved, the old cat made his way outside. *Best to follow you and see what's going on ... need to keep back a ways so the mutt won't sense me.*

Sticking within the tree line, Toby had a difficult time keeping Emma in view. *Time to lose some of this girth!* Toby puffed but had to increase his pace or he was going to completely lose sight of Emma. As he rounded the next corner, Toby saw Emma was at the park and talking to a young woman who appeared to be in distress. He took up a position behind a big maple to keep watch.

Toby watched as Emma assisted the woman off the swing and laid her gently on the ground. *What's going on ... is the girl dying?* Toby darted to another tree for a closer view.

The girl was moaning as though she was in a great deal of pain. Emma was on the phone. *She must be calling for help ... oh dear ... is that girl really dying ... she seems to be in excruciating pain ... she's all scrunched up ... maybe I should run and get Jack ... he can help!*

Toby switched his tail in frustration, unsure what to do. The sound of a distant ambulance siren made the decision for him. *Emma ... good girl ... you got this!*

The ambulance stopped beside the sidewalk, and within ten minutes, the girl was loaded into the vehicle and it sped off to the hospital. Toby was about to return home when he realized Emma was not going in the same direction.

Where are you going, Emma? Home isn't that way.

Toby decided to follow his friend. She took several turns, Duke trotting by her side, and eventually, Emma stopped outside an old wartime cottage. She planted herself behind a big oak and stared at the house.

Why are you here, Emma? Toby placed himself under an ancient blue spruce tree in the yard next door to the house Emma was watching.

Patience wasn't one of Toby's virtues. He was about to turn around and go home when he saw the front door of the house Emma was observing open. A surly-looking man exited. Emma straightened up and clung closer to the tree, pulling Duke's leash tight.

Toby's head tilted to the side. *What are you up to?* He watched as the man got into a beat-up old truck and fired it up. In Toby's opinion, the guy had actually staggered over to the vehicle. *Hope you're okay to drive, buddy ... don't think you are!*

As the truck started to back out of the drive, Emma stepped out from her hiding place and moved quickly up to the driver's side of the vehicle. She smacked the door.

Toby's eyes widened in shock. *What are you doing, Emma?*

The man hit his brakes and rolled down his window: "What do you ... hey, you're the woman who was at the park yesterday."

Emma laughed. Toby detected a hint of hysteria in her tone. "Glad you remembered me. I just want to let you know your girlfriend was just taken up to the hospital by ambulance." With that, Emma turned quickly, and she and Duke raced away.

What the heck! Toby remained in the shadows of the trees for a few more minutes, watching the man in the truck as he hit the steering wheel over and over again. He also appeared to be shouting, his face inflamed with rage. *How does Emma know this guy? What's his connection with that woman in the park? How does Emma know of their relationship? He mentioned he saw her at the park ... but so what ... lots of people go to the park. What happened that Emma would want to confront him ... he looks like a real douche bag!*

As Toby was about to head for home, the guy began to back slowly out of his lane. Toby paused, curious to see which direction he would take, an eerie feeling spreading over him, a feeling that Emma could be in danger. As Toby suspected, the truck took off in the direction Emma had gone, and instead of moving along at a reasonable speed for someone going somewhere, it stayed a discrete distance from where Emma and Duke were jogging.

Toby decided he couldn't leave Emma to the fate of the maniac in the truck—that's what Toby assumed him to be—so, moving quickly out from his hiding spot, the old cat followed the vehicle.

Huffing and puffing, Toby finally turned onto his street. Emma was walking through her front door. The truck sat idling a few houses away, but once the driver saw Emma was in her home, he took off with a roar.

Toby's heart skipped several beats. His Emma was in danger—definitely! *How can I warn you, Emma? There are times I wish I could really talk ... then just think what an even greater detective I would be!*

Twelve

Jack picked up on Toby's agitation as soon as the old cat entered the kitchen. "What's up, old man?"

If only I could tell you, Jack. Our Emma is in trouble. Toby's ears flattened, his tail twitched angrily, and a growl emitted from his throat. *How can I get you there to warn her? I can't tell you what's wrong ... not sure myself ... but I have a deep-seated feline feeling she's in danger ... that much I know!* Toby began pacing around the kitchen, his tail switching sharply.

Jack's brow furrowed worriedly. It had been a long time since he'd seen Toby this agitated and it bothered him. "What's wrong, Toby?" Jack repeated his concern. "What's got you in such a state? Is there something you want to show me?"

Toby ran to his cat door, sat down and meowed loudly.

"Okay, looks like you want me to follow you somewhere," Jack said, heading for the door. "Lead the way, old man," he added as the door swung open.

Toby hurried outside, and down the sidewalk to Emma's house. His heart pounded overtime, and his breathing came in heaving gasps as he raced up the steps to Emma's front porch. Panic was setting in, especially now that since he'd left his friend, the battered truck had returned and was parked across the road. No sign of the guy, though.

Jack came up behind Toby and knocked on Emma's door. Toby paced at his feet, tail jerking anxiously. Finally, after a second rap on the door, Emma cracked it open.

"Jack! To what do I owe this pleasure?" She glanced down. "And Toby! Two handsome men at my door."

Toby thought Emma's voice sounded strained—not typical.

Clearing his throat, Jack paused. In reality, he wasn't really sure why he was there. "Well, Toby wanted to come for a visit and seemed to insist I come along," Jack mumbled, shuffling his feet uncomfortably.

Toby attempted to push his way into the house, but Emma blocked him with her foot. "I'm sorry, Jack," she said, "I'm swamped with cleaning and have everything in my kitchen pulled apart. I need to get it all put back before bedtime. If you don't mind, another time would be better."

You weren't doing any cleaning when I was here, and that wasn't too long ago ... besides, you were out running ... following some guy ... why are you lying? Toby rubbed against Jack's leg and meowed. *Invite her over for supper, Jack ... come on, man ... think!*

As though Jack had read Toby's mind, "Well, if you're working that hard, how would you like to join Toby and me for supper? Just say the time, and I'll throw on an extra plate."

"I don't know," Emma began, but Jack cut her off.

"Tessa's coming over too ... it will be no problem."

Emma hesitated a moment more. Toby meowed loudly. *Come on Emma ... say yes.*

"Okay, can you make it closer to 6:30? That should give me lots of time to finish up here."

"6:30 it is," Jack turned away from the door. "Let's go, old man, and let the lady finish her work."

Toby followed Jack home, despite still feeling that all was not right at Emma's house. *Where's that mutt of yours, Emma? He never misses a chance to bark at me when I come over!*

Thirteen

Emma shut the door and leaned against the wood. "That was a close one," she whispered as she reached to the door leading to the basement. The place where she worked out. The place where the man who loved to beat on his woman was lying unconscious, waiting to see what fate the strange woman had in mind for him.

Emma turned the shower on and tested the water for the correct temperature—hot. She stripped her clothes off and left them in a heap on the floor, then stepped into the tub and let the heat flow over her body. Her mind replayed what had just taken place after Mike had knocked on her door

She'd let him in, invited him to her kitchen, which seemed to puzzle him, but he'd followed her anyway. Then, when his back was turned to her, Emma made her move. He never knew what hit him as he crumbled to the floor. From there, it was easy. She'd dragged him to the basement door, down the steps, and over to the room she'd prepared, plunking him in a chair and securing him with duct tape before he came to.

When he'd regained consciousness, Emma gave him a drink of root beer—spiked with Rohypnol—which, to her surprise, he downed thirstily. She had wondered what she would do if he refused the beverage—how she would administer the Rohypnol to him.

Before the drug took its full effect, Emma found out the guy's name was Mike Sanderson; he was twenty-eight years old; he was laid off from his workplace. However, before she could ask all her question, he'd become sullen and sarcastic, and refused to answer her. Mike told her it was none of her business about his relationship with Janine. Said he'd only wanted to talk to Emma about what she knew, so he could go up to the hospital and see his girlfriend to make sure she was okay. And then, suddenly, Mike's speech became slurred and he shook his head, as though trying to keep awake.

Despite Mike saying he was concerned for Janine, Emma didn't believe him. Men like him always lied. She told Mike that, and he'd called Emma crazy. For such an insult, Emma had sealed Mike's mouth shut with duct tape, then left, locking the door to her secret room. The room where Mike would learn to tell the truth and would be forced to pay for what he'd done to Janine!

And when Emma let him go—if she did—he wouldn't remember clearly anything that had happened to him while incarcerated in her basement!

Fourteen

Jack prepared some chicken thighs for the barbeque, put a pot of rice on the stove, and made a large salad for supper. Toby was watching out the window in anticipation of Emma's arrival. The first guest to arrive was Tessa, and she came bearing gifts—a package of Toby's favourite treats.

Finally, Emma appeared in Toby's line of vision, ambling toward the house. She seemed deep in thought—troubled.

Toby jumped off his perch on the back of the couch and raced to the door, reaching it just as the knock came. Jack hurried from the kitchen to answer it.

"Welcome," he greeted.

Emma smiled and stepped inside. "Something smells good." She reached down and patted Toby on the head. "Hey there, my furry friend." She followed Jack through to the kitchen. "Anything I can do to help?" she asked.

Jack shook his head. "Nope, just waiting for the chicken to be finished; Tessa's watching the barbecue for me. Table's set. We can eat in about five minutes."

Toby rubbed around Emma's legs, trying to get her attention. *What's up, girlfriend? You usually pay me a lot more attention than this.* He looked up at Emma and meowed. *Something is definitely amiss with you!*

Emma finally took more notice of Toby and, reaching down, she scooped him up in her arms for a big hug.

Now this is better. Toby burrowed as far into his friend's arms as was possible.

Jack and Tessa came through the back door, Jack carrying a tray of steaming barbequed chicken. He set it in the middle of the table while Tessa retrieved the salad from the fridge.

"Shall I get the rice?" Emma asked, noticing the pot still sitting on the stove.

"Sure," Jack returned with a smile.

After the meal, the three adults and Toby retired to the living room. During their supper, the sky clouded over and it had started to rain.

Tessa opened the conversation: "When might you like to go see your brother again, Emma? I could take you if you like; my time is quite flexible at the moment—no big cases on my plate."

Toby noticed Emma swallow hard and her hands were trembling slightly. *Poor Emma ... my sweet friend.* Toby glanced at Tessa, who was waiting for an answer. *I don't think Emma wants to see Camden right now ... why should she? After what he did to her ... to all those innocent people he killed ... leaving her alone.*

"I have no plans to see Camden any time soon," Emma finally replied to Tessa's offer. "I'm trying to put my life together—without him—and seeing him would just make it harder for me at the moment."

Toby detected a frosty edge to Emma's tone, unusual for her.

Tessa smiled. "Well if you change your mind, let me know."

"I will ... for sure," Emma whispered, not looking Tessa in the eyes.

"So, what have you been doing to move on?" Jack joined the conversation.

Emma cleared her throat. "Actually, I've been teaching myself self-defence. I bought a tape and have been working out every day."

"Good for you," Jack remarked.

The conversation turned to general issues of no great importance, and after about another half an hour, Emma stood. "I'm feeling tired and think I'll head home now. Cleaning too much, I guess. Thanks for having me over, Jack; the meal and company were lovely."

"Would you like an umbrella?" Jack suggested, looking out the window at the rain, which was falling harder now.

"I'll be fine; I don't live far."

Toby followed Emma to the door, but it was as if she were ignoring him again. *You didn't even say goodbye to me!* He jumped on the back of the couch and watched through the window as she raced down the sidewalk to her house. He noticed the man's truck was still parked on the street, and his heart throbbed in overdrive.

After Tessa left around eleven, Jack decided it was bedtime. "You coming, old man?"

Toby stayed put on the back of the couch, ignoring the offer. *I need to keep watch and see when that guy leaves ... no way he belongs in this neighbourhood ... never seen his truck here before ... and he was questioning our Emma about something.* Toby glanced at Jack, then laid his head back on his paws, his eyes watching the street where the truck was parked.

"Okay, old man, have it your way. Sleep tight." Jack disappeared down the hallway.

Fifteen

Emma knew she had to get Mike's truck off the street and back to his place. She hoped the rain would let up because she'd have to jog back home. "I should take Duke with me but I don't want his hair to be in the cab if, or when, the police investigate the creep's disappearance," she mumbled. "Best I leave Duke here, run home, and pray I don't meet up with any undesirables … best to wait until after all the bars are closed … all the drunks will be home in their beds then."

Thinking she should at least check on Mike and give him something to eat, Emma made a piece of toast—plain—and poured a glass of water for him, dropping another pill in the glass. As she watched the pill dissolve, Emma smiled, but it was not the usual sweet, shy smile her friends were used to seeing on her lips.

Approaching Mike, Emma set the toast and water on a small table within arm's reach of where her prisoner sat. She reached to his face and ripped off the duct tape, freeing his mouth for the meagre meal she'd brought him.

"Bitch!" was the first word through Mike's lips, followed by, "Do you actually think you're going to get away with this?"

The drug must be wearing off … didn't last long… Emma smiled—again, not sweetly—her lips curling sarcastically.

"Get away with what, Mikey?" Emma thought to test the drug and see if he actually remembered any of what had happened to him a few hours ago.

Mike shook his head in confusion. He couldn't figure out why he felt so funny. He knew he was tied to a chair with duct tape, but how he got there, he had no idea. Mike felt the muscles in his legs and arms convulsing. He felt light-headed—dizzy. Finally, he managed to get words out again but really didn't know what he was saying because he couldn't hear himself speak. He couldn't even hear clearly what Emma was saying.

"Doesn't really matter if I get caught. In fact, when I am finished with you, I might even just turn myself in." Emma leaned down in front of Mike, her hands resting on the arms of the chair he was sitting in. "Nevertheless, no matter how this plays out, there's one thing I can guarantee you … you will not ever be able to, or want to, hurt another woman again!"

As Emma tried to feed Mike his toast, he spit in her face. Emma's face turned red with rage, and she back-handed Mike across the face. His nose caught the brunt of the strike and blood trickled down his chin. Emma dropped the toast to the floor and ground her heel into it. She took the cup of water and splashed it on his face, then ripped off another piece of tape and resealed Mike's mouth. She'd give him another drink later, one he'd be so thirsty for that he'd not refuse it.

"Have it your way. I was trying to be nice, make sure you didn't starve," Emma grinned before adding, "before I begin your interrogation." With that, she left the room. When she reached the stairs, she could still hear Mike's struggle to get free—the chair legs banging on the cement floor, and his muffled words that couldn't escape the tape.

Emma rose from the couch at 3:00 a.m., the time she'd figured it would be safe to get rid of the truck. She'd decided she would call a cab to pick her up and bring her home, instead of running back. Safer. Duke raised his head as his mistress walked past him.

"Go back to sleep, boy; I won't be long," Emma said, grabbing the truck keys she'd taken from Mike after she'd knocked him out.

The truck almost didn't start, but finally the engine sputtered and she put the vehicle into gear. "Perfect," she grinned. "As far as anyone knows, I don't drive. So much that people don't know about me!"

Sixteen

Toby hadn't wanted to fall asleep, but he was a cat, and that is what cats do a lot of—sleep. He was awakened by the sound of a vehicle engine. Sitting up quickly, he looked out the window and saw the truck pulling away from the curb. However, he hadn't been able to see who was in the driver's seat as the vehicle moved away from Emma's house.

I hope my Emma is okay.

Gazing over at Emma's house, Toby saw it was in darkness. *Maybe the guy was visiting someone else on the street. Nothing more I can do here.*

Toby jumped off the couch and headed to the bedroom where he shared a bed with Jack—well, the foot of the bed, at least.

Seventeen

Emma parked the truck in Mike's driveway, got out and pocketed the key after locking the door. She pulled out her phone and called for a cab, walking a block and giving a random address for her pickup location.

When the cab arrived, the cabbie was curious. "Late night for a pretty lady like you." His grin showed a couple missing teeth on the right side of his mouth. "Where to?" he asked, as though an afterthought.

Emma gave the address of the all-night gym just down from her house—the same one where her brother had worked and chosen his victims.

"That's the gym, isn't it?" the cabbie asked as he turned the metre on.

"It is."

"Early workout?"

"Yep."

"Surprised you're not walking or running there; it isn't that far."

"I feel safer taking a cab this time of night," Emma replied tersely, annoyed with the man's probing conversation.

"Where's your gym bag?" he continued annoyingly.

"In my locker at the gym," Emma replied quickly through pursed lips. *When is this guy going to shut up? He's so irritating!*

Her answer seemed to satisfy the driver, and within a few minutes, he pulled to a stop in front of the gym. Turning around to her, "Six dollars."

Emma dug in her pocket and pulled out a ten-dollar bill. "Keep the change," she said and got out of the cab before the man could ask her any more pointless questions. She headed for the door and stepped inside the building, pausing long enough in the foyer for the cab to drive away.

Then Emma exited the building and ran home.

Eighteen

Toby slept late in the morning. *What the heck! This isn't like me. Must be all the worrying I'm doing over Emma—tiring me out.* Stretching, Toby stood on the end of the bed, getting his grounding before jumping off and meandering to the kitchen for breakfast. *Jack better have my bowl filled by now. I'm starving.*

The man of the house was sitting at the kitchen table, drinking coffee and reading the morning paper. "Dish is full," Jack laughed when he noticed Toby walking to his food corner.

Toby swished his tail and muttered a "thanks" meow, then dug into his breakfast. He ate faster than usual, and when he was finished, he walked toward the cat door. Pausing at the entrance, he looked back at Jack and meowed.

"Going to see your Emma, Toby?" Jack chuckled.

With an affirmative flip of the tail, Toby slipped out his door.

When he arrived at Emma's, all seemed too quiet. Emma never slept in. Toby crept into the backyard, using his partially dug out spot under the fence, and made his way cautiously up to the three-season room door—just in case Duke had been let out and was lurking behind a corner, ready to pounce on his feline enemy.

My lucky morning ... no sign of the mutt ... or Emma, for that matter. This is getting stranger and stranger. By now, the mutt would've sensed me out here and been barking up a storm. Hmmm...

Toby circled around the three-season room, meowing as he went. Still no sign of anyone—human or dog. He made his way to the front of the house and jumped up on the windowsill that looked into the living room. Emma hadn't pulled the curtains across yet.

Jumping down, Toby went to the door and began scratching it and meowing as loud as he could. As he was about to give up, Toby heard a sharp bark and the clip of dog feet approaching the door.

"Hush, Duke," Emma called out from where Toby thought was the kitchen—he was estimating the distance. Her voice got closer. "Who could it be?" she said as she cracked the door open, keeping the chain lock secured. "No one, Duke … oh," she said, looking downward. "It's Toby. What are you doing out and about so early?" Emma asked, but not opening the door wide enough for him to enter.

What's up, Emma? You always let me in when I come over in the mornings ... or anytime.

Emma started to close the door, and Toby let out a sharp meow, followed by a guttural growl from deep in his stomach.

"Sorry, Toby. I have some things to do this morning. Maybe I'll see you later if I get my work done." The door shut firmly, leaving Toby alone on the veranda.

Toby swished his tail angrily and made his way down the steps to the sidewalk. He was going to go home, but at the last minute turned and made his way back into Emma's yard. Once there, he found a thick bush to hide under.

I know you're in trouble, Emma. Your Toby is on the job. I'll save you from whatever it is that is making you so different from my gentle friend!

45

Nineteen

Emma prepared Mike another piece of toast and poured him a cup of coffee. The Rohypnol dissolved quickly in hot water. "He'll think twice about spitting at me if I'm holding a hot beverage in my hand, won't he, Duke?"

Mike was dozing in the chair when Emma approached. She kicked his leg. "Time to wake up, Mikey!"

"What the..." Mike tried to sputter, before realizing where he was and that his mouth was taped shut. The moan that gurgled in his throat sounded desperate.

Emma pulled up a stool and sat down in front of Mike. She ripped the tape off his mouth. "Shall we try this again? You must be starved by now. I brought you a cup of coffee, too." Emma grinned coldly. "Oh, and I'd suggest you rethink spitting this time—hot coffee will definitely stain your shirt." Emma paused and put a hand to her mouth, a meagre attempt to hide the smile on her lips. "Oh, dear ... have you soiled yourself?"

Mike struggled with his restraints. "You're crazy, lady! Why are you doing this to me? You don't know me!" There was pain riddling through his voice ... and terror.

Emma stood and circled Mike's chair. "Oh, there you're wrong, Mikey," Emma's tone was hostile. "I know your kind. I saw what you did to your girlfriend, Janine, in the park that day. I was witness to what you must have continued doing after you dragged her home. I sat beside her on the grass as she doubled over in pain, losing the baby you put in her belly. Her body so bruised. Her spirit so broken.

"Yes, I know your kind. I've met your kind many times. I was victimized by your kind. Arrogant. Aggressive. Brutal. No conscience. Scum of the earth." Emma paused. "Need I go on?"

Emma walked out of the room toward a laundry tub. She filled a small pail with water. When she returned to her victim, Mike screamed in shock as Emma splashed the cold water on his pelvic area.

"There," she snorted, "that ought to cut down on the smell." Emma set the bucket down and picked up the plate with the toast on it. "Ready for a bite? Like I said, you must be starving by now. If you hurry and eat this like a good boy, the coffee I brought you will still be warm."

Mike stared at the woman tormenting him. There appeared to be nothing to her. She was fragilely built, probably didn't weigh more than 110 pounds. She had the face of a child, sweet and innocent, upon first sight; however, when Mike peered into her eyes, he saw the crazy there! He felt if he were going to survive whatever she had in store for him, he'd need his strength. Mike opened his mouth to receive his meal.

The toast was cold and dry, but it was food. Mike chewed slowly, savouring each bite, prolonging his meal, hoping the delay would give him the feeling of fullness. When he finished the bread, Emma put the cup to his lips. The coffee was lukewarm but Mike was thirsty, so it went down quicker than he wanted it to.

The last drops of coffee dribbled down Mike's chin, Emma having tipped the cup too quickly. His tongue reached out to get the stray bits of liquid gold.

"Well now," Emma stood back and glared at Mike. "Feel better?"

"What if I need to shit?" Mike asked, ignoring Emma's actual question.

She chuckled. "Hmm … that will present you a problem, won't it?" She took a moment to study her prey. "Tell you what … if you answer all my questions to my satisfaction, I might just let you go before you have to shit!"

She's not going to kill me then! I just have to play her game, whatever it is, and the crazy bitch will let me go. I can do this. I have to do this. I don't want to die. "What do you want to know?" Mike asked, his speech already beginning to slur again. His head was spinning too, and he looked around the room in confusion, as though trying to recall where he was now.

Emma glanced at her watch. "Oh, dear. I have somewhere I need to be shortly. I do hope you can hold it for a while." Her laughter echoed in the basement, interrupted only by the tearing off of another piece of duct tape.

Before she placed the tape on Mike's mouth, "Is this necessary?" he asked.

"Very. I do have neighbours, and it would be disastrous for you to call out to them. I'd have to explain the voices to my friends. Then, I'd have to punish you." Emma grinned. "So, you see, I'm just trying to protect you from yourself." A pause. "And if my friends thought you were someone who was going to hurt me, I can't be held responsible for what they might do to you. They love me. They protect me." Emma finished with a harsh laugh.

Mike's shoulders fell in defeat, and he grimaced as the tape closed over his lips. His stomach was churning and he prayed he didn't vomit.

Emma fixed herself some brunch, after which she intended to go up to the hospital to check in on Janine. She was hoping the young woman was still there; Emma had a lot of questions for her.

She cracked the door to the cellar to allow the smell of her meal to waft down to Mike—a form of torture. When she finished eating, Emma shut the door and then let Duke out to the backyard.

"I'll be back shortly, buddy; make sure no one comes snooping around."

Duke moaned, as though he didn't want to be away from Emma. He hesitated in the doorway, looking back at her, before trotting out to the yard to find a shady spot to take up his vigil.

Twenty

Half an hour later, Emma was standing at the information desk asking if there was a young woman named Janine still in the hospital. Emma explained the situation and how she was connected to it.

Luck was with her; Janine was still in the ER in room two. Emma slinked down the hallway, moving with purpose, and hoping no one else was visiting Janine when she arrived.

"Hello, Janine," Emma greeted, approaching the girl in the bed.

There was a flicker of recognition in Janine's eyes. "You're the girl from the park—the one who called the ambulance for me, aren't you?" Her voice was raspy, barely a whisper. "How nice of you to come and check on me."

"My pleasure," Emma smiled amiably. "How are you feeling?"

"Been better."

"The baby?"

Tears collected in Janine's eyes. She shook her head. "A little girl," was all she could manage to say before the tears released.

Emma grasped Janine's hand. "I'm so sorry."

"Probably for the best ... my boyfriend and I just split up."

"Did he do this to you?" Emma pointed to the bruises on Janine's arms and face.

Janine squeezed her eyes shut, turned her head away and nodded.

"Did he beat you often?" Emma pushed for more information.

Janine opened her eyes, and a puzzled look crept across her face.

"I'm sorry ... I don't mean to overstep. I just feel so bad for you." Emma pushed a few tears to the corners of her eyes, squeezed hard and allowed them to fall onto her cheeks.

Janine began crying again. "I don't mean to be rude," she stuttered between heaving sobs. "I'm just so embarrassed ... I wasn't raised to accept such behaviour from a man ... he was so sweet at the beginning ... everything was going great ... we talked about the future about having a family ... then, he lost his job ... well, he got laid off ... and after a couple weeks of being home with nothing to do, he started drinking heavily."

Emma laid a hand on Janine's shoulder. "It's okay. You don't have to tell me any more. I'm sorry I pushed..."

"No, no. I need to talk to someone; I've been silent far too long." Janine hesitated and drew in a deep breath. "I kept telling myself that he wouldn't hit me again because he said he wouldn't. But he did. The longer Mike was laid off, the more frustrated and violent he became..."

"His name's Mike?" Emma asked innocently.

Janine's head tilted to the side and for the second time in the visit, she looked puzzled. "You know Mike?"

"Oh, no ... no, not *your* Mike, I assume. I know a Mike, but probably not the same one ... the one I know lives out West," Emma lied. "When do you get out of the hospital?" Emma changed the subject. She needed to know where Janine lived because if she lived with Mike, it could present a problem. "Will you need help when you leave here?" Emma added.

Janine almost started to cry again but checked her tears with a surging sigh. "I'll be okay ... thanks. I'll be staying with a friend until I find a new place to live." *This woman doesn't need to know I have no place to go ... no friends ... no family.* "As soon as I'm out of here—not sure when that will be—I have to call the police and get an escort so I can get the rest of my stuff from Mike's place."

Alarm bells went off in Emma's head. She was going to have to move quicker than expected. *How can I buy more time? Janine will know he's missing, especially now that Mike's truck is there at his house ... maybe I should move it ... leave it somewhere it won't be found for a while ... she'll think he just ran off because he was so broken up from her leaving him...*

"Are you okay?" Janine broke into Emma's rambling thoughts.

Emma gave her head a shake. "Sorry, I drifted off in my thoughts, thinking about your situation, I guess." Pausing a moment to decide if she should divulge anything more—truth mixed with fiction—Emma finally decided to plunge forward. "I know how you feel, Janine. I've been in a similar situation. The most important thing is not to go back to him. I went back to mine several times, but finally broke free after he almost killed me."

Janine was listening intently as Emma continued with a horror story about her life. By the time she was finished, Emma was sure Janine would never return to Mike—for more reasons than one.

Emma stayed a few more minutes, then finally stood and said it was time for her to leave. Instead of giving Janine her phone number, Emma asked for hers and promised to call her in a few days—a promise she had no intention of keeping. The visit had just been to gain information on Mike, to ensure he was as much of a scumbag as she thought him to be. Janine would survive. Mike—maybe not.

Twenty-one

It was late afternoon when Toby noticed Emma returning home. He'd been worried, having seen her leave around lunch without Duke—unusual for her when she left her place. Toby had taken a jaunt to check out the house, but Duke was keeping guard in the backyard, so Toby returned home to his lookout from the back of the couch.

Seeing Emma walking up the sidewalk, Toby hurried out his cat door, hoping to meet her before she entered her house. He reached Emma's porch at the same time she did, utterly out of breath.

Emma was shocked. "Toby! What's got into you? Twice in one day," Emma stated as she put her key in the door.

Toby rubbed around Emma's legs, watching judiciously for a chance to slip inside the house and check out what was going on. As the door cracked open, Emma didn't anticipate that Toby would enter uninvited. He rushed past her, into the kitchen.

Doesn't look like she's been cleaning like she said! Still a bit of a mess ... no cleaner smell.

"Toby! What are you doing?" Emma shouted. "I don't have time for you right now," she added harshly as she entered the kitchen.

Toby meowed loudly, taking offence with Emma's statement, especially her tone.

Emma, realizing she'd hurt her friend's feelings, "I'm sorry, Toby ... I just have a lot going on at the moment and I've been out all afternoon." She knelt down and rubbed Toby's back. "There, is that better? However, you need to go home now; I have to let Duke in, and you guys don't get along."

Before Toby realized it or could stop her, Emma scooped him up in her arms and walked to the front door. Within seconds, he found himself outside and heard the lock click into place as the door closed before he could turn around and push his way back in.

Toby sat down and stared at the door, his tail quivering angrily. *What's wrong with you, Emma? This is not like you. You're changing ... you're not acting like the sweet girl who moved in here. Your brother is a low-life, but not you. Not you, Emma!* Toby gulped down the tears that were welling in his throat, turned toward home.

Twenty-two

After disposing of Toby, Emma let Duke into the house. "We've got work to do, boy," she said as she plugged the kettle in to make Mike another *special* coffee. As she dropped one Rohypnol into the hot liquid, Emma wondered how much of the drug it would take before Mike was addicted to it.

Maybe that will be my revenge ... I don't have to kill these guys ... I really don't want to go that far ... I just want to ensure they don't—can't—ever hurt another female again!

Emma made her way to the basement door, cup in hand. Duke followed her faithfully. She found Mike awake, and even though he was staring hostilely at her when she approached him, Emma noted the confusion in his eyes. She ripped the tape off his mouth. "I brought you a drink," Emma stated, putting the cup up to Mike's lips.

Mike sipped at the coffee, thankful for the small mercies his torturer was giving him. His mind was confused about where he was. He couldn't remember how he'd gotten tied up. He couldn't remember why he'd come to this house in the first place. Who was this woman? The last drops of coffee went down smoothly.

"I thought I heard voices upstairs ... who were you talking too?" he probed, his words slurred, his voice strained with pain.

"Just my neighbour's cat," Emma replied. "No one to swoop in and save you, if that's what you might be thinking," she added with a wicked grin.

"A cat?"

"Yes, a cat. He comes over all the time to see me, but at the moment, as you might well realize, I don't have time for him. I sent him on his way." Emma paused the conversation and ambled around Mike's chair.

"Your girlfriend lost the baby," she stated blandly.

"Girlfriend? Baby?" Mike looked bewildered.

"Yes, your girlfriend … and your baby. But you must not have given a shit about either one, the way you beat her. Which is why she lost the baby." Emma leaned over Mike's chair and ran a fingernail down his cheek, leaving a red welt in its wake.

"How do you know all this?" Mike's mind zeroed in on a foggy memory of his girlfriend. He squeezed his eyes tight and saw a vision of her … of Janine.

"I paid her a visit at the hospital," Emma filled Mike in further. "She's still in the ER. You beat her pretty badly. I'm sure the authorities have taken note of that."

"What's all this to you?" Mike demanded. "You're a stranger to Janine and me," he scowled.

"Oh … finally … you remember her name!" Emma chuckled madly and leaned over Mike's chair, looking him directly in the eyes. "But I'm not a stranger to your kind," she snapped.

"You don't know nothin' about me, lady," Mike spit angrily, his voice tight with aggression. He struggled against his restraints. "If you let me go now, I won't say anything to anyone."

"No can do, Mikey. You need to pay for your sins."

"And I supposed you're the one who's going to make me pay?" Mike was still confused about what was going on and what the woman in front of him had to do with his life, but he was attempting to make her see he wasn't afraid of her.

"Yep. Cops won't do anything for your girlfriend … they're useless when it comes to protecting abused women."

Mike developed a genuinely sick feeling in the pit of his gut. *This woman is totally off her rocker ... I need to get out of here, but she has this tape so tight on me ... cutting off my circulation ... can barely feel my arms and legs...*

Emma turned her back to Mike. "No way you're getting out of this," she smirked as though she'd read his mind. "However, if you answer truthfully, I might just let you out of here alive. Confession is good for the soul, Mikey. Want to confess anything to me?" Emma leered. "And remember, I've just come from talking to Janine. She told me everything." A pause for effect. "Everything!"

Mike's face blanched. He was tired and hungry. And terrified. He was confused, and he felt sick to his stomach. *Best I come clean ... at least that way, there's a chance I'll get out of this alive.* "Okay ... okay ... Do you want me to say that I've been a terrible boyfriend? I have." Mike gave his head a shake, trying to remember more about Janine. *Why is my brain not working?* Mike looked at the coffee cup. *Fuck! The bitch must be drugging me!* He tried to speak again, his speech slurring: "I never hit Janine until I lost my job ... I started drinking heavily ... even did a few drugs ... shouldn't have done either—the booze and the drugs ... oh God ... oh God..." Memories of what had gone on between him and his girlfriend surfaced hazily in his mind.

"Excuses! Excuses! Always excuses for bad behaviour!" Emma cut Mike off.

"No! Not excuses. The truth." Mike was breathing heavy, his heart rate accelerating. "I'm sorry ... is that what you want to hear?" he added, looking downward.

"Are you really? How many times, after you hit Janine, did you tell her you were sorry?" Emma glared at Mike, knowing what the truth was. "Let me guess and you tell me if I'm right: you apologized after each brutal session and then were on your

57

best behaviour for a few days before losing it again. Is that correct?"

Mike remained quiet. His head was vibrating painfully. *Was this woman right? Were his behavioural patterns so bad that God had sent this woman to punish him? Does she know about the others? Does she know how all my relationships ended? Does she realize I didn't want this for Janine and me? I loved her ... love her. Janine was going to be the one ... maybe she can still be if I ever get out of here ... I'll tell her how sorry I am ... I'll even go to AA ...*

A sharp smack across his face brought Mike out of his wandering thoughts. "Answer me!" Emma shouted.

Mike nodded: "Yes ... yes ... you're right. I've been a terrible person ... I want to do better..." Mike stumbled over his words.

"Want?" Another slap.

"I ... I'm going to d-do better. I ... I'm going to g-get help."

Smack!

"Please ... don't d-do this t-to me," Mike pleaded, holding back his tears, hazy memories of his parents' abuse intensifying in his mind.

"Do what?" *Smack.* "How do you like it? How many times did your girlfriends plead for you to stop?" *Smack.*

Mike shook his head, trying to shake off the pain. "Too many," he gasped.

Emma's fist drove into Mike's stomach, doubling him over as much as he was able to bend due to his constraints. She continued her assault, strolling around his chair, striking him from all directions. Blood trickled from the wounds as Mike's skin cracked open.

"Please … stop!" Emma's victim managed to choke out. Still, no tears. He wasn't willing to give her the satisfaction. "Just tell me what you want, and I'll do it."

Emma laughed hysterically. "I want you to feel their pain. Really feel it! Then, I am going to release one of your hands, and you are going to write a letter of apology to each one of the women you violated with your fists and any other ways you may have hurt them in." A pause. "And don't even try to fool me by saying Janine is the only woman you've beaten!"

"Yes … yes … anything." Mike's eyes looked pleadingly to Emma. He could barely keep his eyes open.

Without warning, she struck him again—hard—knocking his head back. Emma stepped back to view her handiwork. "Okay, Mikey. I'll give you this one opportunity to make it good."

Emma leaned over Mike's chair from behind and wrapped her arms around his neck, squeezing hard, cutting off his breath. "But let me warn you," she whispered in his ear. "If I read one word in these letters that I feel is insincere, we start over. Understand?" Emma released her hold.

Mike nodded.

Twenty-three

The nurse who had admitted Janine into the hospital stood by her bed, clipboard in hand, a concerned look on her face. "The doctor has said you can be released today, but there are a few things I need to talk to you about." The nurse hesitated, not wanting to push the young woman. Taking a deep breath, she plunged forward.

"You've had more than one shock to your system," she began. "You've not only lost a baby but your body has been battered; and, if I might be so bold to add, on more than one occasion.

"I am hoping you're not going back to the monster that is doing this to you." The nurse took some pamphlets from her clipboard and laid them on Janine's bedside table. "These have information about some community resources to tap into where you can get counselling for the abuse you've been through. I strongly suggest you follow up on this.

"Many women feel they can handle their situations, but too many—more than you might believe—go back, time after time. Some finally break the chains—too many others don't. The ones who don't either show up here regularly or end up in the morgue." The nurse paused. "I would suggest you charge your boyfriend with assault, and even the death of your baby," she added.

Janine was listening carefully. She knew enough that she was going to need some sort of support. She had a handful of friends from work—more acquaintances than bosom friends she could call on under her present circumstances—and the only family she had were old and wouldn't be much help for her.

Janine's parents had been killed in a car crash about a year before she'd met Mike and Janine was an only child. Therefore, she knew if she weren't going back to Mike, she'd need help.

Reaching out, Janine picked up the brochures. "Thank you," she whispered, without looking at the nurse.

The nurse nodded. She had a soft spot for women like Janine, being a survivor herself. Reaching into her pocket, she pulled out a piece of paper. "This is my number if you ever need someone to talk to."

Janine took the note and slipped it inside one of the brochures. She swallowed hard, almost choking on the tears engulfing her throat. Before she had a chance to thank the woman, the nurse left the room, leaving Janine alone with a lot to think about.

With her meagre possessions packed into a bag, Janine left the hospital. She wasn't sure where to go first but was anxious to retrieve the rest of her belongings from Mike's place before he threw them out or destroyed them. Janine assumed her car was still parked beside the park where she'd collapsed, so she called a cab to take her there.

"Nice day," the cabbie attempted a conversation, after moving out into the traffic.

Janine just nodded and looked out the window, not wanting to be bothered with meaningless interactions. She noticed the cabbie watching her from the rear-view mirror. Once he realized his passenger wasn't in a mood for conversation, he shrugged and focused on getting Janine to her destination.

As the cab approached the park, Janine breathed a sigh of relief when she saw her little red Volkswagen still parked on the roadside. After paying her fare, she dug her keys from her purse and proceeded to her car.

Sitting behind the steering wheel, motor purring softly, Janine burst into tears. She loved Mike—the old Mike. But the brochures in the plastic bag were glaring at her. Still, there was no way Janine was going to have him charged. She just wanted to get on with her life and put him behind her.

Slowly, Janine put the car into gear and drove to the police station.

Twenty-four

As Jack and Toby pulled into the police parking lot, they noticed a young woman leaning on her car, staring at the front of the building. She appeared to be crying.

Jack, forever the gentleman, and Toby, forever the cat with a good nose for picking up on a problem, walked over to see if there was anything they could do to help out.

"You okay, miss?" Jack queried. Toby stood by his side, studying the situation.

Janine looked up, shocked and embarrassed that a stranger had caught her in a moment of distress.

Before she could answer Jack, though, he asked, "Do you need help to walk across this parking lot and through those doors?" He'd observed the bruises on her face, which alarmed him, and indicated that the woman might be in trouble.

Good man, Jack ... just looking at the girl, we can tell she's tormented by something!

Janine wiped the tears from her face. The man in front of her looked safe enough. She looked down at Toby. *A cat ... the man brought his cat to a police station?*

Jack, noticing where Janine's eyes had wandered, decided to introduce himself. "It's okay, miss. My name's Jack Nelson; I'm a semi-retired police officer," Jack informed, no longer considering himself fully retired because Captain Bryce Wagner kept calling on him to help out with cases. "And this is my cat, Toby—Detective Toby—as he would like to be known."

For the first time since their initial interaction, Janine smiled. "A cat detective ... how strange."

Jack chuckled: "You have no idea!" He paused. "So, can we two gallant old men be of any assistance to you, miss?"

A semi-retired cop and an old cat ... sounds safe enough. Before she realized it, Janine was confiding to Jack her predicament.

"So, you see," she said, finishing her story, "I need to get my belongings from Mike's place, but once I have them, I don't know where I'm going to go. I gave up my apartment when I moved in with him."

Jack ran a hand through his hair, thinking. "Well, first thing, I believe you should file a report on this Mike and have him charged."

Janine was quick to reply. "No, I don't want to charge him; I just want to leave. He's not a bad man; he's just in a bad place right now."

Not wanting to push the issue, Jack proceeded in another direction. He couldn't remember the number of times he'd heard those words from a woman when he was working the streets, investigating domestic disturbances. "Okay then, let's go in and see about getting you a police escort to pick up your things."

Come on, Jack, you can do this ... we can help out this poor girl. Toby pushed up against Jack's legs.

As though reading his cat's thoughts, Jack said, "No, Toby. We can't."

Janine looked puzzled. "You can't what?"

Jack grinned. "Believe it or not, Toby wants us to help you."

"Really? How do you know what he wants?" Janine's eyebrows rose questioningly.

"Really ... you have no idea," Jack commented for the second time. Looking down at Toby, "We have to do this right, old man—by the book!"

Twenty-five

An hour later, Janine was following Jack to his house. The captain, Bryce Wagner, had assured Janine that Jack and Toby would be able to help her get her belongings out of her ex-boyfriend's house. The captain was short-staffed at the moment, due to a series of break-ins in the city's North End, and if she needed to expedite the collection of her possessions, Jack and Toby were her best option.

On the way out to the parking lot, Jack heard Janine's stomach rumble. "Why don't we stop by my house for a bite of lunch? We can also discuss further what to do with your stuff once we fetch it."

Janine smiled faintly. "That sounds wonderful ... you are too kind."

Despite not having eaten since the skimpy breakfast at the hospital, Janine picked at the plate of eggs, bacon, and hash browns Jack prepared for her.

"So, do you have any friends you can bunk with until you find your own place?" Jack opened the conversation after swallowing a piece of egg on toast.

Janine shook her head. "Lots of acquaintances, but no friends around here that would be able to take me in—or want to."

"Parents?"

"Dead."

"I'm sorry."

"Car accident a couple years ago."

"Siblings?"

"Only child."

"Other relatives?"

"Too old."

We got lots of room here, Jack! Toby, having polished off his kibbles, pushed against Jack's leg again. *We can't turn her away ... or, maybe, Janine can stay with Emma! Now there's a thought, Jack. Emma could use some company; she seems lonely since her no-good brother went to jail.* Toby meowed, looked from Jack to Janine, then jumped up on the sill of the window that afforded a view of Emma's house. He meowed loudly again.

Jack, picking up quickly on what Toby was indicating, "We can ask, Toby, but from what I've observed, Emma seems to like living alone."

"Emma?" Janine's eyebrows rose questioningly, wondering if this might be the same Emma who had saved her in the park and then visited her in the hospital. Probably not.

"You might still be having a difficult time believing how this cat can communicate, but Toby thinks our neighbour, a lovely young woman who lives alone, might be able to take you in until you can find a place of your own." Jack was almost ready to tell Janine why Emma was living alone—that her brother was a murderer—but second-guessed himself. What did it matter if Janine knew Camden was a serial killer, murdering several people in Brantford and on the West Coast?

Toby, having gotten his point across, smiled his cat smile, jumped down to the floor, and went and sat between Jack and Janine. He stared up at Janine. *Gosh, I'm a sucker for a pretty face!* Toby meowed and made his way to the cat door, meowed again, and looked back at Jack.

"Okay ... okay, Toby. Give us some time to discuss this, and finish our lunch. Janine has to be comfortable with the situation—meeting our Emma—before she accepts. That is, too, if Emma is agreeable."

Toby flattened his ears and switched his tail impatiently. Not only did he think it would be good for Emma to have a house guest for the company, but he was also worried about his friend. Toby was anxious to get over to Emma's and check in on her. However, he'd prefer it if Jack were with him this time.

I guess I'll have to wait until Jack is ready to make his move ... trouble is, he doesn't realize the importance of what I'm trying to accomplish here! Of the danger our Emma might be in!

Toby laid down beside his cat door to wait for Jack, his eyes slit in a half-sleep cat nap, ready to leave as soon as his partner indicated it was time to head out.

Twenty-six

Emma was tired. It had been a long morning. Before going upstairs, she'd secured Mike's left hand behind the chair so he wouldn't be able to reach it with the hand she was partially freeing to enable him to write his notes.

"Just an assurance you won't try to escape," Emma stated as she double-taped Mike's left wrist to the chair and then wrapped more tape around the actual hand.

Stepping back, "How much time do you think you'll need to accomplish this task?" Emma put to him.

Mike wasn't sure; he had so many failed relationships in his past. However, much of what he had to say to each of them would not be different one from the other. Only Janine's would have to be markedly different, filled with the deepest regrets, and begging her forgiveness. Janine was the one who truly mattered to him, but he got the impression his torturer wouldn't differentiate between the women in his life.

Emma stood impatiently, tapping her foot, waiting for Mike's answer.

"Give me a couple hours," Mike finally answered, hoping that would be enough. His eyes were half-closed; he was so tired. *I don't even know if I'm going to be able to do what the bitch is asking ... I just want to go to sleep.*

Emma grimaced. "Two hours then, Mikey. Write carefully ... weigh each word you put on these papers." With that final statement, she turned, snapped her fingers for Duke to follow, and left, leaving Mike alone with his terror of ensuring he could write his confessions and apologies to the satisfaction of the crazy woman who'd overpowered and imprisoned him!

Twenty-seven

"How much do you need to pick up from your ex's place?" Jack inquired. "We can take my truck if you have any big furniture."

"No," Janine replied, shaking her head. "I just have a few things, mostly clothing and mementoes. Mike can keep the furniture; none of it's mine. I sold my stuff when I moved in with him."

Jack glanced at his watch. Two o'clock. "Maybe, we should go now, before your ex gets too far into his bottle," he suggested.

"We would have had to be there before lunch for that to happen," Janine replied, a hint of hurt sarcasm in her words. "But, better now than later, I guess. I just want to get this over with."

Toby, hearing the way things were going to play out, decided he still needed to go along for the ride. Jack suggested to Janine that they take his truck anyway—more room for everyone—especially in case she decided to take some of the larger items. Janine finally agreed.

When Jack stopped in front of Mike's place, Toby's heart began beating overtime. *What the heck is that truck doing here? This is getting so weird ... weirder by the minute.* Toby glanced at Janine, noticing her hands were shaking and her face had blanched. *She must be terrified of this guy ... and, what's his connection with Emma? Why was she following him that day after meeting him in the park?*

69

Toby studied Janine harder. *Are you the woman the ambulance took away? I didn't really get a good look at her. If so, that means Emma knows you!*

Jack noticed that Janine seemed frozen in her seat. "It'll be okay, Janine," he told her. "I have a badge I can flash if Mike decides to give us any trouble," he added, getting out of the truck.

Going around to Janine's door, Jack opened it for her and assisted her out of the vehicle. Together, with Toby following close on their heels, the retired cop and the young woman made their way to the front door.

Janine hadn't bothered to pull her house key out. "I assume he's home," she stated. "The truck is here."

Jack rapped on the door, for courtesy sake, then stepped back and waited. Janine and Toby stood behind him. After a few seconds, Jack knocked again.

"Highly unlikely, but maybe he went for a walk," Janine suggested. "Here, I'll just use my key." She sounded relieved that Mike might not be home.

Stepping into the house, silence greeted them. Janine gazed around, her brow furrowed in worry. "Doesn't look like Mike has been here for a couple days," she noted, looking around.

"Well, why don't we take advantage of his absence and get your stuff out of here?" Jack said, matter-of-factly. "Hopefully, we'll be finished and out of here before Mike shows up."

Janine made for the bedroom, Jack following on her heels. "What can I do to help?" he asked.

"Not much, except maybe taking things out to the truck for me; you don't know what's mine and what isn't."

Toby sat nearby watching the two humans work, then, bored, began to wander around the house. *What a mess ... I bet it wasn't made by Janine.* Toby noted the empty beer and liquor bottles in the living room; broken picture frames on the floor; the couch in disarray, more than one of the cushions looked as though they'd been ripped open with a knife.

"Are you sure you have everything?" Toby heard Jack ask Janine as the two of them walked into the living room.

A sad look crossed over Janine's face as she gazed around at the mess. Finally, tears in her eyes, she managed to nod. "Yes," she muttered. "There's nothing left for me here."

Twenty-eight

Mike tried his best to write on the pieces of paper Emma had left for him, but he just wasn't able to hold the pen … He startled awake when he heard the basement door open. He looked at the paper in front of him and wondered what they were doing there. *Was I supposed to be writing something? Why am I tied to this chair? Who is doing this to me?*

Mike tried to focus his eyes. Footsteps were pounding down the steps and across the basement floor. The door to his prison opened, and there she stood. Mike wondered who this woman was and why would such a beautiful woman tie him up. He glanced down at his bare arms, where there were numerous cuts and the beginnings of several bruises. *Did she do this to me? God! Why can't I remember?*

"Still writing, Mikey?" Emma's eyes glared with sarcasm. "Your two hours are up," she added as she approached Mike's chair.

"Two hours … writing what?" Mike looked at the papers with confusion. Glancing down to the floor, he noticed a pen.

Emma detected the strain in Mike's voice. She sauntered around to the back of his chair and leaned over to observe what he was working on. "You haven't written anything, Mikey," Emma noted a few half-attempted scribbles on a couple sheets of paper. The rest were blank. "And your time is up." She laughed manically. "How am I to know you are on the path to redemption if you don't do as you're told and write these letters?"

"Please," Mike pleaded. "I don't know what you're talking about. What letters am I supposed to write … and to whom?"

Emma dug her fingers into Mike's shoulders. He winced in pain, feeling how powerful she was, especially in his weakened condition. *She's so tiny ... how the hell did she manage to overcome me and tie me up in this room?* Mike had no idea.

Emma re-evaluated the situation, realizing what the problem was. Mike was over-drugged. If he was going to be able to even think enough to write the notes she wanted him to, she was going to have to lighten the drug dosage or eliminate one dose altogether.

Emma released her hold on Mike's shoulders, then reached over and straightened out the papers. She picked up the pen from the floor and set it on the little table. "Tsk ... tsk, Mikey ... I guess I'm going to have to give you another chance to make things right." For the second time, she explained to him what he had to do before walking out of the room. The door to Mike's prison closed, once again.

Mike's head dropped to his chest and for the first time in a long time—since he'd last seen Pastor Dale—Mike prayed to God for a saviour.

Twenty-nine

Toby was disappointed Jack didn't take Janine directly over to Emma's when they arrived back to the house.

"You look exhausted, Janine," Jack stated, noting the drawn paleness of her face. "Maybe you'd like to rest a bit before we go over to Emma's," he continued as he helped her down from the truck. "We can leave your things in the back for now; they'll be safe. I'll lock the camper door," Jack added.

Janine looked up at Jack. She couldn't believe how fortunate she was to have bumped into such a caring man. Jack reminded Janine of her father.

"Thank you," Janine said. "I am exhausted. It's been a long few days."

Toby scowled on his way to the cat door, but after observing Janine a little closer himself, Toby realized the girl would probably collapse if she didn't get some rest before going to speak with Emma.

I could use a nap myself ... and a snack, if Jack obliges me. Studying his empty dish, Toby scowled again. *I guess I'll just have to sit here to ensure Jack notices my bowl needs replenishing!*

Footsteps were approaching the kitchen, and within seconds, Jack and Janine appeared.

"I'll make you a cup of tea," Jack was saying, "and then you can lay down for a bit. There's a spare room just down the hallway."

Toby let out a meow, then looked at his dish.

Jack chuckled. "Of course, Toby; just let me plug the kettle in for the tea first."

Toby swished his tail impatiently.

Thirty

Emma was frustrated with the way things were going. She hadn't anticipated Mike wouldn't be able to write the notes; hopefully, with not giving him another dose of medication, he'd be able to accomplish the task.

A sharp pain shot through her head. "Not now," she grumbled, pressing her hands to her temples. It had been months since she'd had a migraine. The last one was just before Camden's arrest. Emma pushed back from the table and made her way upstairs to her room.

Opening the top drawer of her dresser, Emma dug around in the back until her fingers closed over the bottle of pills. She dumped two of them into her hand, replaced the container to the drawer, and returned to the kitchen. Going down the stairs, Emma had to grab the railing to prevent herself from tumbling to the bottom.

After swallowing the pills with a large glass of water, Emma made her way into the living room and lay down on the couch. Duke, sensing his mistress was not well, lay on the carpet beside her, looking up at Emma with his concerned dog-eyes.

Burying her head between two pillows and pulling a crocheted blanket over her body, Emma fell into a dream-filled sleep…

"Emma darling … come here, sweet thing. Don't be afraid … I won't hurt you … this is what little girls do for their daddy."

"But you're not my daddy."

"Of course I am, sweetness … not your real daddy, but I'm the one taking care of you now, and I have the responsibility

of teaching you about relationships between daddies and their little girls."

"I want my brother; I want Camden."

Camden is busy right now ... this is our time ... our secret time ... do you understand that ... no one must know the secrets between a daddy and his little girl! Camden will have his time with me later and I will teach him what he needs to do to grow up and be a good daddy."

Emma's eyes opened wide with terror as she looked around, desperately hoping her brother would materialize and save her. But the man was holding her hand, leading her toward a large barn. The smell of fresh-cut hay wafted into her nostrils as the man dragged her up the stairs to the loft. Emma struggled to get away, but the 'daddy' was too strong. Tears streamed down Emma's cheeks. She was so frightened. She was only ten.

Folding her into his arms, the man began stroking Emma's hair, then her back. He cooed softly to her and told her everything would be alright; he'd take care of her. He'd teach her everything she needed to know.

Emma began to relax against him, the sound of his voice lulling her to sleep; but then, suddenly, she felt his hand reaching under her dress and pulling at her panties. Emma's body went rigid with terror.

"Don't be afraid, sweetness ... Daddy is just teaching you about daddies and their little girls ... you need to know these things."

Emma began crying again. She was trying to scream ... scream for her brother, but a large hand covered her mouth, while another hand ripped off her panties. Emma felt rough fingers pushing into her vagina. Pain shot through her—pain like she'd never experienced before!

Finally 'daddy' removed his fingers from inside her, wiping them on her trembling flesh. But an inner voice whispered to Emma that her nightmare wasn't over yet. As she opened her eyes, she saw 'daddy' fumbling to remove his pants. She tried to get up, but 'daddy' slapped her hard.

"Don't move!" he hissed. "The lesson isn't finished yet!" His eyes flamed with madness.

Emma lay on the straw, biting back her tears now, trying to go someplace in her mind that would protect her from the monster. But all the doors kept closing around her. No one was willing to let her in—willing to help her.

When 'daddy' shoved his penis into her body, her screams were lost in the palm of his hand. Upon finishing his business, he reached for a cloth that was in the pocket of his jeans and wiped the blood from Emma's legs. Then he took her gently in his arms again, rocked her, brushed away her tears—the tears he'd pillaged from her.

"Hush, hush, sweet Emma. The first time is always the worst. I promise you that it won't hurt like this next time!"

Emma bolted up from the couch, tears streaming from her eyes—from her heart. The pillow was soaked; she must have been crying for a long time—a lifetime of tears shed in the dream.

The foster daddy had lied. It did hurt—always hurt—emotionally. Emma couldn't tell her brother about what any of the daddies did to her because they all said it was a secret and if she told anyone, they would be most displeased and they would hurt Camden.

Emma continued to bare her pain in silence—until the day she turned sixteen and Camden had come looking for her to give her a birthday present—until he had found their newest foster father on top of her—the day Camden took her away from the monsters!

Duke sat up and whined worriedly. He shoved his nose at his mistress, trying to comfort her. Emma stroked his head absentmindedly.

Her dreams had hibernated for a while, but now it seemed they were rearing their ugly heads, striking terror into the heart and mind of a young woman who had tried so hard to lock away her inner child. To rid herself of the ghosts of the past.

Thirty-one

Toby curled up on the back of the couch where Janine was sleeping peacefully. She hadn't wanted to mess up the bed in the spare room. Jack was busy cleaning in the kitchen, trying to keep the noise down as he put dishes and pots and pans away.

Janine stirred on the couch, moaned, then settled back. Toby looked out the front window and, not seeing any action on the sidewalk or near Emma's house, decided to catch a catnap before going to pay her a visit.

Jack, finished with the kitchen chores, joined the sleeping pair in the living room, stretching out on his comfortable chair. Looking at Janine sleeping so soundly, a frail, innocent child, Jack pondered on the evils in the world before he closed his eyes and drifted off into a dreamless nap.

Thirty-two

Emma rose slowly from the couch and made her way upstairs to the bathroom. She turned the water on in the shower, stood for a moment leaning on the sink, then gazed into the mirror.

Dark circles surrounded her eyes, and her face was blotched from the tears she'd shed. Standing back from the sink, Emma removed her clothes and stepped into the shower, letting the steaming hot water pour over her body. She reached for the sponge and squeezed some liquid soap on it before scrubbing her body from top to bottom until every inch of her skin was red and raw.

Finally finished, Emma turned the shower off, stepped onto her bath mat, and patted the beads of water from her body. She walked naked to her room and dressed in a clean pair of jeans and a T-shirt—no underclothes, no socks. Her feet left damp footprints on the hardwood stairs as she made her way down to the kitchen.

Emma stood at her kitchen window and gazed out into the back yard, thinking about how she was going get Mike out of her house and back to his place. She knew she couldn't keep him forever. Sighing, Emma walked out into her three-season room where her plants were—all except for the Castor bean, which the police had confiscated when they'd arrested Camden.

Duke wandered into the room and stood by the back door, whining to be let out. Emma opened the door and decided to join him for a bit in the yard. Duke grabbed an old ball that Emma usually threw for him and brought it to her. She stroked his head. "Not now, boy. I'm not feeling well."

Dropping the ball at his mistress' feet, Duke sat down and wagged his tail, a pleading look in his eyes. Emma smiled. "Sorry, boy, I'm just not up to it today."

Finally, Emma had enough of outside and headed back into the house. Duke, not getting to play, decided to follow her. Emma walked to her fridge. She wasn't starving but knew she needed to eat something to maintain her strength for what she was going to have to do.

The sandwich Emma made continuously stuck in her throat though, despite the moistness of the egg salad. As she took her last bite, she was startled out of her thoughts by a knock on her door.

"Not now," she muttered, thinking about whether to answer or not.

The knock came again, harder this time, followed by the sound of Jack's voice calling her name.

"What's up with you, Jack?" Emma questioned the empty space while walking through her living room. She opened the door a crack, but shut it quickly, her breath coming in gasps as she leaned against the door. *What's Janine doing with Jack!*

"Emma," Jack called out worriedly. "Emma! Are you okay?"

Emma choked in a deep breath, trying to calm herself down, then reached to the handle and swung the door open. She stepped out onto the porch, closing the door quickly behind her. She smiled.

"Janine—what a small world. I had no idea you knew my neighbour, Jack." Emma paused. "What brings you over here, Jack … and, dearest Toby … always a pleasure to see you." Emma leaned over and patted Toby on the head.

Toby sensed the strain in Emma's voice. *Hmm, you weren't so happy to see me the last couple times I showed up … and your greeting now seems forced … how do you know Janine*

... ah ... she was the woman in the park ... and Mike's truck ... it was near your place ... now it's back at his house but he isn't there ... what's going on, Emma? What aren't you telling us? What—who—are you trying to hide? Toby's cat whiskers twitched, anxious to solve another mystery.

Janine appeared as shocked as Emma. When she thought about it, the woman who had saved her life that day in the park, and then visited her in the hospital, had been evasive about who she was, other than giving her first name as Emma. Janine had given out her phone number but it hadn't been reciprocated.

Jack picked up on the discomfort between the two young women. "You ladies know each other?"

Emma remained silent. Janine offered an explanation: "Emma is the woman who found and helped me the other day in the park." She paused. "I'm so happy to meet up with you." Another pause. "You never gave me your phone number when you visited me in the hospital," Janine added accusingly.

A look of concern entered Emma's eyes. "I guess I was just so upset about your condition that I never thought to mention my number—but I did have yours," she added.

"But you never called." Janine had no idea why she said that.

"Sorry. I've been busy." Emma quickly turned her attention to Jack, and tilting her head to the side, "So, what can I do for you?" she asked again.

Jack cleared his throat. "Well, as I am guessing now that you already know, Janine is going through a rough patch. She needs a place to stay until she can find her own apartment. Toby is actually the one who pointed us in your direction—you know how he can get points across despite being a cat!" Jack chuckled and looked down at the old cat, which scowled back.

"Really," Emma said through pursed lips. "So you want Janine to stay with me?"

Janine was quick to pick up on Emma's discomfort. "If you don't want to host me, I understand. It is quite an imposition to ask of anyone; after all, we've just met." Janine cleared her throat, swallowing her pride. "I'll be okay … there are hotels with suites where I can cook my own meals."

Emma's heart sank; she felt terrible. Janine was a victim—like her. "It isn't that I don't want to," she began. "If you could give me a day or two to prepare a room for you, you can stay here for as long as you need." Emma smiled. She thought that would give her time to dispose of Mike—one way or another!

Toby fixed a stare on Jack. *Come on, Jack … just offer for Janine to stay with us until Emma gets a room ready for her.*

"Well, that sounds good, Emma," Jack remarked, and turning to Janine: "I guess, if you don't mind hanging with a couple old bachelors, you can stay with Toby and me until Emma gets your room ready."

Good man, Jack … I knew you'd pull through for the girl.

Everyone was shuffling their feet uncomfortably on the porch, each one not sure of what to do next. Finally, Emma spoke up: "Well, if you don't mind, I need to get back to what I was doing before you came over." She opened the door. Turning back for a moment, "I'll call you as soon as the room is set up."

No one noticed Toby slip inside.

Thirty-three

Toby hid under the couch until he was sure everyone was gone, including Emma to another room. There was something up with her and Toby was bound and bent to uncover what it was. Duke was growling and looking in Toby's direction, but Emma grabbed him by the collar.

"Come on, Duke; Toby's gone home and it's time for you to take a trip to the back yard."

While Emma was letting his arch-enemy outside, Toby slipped into the kitchen and hid in an obscured corner where he could observe but not be seen.

Emma returned from the three-season room without Duke and sat down at her table. She just sat there, shaking her head, in a trance-like state.

"Terrible … disgusting … what a prick…" Emma kept verbalizing over and over.

Finally, she rose from her chair and pushed it back from the table. Toby watched her walk to the basement door, and noticing she left it cracked open, he slunk from his hiding place and followed her.

Pausing at the top of the stairs, Toby watched Emma go all the way to the bottom before he made another move. Being a cat, despite being slightly overweight, Toby made not a sound as he descended into the basement.

Emma has quite the setup down here … I had no idea she worked out on a punching bag … maybe it was Camden's and she just hasn't gotten rid of it. She did mention she was doing some kind of training—but this?

To Toby's surprise, Emma began dancing around the bag, striking out at it every few seconds. This went on for about five minutes before Emma walked to the laundry sink and splashed cold water on her face, then she turned and proceeded to the far end of the basement where there appeared to be a room. Toby crept closer.

Emma opened the room's door and stepped out of view. Luck was with Toby again: the door was left partially open. He heard Emma talking to someone.

I had no idea Emma had a boarder ... I wonder why she wouldn't have mentioned that.

"Well, Mikey," Emma's voice sounded harsh and cold. "We have a bit of a problem; I am going to have to finish up quickly here and get you out of my house—one way or another." The laugh that followed sounded hysterical to Toby's ears.

Toby's eyes just about popped out of his head when he peeked into the room. *It's the guy! Tied to the chair with duct tape! What are you doing, Emma? What's happening to you? You're not like Camden ... please don't be like him ... you're my sweet Emma.* Toby's tail jerked nervously as Emma continued her barrage of words to Mike.

"From the looks of the number of notes you have here, you've abused a lot of women, Mikey, and I'm unsure if I'm willing to forgive you for such atrocities."

Toby watched as Emma ripped the tape from Mike's mouth. He saw the man grimace in pain but not cry out. Despite wanting to get out of the house and fetch Jack, Toby felt he needed to stay a little longer to really see what Emma was up to.

"*You* aren't willing to forgive me?" Mike spoke up. "I thought all you wanted was for me to apologize to the women. What did I ever do to you to make you so pissy?" Not being under the full influence of the drug Emma had been giving him was giving Mike more awareness of what was going on—not entirely, but enough to provide him with a bit more fight-back.

Emma's tone was icy when she replied: "To me? Nothing directly. However, every time you strike a woman, you're abusing all women, so I need to punish you for your crimes!" Emma gathered up the notes and began flipping through them, reading the names in her mind.

Toby's ears flattened. *Emma, what the*... The next thing he heard was a slap, and then a grunt from Mike.

"That was for Karen," Emma shouted.

The slaps continued, and women's names followed each one. Toby couldn't believe his eyes as he watched his beloved Emma beating on the guy in the room.

Oh, Emma ... what has happened to you ... have I been blind to who you really are? This just doesn't seem right!

Toby was even more dismayed as he noticed the blood on Mike's face and saw how limp he'd gone in the chair, his head lolling to the side.

Are you going to kill the guy, Emma? Please don't go that far ... stop ... now ... before it's too late. I know he's a scumbag, worse than an old alley cat ... but you can't kill him, Emma ... you can't go to jail ... come back to me, sweet Emma!

Toby was shaking inside. His fur stood up on his back. His tail twitched in frustration. He feared that by the time he got to Jack—if he could get him back to Emma's and down to her basement—it might be too late for Mike. The woman in the room was not Toby's Emma!

At length, the commotion ceased, and Emma was heading to the door, the notes in her hand. Toby caught a glimpse of Mike, unconscious in his chair. He had to hide before Emma left the room; there was no way he could have her see him. Toby needed—more than ever now—to find a way out of the house—

quickly—and figure out how to get Jack back to Emma's house and down to the basement.

Slinking behind a stack of close-by boxes, Toby watched Emma climbed the steps before he crept cautiously across the basement. When he was positive Emma was upstairs, he climbed up the steps, only to discover the door was closed tight!

Toby heard Emma moving around in the kitchen. The smell of coffee wafted through the crack at the bottom of the door. The cat realized the only way to get out of the predicament he was in was to cause a commotion that would get Emma back to the basement, leaving the door open, giving him a chance to escape—at least into the central part of the house. From there, he'd figure out a way to get back to Jack.

Looking around for something large enough that if knocked off the landing it would make a big noise, Toby noticed a small box in the corner. He approached it cautiously and peeked inside. *Good. Looks like a bunch of assorted dog toys ... they should make a big enough noise if I can push them to the bottom of the stairs.*

Toby gave the box a good shove with his nose and it slid across the landing, stopping at the edge just before the first step. Another shove sent it catapulting to the bottom, landing with a shattering crash. Toby heard Emma's chair scrape across the floor and then her footsteps approaching the basement door.

"What the heck," Emma commented, looking into the basement, searching for the source of the noise.

Toby hunkered in a corner, hoping Emma would venture further down the stairs. Once again, luck was with him as Emma made her way down to the fallen box and its spilled contents. As she bent over to pick up the dog toys, Toby slipped through the door. As he crossed the kitchen floor, he noticed one of the notes on the floor.

Maybe there will be a clue on this paper ... I need to get it to Jack! Securing the note in his mouth, Toby made his way to the living room, taking up residence once again under the couch, hoping for a moment when he'd be able to escape.

Thirty-four

As Toby waited under the couch for his next opportunity to get completely out of the house, he heard Emma reading aloud from a book on hypnosis. She was reading slowly and repeating each paragraph four or five times before moving on to the next section.

Toby's tail swished slowly on the floor; he thought he heard his stomach growl and hoped Emma hadn't heard it too.

A click reached Toby's ears, and the room lit up. Footsteps. Emma was pacing around the room. Toby dared to peek. His friend had a crazed look about her—like her brother.

Oh no! My poor Emma. I must save her. But how to get out of here?

A sharp barking started up from outside.

Great! Possibly my chance to escape ... Emma will have to let the mutt in, giving me the opportunity I need. Toby inched closer to the edge of the couch. He was thankful for the raised legs on it and the crocheted blanket that draped to the floor.

"Okay, Duke ... I'm coming," Emma muttered, heading toward the three-season room.

Toby took his chances and followed, sticking close to the walls where it was the darkest, the note secure between his lips. Once again, luck was with him; Emma left the adjoining doors open while letting her dog in. Toby dashed through and darted for cover in the yard, narrowly missing being seen by his enemy, Duke.

Duke began growling, sensing a disliked presence in his domain. Emma hushed him, ordering her companion into the house. Toby heaved a sigh of relief and quickly made his way to the small opening under the fence where he usually came and went to visit Emma.

Thirty-five

J ack and Janine were watching T.V. when Toby arrived home. He made his way straight to his dishes, diving ravenously into his kibble, washing the dryness down with the fresh water Jack had filled in the second bowl. *The note can wait until I eat ... can't be doing too much detective-ing if I'm starving!*

Footsteps approached. "Toby!" Jack exclaimed. "Where you been, old man? I was beginning to get worried."

Toby looked up briefly from his meal. *You have no idea, my friend ... no idea. Emma is falling off her rocker, as you humans might say. I need to get you over there and save that guy she has tied up in her basement, even if he's a scumbag! You can have him appropriately charged later, Jack; he's the filthy pig who hurt Janine ... I need to get you back there ... to the basement!*

"Hunting wasn't very profitable, I see," Jack chuckled as he walked to the fridge and took out a beer and a ginger ale. Turning back to Toby, "Going to join Janine and me when you're done there?" Jack asked. "Our favourite show, *Law and Order*, is on."

Toby flipped his tail up, then finished off the last few kibbles in his dish. Securing the note in his mouth, he followed Jack to the living room, jumped up onto the couch, and dropped the message on Jack's lap.

"What's this?" Jack asked, picking up the piece of paper. He turned it over in his hand and studied the writing, which was barely legible.

Karen ... I'm sorry for what I ... The words trailed off to a bunch of illegible squiggles.

"Where did you get this, Toby?" Jack queried, not expecting an actual answer. "Did you find it on the sidewalk?"

Toby made his way to his spot on the back of the couch and looked in the direction of Emma's house, hoping Jack would get the message. However, when he glanced back to see if Jack was watching, Jack had already set the note on the coffee table and returned his attention to his television program.

This isn't good ... come on, Jack ... you need to take the note seriously! Toby glared at Jack and meowed, then growled.

Jack looked away from his T.V. show, annoyed. "What's got into you, Toby? Chill out, old man."

Toby swished his tail angrily, another growl directed toward Jack. He turned his back on his friend, deciding to keep watch on Emma's house while he tried to formulate another plan to get Jack to pay attention to the note. Within seconds, though, Toby was emitting tiny cat snores.

"Poor kitty," Janine commented to Jack.

"Yeah, looks like he's had a rough time in the big jungle out there," Jack snickered. "Not like him to be gone so long from the comforts of home—unless there's something wrong and he's on the job," he added.

"On the job?" Janine looked puzzled.

"Oh, yes ... if you remember, I mentioned that Toby is a detective and the only time he misses a meal is when he's investigating something." Jack paused. "Come to think of it, the old man has seemed upset about something lately ... Emma ... I think he's worried about her for some reason," he added. The piece of paper Toby had dropped in his lap, though, didn't even cross his mind.

Janine smiled, groaned, and stood. "It's been a long day. If you don't mind, I'd like to turn in for the night. I can't thank you enough for helping me, a complete stranger."

Jack motioned down the hallway: "First door on the left past the bathroom," he informed. "I set out some towels for you at the end of your bed. Rest well; tomorrow is another day."

"Thank you. Goodnight," Janine said as she left the room, leaving Jack alone with his thoughts—and a sleeping cat.

Thirty-six

Emma's mind was in turmoil. She'd never thought she would ever actually cross the line and murder someone. But this guy—Mike—he was the personification of abusive men. His written notes, as scanty as they were, were proof of that. And how was she going to handle the situation now she'd gone this far? There was no way Mike—if he remembered anything about what was happening to him in her house—was not going to charge her if she were to let him go. The drug was powerful, but would it erase all memory of the events that took place in her house? And, to top it off, now she'd gone and said she would take the guy's girlfriend in until she found a place to live permanently.

Timing was of the essence. Emma could no longer keep Mike in her basement. She needed to get him out of her house and back to his place. That meant giving him a super dose of the drug, which would hopefully immobilize him so she could move him. That also meant going back to get Mike's truck to transport him and doing it in the dead of night, praying no one would see her dragging a dead-weight body into his house.

Emma closed her eyes. It was still early. She needed to get some rest before she made her next move. Duke lay down on the floor beside the couch, resting his head on his front paws but keeping his eyes on his mistress. Emma, sensing her dog's concern, reached a hand down and rubbed the top of his head.

"It'll be okay, boy. We'll get through this. I'm learning from the mistakes I made this time, and trust me, I won't make them again!" Emma sighed and allowed her body to succumb to slumber.

Thirty-seven

Toby woke up in the middle of the night. He looked around the room and noticed everyone had cleared out. He was surprised Jack hadn't tried to wake him. Looking over at Jack's chair, Toby noticed the note sitting on the end table beside it.

I need to figure out a way to get Jack to have another look at that note, and then try and make him understand where it came from! Time is of the essence here. I need to ensure that the scumbag is okay, but more than that, I need to stop Emma from stepping over a line that there will be no return from!

Toby made his way across the couch and down to the end table. He picked up the note in his mouth and returned with it to his spot on the back of the sofa.

Why do I keep getting this feeling that something terrible is going to go down tonight?

Toby glanced out the window, gazing in the direction of Emma's house.

What he saw terrified him.

Thirty-eight

Emma awoke around two o'clock in the morning, refreshed and ready to get Mike out of her house. Duke followed her up the stairs to her room, where she changed into a black jogging suit and tucked her long, blond hair into an over-sized ski-cap.

Back in the kitchen, Emma prepared a drink for Mike—a double dose of the Rohypnol. She figured that should be enough to enable her to handle him out to the truck and then into his own house. Emma still hadn't decided whether, once she got him there, she was going to tie him up again or just take her chances that he wouldn't remember anything that had happened to him over the past few days. If he did remember, hopefully, he wouldn't be inclined to go to the police. After all, they wouldn't take too kindly to the stuff he'd done to all his past girlfriends—and to Janine, which was a current victim. All it would take to expose him was to send copies of his notes, along with an anonymous letter explaining the content, to the police.

On the other hand, maybe she could just give him another dose of the Rohypnol, enough to end it all for him. She could leave a suicide note beside him, along with the hand-written ones. Emma smiled as she thought of what she could write on his behalf. How she could tell everyone how sorry he was for abusing all those women, especially Janine!

Emma didn't have to decide just yet. She put the bottle of pills, along with Mike's truck keys, into the zippered pocket of her jogging pants and headed toward the door to leave and get Mike's truck. Duke whined at the door, wanting to go with his mistress.

"Not this time, boy," Emma patted him on the head, as she closed him in the house and jogged into the night.

A half-hour later, Emma pulled up in front of her house. Luck was with her that there was no moon, and a heavy blanket of clouds covered what stars would have lit the night sky. Duke wagged his tail anxiously when Emma entered the house, and he followed her into the kitchen where she'd left Mike's drink. Picking up the cup, Emma made her way down to the basement and over to the room where Mike was tied up.

Mike looked up when Emma entered the room, an indifferent look in his eyes.

"Brought you a drink, Mikey," Emma said, approaching him.

To her surprise, Mike shook his head and looked away from her, an indication that he might not be so receptive to drinking the beverage this time. Emma ripped the tape from his mouth. "You not thirsty, Mikey?"

"Nope ... not drinking anything you're giving me ... not eating anything you might give me either." Mike's face suggested he was ready for a fight. "What are you going to do about that, lady?" he added.

Emma stepped back and observed her captive. Duke growled softly, not liking the tone of the stranger who appeared to be threatening his mistress. Suddenly, Emma laughed—harsh and hysterical.

"Let me see ... what should I do with you?" Emma's lips curled menacingly. Emma's brain went over the numerous Rophypnol side effects ... aggression was one of them. Mike was definitely exhibiting aggressive behaviour at the moment. *He must be coming down from the last dose I gave him ... guess I'll have to force him to drink this.*

Emma set the cup down and walked around Mike's chair. His eyes followed her movements as best he could. Suddenly, Emma grabbed hold of Mike's hair, jerking his head back. She stared into his eyes, which had opened wide in shock. "You will do as I say, Mikey," Emma hissed, "Or pay the price with your life. You will drink this drink I brought you, and when you wake up, you will be in your own home and will never have to see me again. Choose not to drink it, I'll let you rot here in this chair and no one will ever find your body!" Emma thrust Mike's head forward.

Mike began to shake uncontrollably. *This bitch is totally crazy! I need to get out of here, any way I can. Maybe, I can convince her just to let me go ... tell her I won't say anything to anyone ... tell her whatever she wants to hear ... anything to get out of here alive!* Survival raced through Mike's mind, but for some reason, he held his tongue, fearing what Emma would do to him.

Emma picked up the cup and held it out to Mike: "Ready for your drink, Mikey?" Her eyes glowed with madness.

Whatever willpower Mike had found to fight against Emma when she first walked into the room dissipated. The will for survival was much stronger. He opened his mouth to receive the liquid. Emma put the cup to Mike's lips, and he gulped down the coffee. When he finished, Emma patted his cheek.

"Good boy, Mikey. Don't you feel better now?" Emma laughed. Her insanity saturated the room.

Emma returned to the basement half an hour later. Mike was out cold, and even though Emma was pleased with the result, she also worried that she might have given him too much. She checked for a pulse. It was there, though faint.

Pulling a knife from her pocket, Emma cut Mike's tape away, then lifted him effortlessly and climbed the stairs, his body slung over her shoulder. Duke paced around her, hoping to go out for a run, despite it being the middle of the night.

"Stay, boy. You can't come with me right now. This is something I have to do alone."

Duke growled low in his throat. He wasn't pleased; he felt the need to be with his mistress. He didn't like the man who was slung over her shoulder, despite him being immobile.

Emma finally managed to get out the door, leaving a worried Duke behind. She made her way to the truck and clumsily thrust Mike into the front seat. He slumped sideways like a wet rag. Climbing into the driver's seat, Emma shoved his head away, started the truck, and backed out of the driveway, totally unaware of the eyes that were watching her from the next door living room window.

Five minutes later, Emma pulled into Mike's driveway. Awkwardly, she pulled Mike from the truck and shoved the door shut with her foot. Emma's heart was thumping as she made her way up the sidewalk and steps to the front door, her eyes searching the neighbourhood for any lights or walkers. So far, so good.

Twenty minutes later, Emma was jogging home, having left Mike asleep on his couch. She'd opened a bottle of whiskey and poured a glass of it, spiking it with another dose of Rohypnol, leaving both on the coffee table. She'd heated a frozen dinner in the microwave, scraped some of it in the garbage, and put the rest of it on the coffee table with a fork in it. Emma wanted to make it look like he'd been having supper and a drink. Before leaving, she'd looked around, then turned on the T.V. and set it to the American Movie channel, which she assumed a guy like Mike would watch. As she opened the door to leave, Emma noticed a key hook on the wall, and she placed the truck and house key ring on it before leaving Mike's house.

Duke greeted his mistress at the door, his tail wagging furiously. Emma took her gloves off and threw them in the garbage, then patted him on the head. "He's gone, boy. But now, we have to get rid of the evidence that he was even here. I need to clean up the room and put some boxes and other junk in there ... make it look like a storage room.

Two hours later, the room totally transformed, Emma went up to her room to get some sleep. The sun would be up soon. When she got up, she would prepare Camden's room for Janine, then give Jack a call and let him know she was ready to take in her guest.

Thirty-nine

Toby kept vigil, waiting for Emma to return. When she did, she was on foot. *What are you doing, Emma? What have you done with Mike? Why did you have him in your house in the first place? Why were you torturing him?*

It was still too early to wake Jack up, so Toby closed his eyes to wait for the sun. The note was safely tucked under his front paws. Emma's house was in darkness now. Toby had observed the lights turn on in the basement, then off. Then one turned on and off upstairs.

The warm sun sprayed in the living room window, landing on the spot where Toby was sleeping. Lazily, he opened his eyes, stood up, stretched, and yawned. Picking up the note in his mouth, Toby made his way out of the living room and down to Jack's bedroom, jumping up on the bed. Jack groaned groggily.

"Toby. What's up, old man? It's too early," Jack's voice was still drunk with sleep. He rolled over and put a pillow over his head.

Don't be so lazy, Jack ... you're not a cat ... I'm the one who's supposed to sleep sixteen to twenty hours a day! Time to get up. We got things to do.

Toby began to knead the blanket on Jack's back, digging his claws in as far as possible. Jack stirred and rolled over again, throwing the pillow at Toby. Toby ducked, and almost lost the piece of paper he was still holding in his mouth.

Jack sat up in bed. "What's this?" he asked, reaching out for the note. "Is this the same one you dropped on my lap last night?" he queried.

Toby meowed and rubbed his head against Jack's hand.

Jack, realizing Toby might really be trying to tell him something important, got out of bed. Walking to the bathroom, "Give me a couple minutes, old man, to get freshened up and have some breakfast and a coffee, and then you can tell me all about it, okay?"

Toby, recognizing he had no choice but to wait, picked up the note in his mouth and went to the kitchen to wait for Jack. *No way am I letting this note out of my sight until I convince Jack to follow me to Emma's. I want to see the look on her face when she sees it!*

A few minutes later, Jack entered the kitchen, looking only slightly more awake. Toby noticed age crawling over his friend, much like he felt the time in his own bones.

"First things first, eh Toby," Jack said, going to the cupboard where he kept the cat food. As he leaned over to pour kibble into Toby's dish, he noticed the note on the floor. "This must be really important to you," he said. "However, two hungry men can't do much without a good nutritious breakfast. Eat up, and then I'll follow you wherever it is that you are trying to take me." Jack paused. "And take your note with us," he added with a grin, still not sure how seriously to take it.

Toby looked up from his dish for a few seconds, glaring at Jack. *Don't think for a minute, Jack, I am unaware that you think I'm off-kilter right now, but you'll see soon enough. Why do I have to convince you every time something terrible happens that I'm the one who solves the crimes—not you or the cops? Me! Detective Toby!*

A shadow entered the kitchen.

Damn! I forgot about Janine. She could complicate things for me here. Hopefully, Jack won't have her accompany us when I take him over to Emma's.

"Good morning, Jack," Janine addressed her host.

"Morning," Jack returned. "Sleep well?"

"Yes, thank you."

"Coffee?" Jack held up a coffee cup.

"That would be nice."

"How about some breakfast?' Jack asked as he poured Janine a coffee.

She shook her head. "No, thanks. I don't usually eat this early. I'm not really hungry right now."

Jack popped a couple pieces of bread in the toaster for himself. "Well, I can't go without something to eat as soon as I'm up and about." He walked to the fridge and took out a jar of marmalade. "Toby and I have a little errand right after we eat. I don't think we'll be long, but if you get hungry before we get back, just help yourself."

Janine smiled. "Thank you, Jack. I don't know how I'll ever be able to repay you for everything you're doing for me."

"Always been a sucker for a damsel in distress," Jack grinned as he took his toast out of the toaster.

"Is it okay if I watch some news while I have my coffee?" Janine asked.

"Be my guest. The remote is probably on the end table by my chair." Jack spread the marmalade on his toast and sat down at the table.

It didn't take Jack long to down two pieces of bread and a cup of coffee, and when he was finished, he stood and looked down at Toby, who was waiting patiently by the back door, the note secure between his teeth.

"Okay, old man, lead the way."

Toby darted out his door, heading in the direction of Emma's house, Jack close on his heels.

Jack was puzzled when he watched Toby race up Emma's sidewalk and onto her porch. He paced in front of the door, looking up at the doorbell, the note still in his mouth.

"Does that note have something to do with Emma? Is she in trouble, old man?" Jack reached out and pushed the bell, then reached down and took the piece of paper from Toby, studying it with a perplexed look on his face.

Toby and Jack waited for Emma to answer the door. Jack checked his watch. "Maybe she's still in bed," he suggested.

Toby meowed and looked up at the doorbell again.

"Okay, one more time," Jack said, "and if Emma doesn't answer within a minute or so, we go home and come back later."

Just as Jack was about to give up, he heard Duke barking and footsteps—dog and human—approaching the door.

"To what do I owe this pleasure?" Emma asked, opening the door while holding tight to Duke's collar. She glanced at her watch, a scowl crossing her face.

Jack noticed Emma's discomfort immediately. "Sorry to bother you so early, but Toby is agitated about this," Jack handed Emma the note, "and when I told him I would follow him to where he found it, he led me here. Is this yours? Are you in some kind of trouble, Emma? You know, you can always turn to us if you need help." Jack looked deep into Emma's eyes, his own filled with concern.

Toby watched Emma's reaction to the note closely. Her hand shook slightly as she took hold of the piece of paper and scrutinized what was written on it. Slowly, she handed the message back to Jack.

"I have no idea what this is. It's not mine," Emma said, a nervous edge to her voice.

Why are you lying, Emma? I found this at your house! On your kitchen floor! What have you done with Mike? I know you left with him last night ... shoved him in his truck and drove off ... returning a bit later on foot ... I saw it all, Emma! What have you done?

Glaring up at Emma, Toby let out a meow, followed by a low growl.

Jack stooped down and scooped Toby up into his arms. "Come on, old man; I don't know what your game is here, but this note doesn't belong to Emma, so let's leave the girl alone." He paused before turning to leave. "Are you still good with Janine staying with you for a bit? If it's too much for you, please don't be afraid to say so."

Emma shook her head. "I just have a few things to clear out of Camden's room," she informed. "Janine can probably move in later today," she added with a smile.

Jack nodded and held tighter to Toby, who was struggling to get down. "I'll give Janine the good news. Just call when everything is ready."

"Will do," Emma replied, stepping back into her house and shutting the door. She watched Jack walking back to his house, Toby still in his arms. She didn't like that Toby was looking back toward her place, and he didn't look happy.

When her neighbours were out of sight, Emma made her way to the kitchen and began pacing. "How did Toby get hold of that note? Was he in my house and I didn't see him? Is that what Duke was so upset about yesterday? And I pulled him away ... I should have listened to my dog ... did Toby see Mike ... did he see or hear what I was doing in the basement? ... The note is definitely one that Mike wrote ... there's no way Toby could have gotten in my house ... maybe Mike had one in his pocket and it fell out when I was carrying him to the truck last night ... but how did Toby get hold of it so quickly? Did Toby see me last night? For God's sake, Emma! Get a grip on yourself! Toby is just a cat! Just a friggin' cat!"

Little did she really know her friend.

Forty

Mike came to, his head pounding. He tried to get up from the couch but his body didn't seem to want to co-operate. He looked around the room at the mess, at the coffee table with an open whiskey bottle and a half-drunk glass of liquor, at the partially eaten dinner, at the television with an old Western playing. He couldn't remember any of this.

A broken picture frame on the floor drew Mike's attention. The picture itself lay beneath the shattered glass. A photo of him and a woman. Mike shook his head, trying to focus on who was with him in the image. He tried, again, to get up, to no avail. It was as though his limbs were made of rubber.

Mike licked his lips, which were dry and cracked. His tongue felt fuzzy and thick. "I need a drink," he mumbled, reaching for the glass on the coffee table.

Somehow, Mike managed to lift himself up enough that he could reach and grip the glass. He lifted it to his lips, his hand shaking, opened his mouth and downed the liquid. When he finished, the glass slipped from his hand and fell to the floor beside the couch, and Mike flopped back on the sofa and closed his eyes.

Forty-one

Jack gave Janine the good news that Emma would have a room ready for her by late afternoon. Janine smiled. "That's wonderful news. She is so kind to be doing this for me. I'll begin looking for a place right away, though.

"Now, first things first; I need to call my work and let them know what has happened and ask if I might take a week of my holidays."

"Sounds like a good idea," Jack remarked. "If you need anything, don't hesitate to ask."

"Just the use of your phone, if that's okay. I forgot to plug my cell into the charger last night," Janine admitted sheepishly.

"No problem." Jack stood and walked over to the coffee pot, which was still warm with the morning coffee. Pulling out the carafe, "Ready for another coffee ... maybe a bite to eat now?"

Janine's stomach growled, reminding her that she hadn't eaten yet. "Actually, that sounds good ... a couple pieces of toast would hit the spot."

Toby was sitting by his dishes in the corner of the kitchen, glaring at Jack. He knew it wasn't Jack's fault that Emma had lied, but now he had to figure out what was going on and how to convince Jack that Emma was still in danger. From herself or others. Of who, Toby wasn't sure of anymore!

Jack left to do some errands after fixing Janine's breakfast. "Coming along, old man?" he directed to Toby.

Toby flipped his tail and walked out of the kitchen. Within a few seconds, he was on the back of the couch, staring out the window. *I need to keep an eye on what's going on at Emma's.* Toby saw Emma and Duke in their backyard. She was working in her flowerbeds; the dog was lying under the maple tree.

Resting his head on his paws, Toby decided there was nothing more he could do about the situation right now. He was exhausted from having stayed awake for much of the night. A catnap was obligatory to refuel his body and his mind.

Janine grinned when she entered the living room and saw Toby sound asleep on the back of the couch. Not wanting to disturb him, she picked up the portable phone and the newspaper and returned to the kitchen to browse through the apartment rentals and make her calls.

The first call was to her workplace. "Janine! We've been so worried about you," Freda, Janine's boss exclaimed. Freda was in her fifties and had managed the office for the warehousing company for her brother-in-law since his wife passed away twenty years ago. Janine was her right-hand in the office. "Are you okay, girl?" Freda added.

"I've been better, that's why I'm calling. I need to take a week of my holidays … Mike and I are no longer together, and I have to find a place to live…" Janine went on to explain to Freda that she'd also just lost her baby—Freda was the only one at the office who knew about Janine's pregnancy—and she needed some time to heal, as well.

"You take all the time you need, girl," Freda returned understandingly. "If you need more than a week, just give me a call. Take care of yourself and keep in touch, okay?"

Janine knew that was her cue to say goodbye and let Freda get back to work. "Will do … thanks, Freda … I'll keep you posted."

After hanging up the phone, Janine leaned back in the chair and gazed out the kitchen window. Freda always sounded concerned, but, in reality, she was all business. She was not anyone's friend in the office—she was the boss. Her kindness only extended as far as she deemed necessary, and Janine was aware that if she prolonged her absence too long, she might just find herself out of a job.

Janine turned her eyes to the newspaper on the table. She flipped through to the real estate section and began scanning down the columns for apartment rentals, circling two or three possibilities.

Toby was startled awake by a light knock on the front door. He looked around, knowing Jack wasn't home, but Janine was. Where was she? In answer to his question, Janine walked into the living room, heading for the door.

"I'll get that, Toby," she grinned.

To Toby's surprise, their visitor was Emma. Toby was disappointed, though, when he saw Duke was with her. *What's up with that ... she never brings the mutt over here!*

"Emma!" Janine sounded surprised to see her. "Jack's not home at the moment," she added, assuming Emma wanted to talk to him.

"That's okay," Emma replied. "I'm just on my way out for a run and thought to stop by and let you know I'll be gone for about an hour. I just finished the room for you and you can move in after lunch if you like." Emma paused. "We can discuss all the details of your stay once you are settled."

"That will be great," Janine returned. "I hope it is not an imposition for you ... me being there ... I have found a couple possible apartments and am going to check them out. They aren't available for a month, though."

"Not a problem at all," Emma smiled sweetly. Duke was growling now that he'd noticed Toby sitting on the back of the couch. "Well, guess I better get on my way; Duke and Toby are not the best of friends," she laughed. "See you later," she called back as she turned and headed down the steps.

Janine closed the door and turned to Toby. "I'm going to pack my suitcase; would you like to join me, Toby?"

Toby jumped down from the couch and followed Janine to the room Jack had hosted her in. It would be good to get the house back to themselves again—a couple old bachelors. However, there was still the issue of what was going on with Emma. *Not only do I have to worry about Emma, now, with Janine living there, I might also have to worry about her, as well!*

Forty-two

Jack couldn't help thinking about how he'd first met Janine, about the story she'd told him in the parking lot. He couldn't get it out of his head that she didn't want to charge her ex-boyfriend with abuse. It didn't sit right in his gut. He also thought how weird it was that Janine and Emma had met in the park, and how Emma had helped Janine. Why hadn't Emma mentioned anything about the incident when she was over for supper? Jack thought that would have been a newsworthy piece of information to share. And Janine hadn't mentioned that the woman who helped her in the park was named Emma when Jack had said who their neighbour was.

And there was the way Toby was behaving. Toby only acted this way if there was something wrong and all the indicators pointed to the fact something was going on with Emma. Jack had noticed the look Toby had thrown Emma's way when she'd denied the note had anything to do with her.

Jack turned onto Gretzky Parkway, heading toward the police station. He felt a need to have a heart-to-heart conversation with Chief Bryce Wagner.

After hearing Jack's concerns, Bryce leaned back in his chair, folding his hands behind his head. Finally, "I hear your concerns, Jack, but you know as well as I, there's nothing we can do unless the girl wants to lay charges." Bryce leaned forward with a grin, "As for what Toby is trying to tell you, your guess would be as good as mine. We just have to bide our time and see what else that old cat comes up with so we can be clear on details. We can't go off half-cocked based on an animal's idea that your Emma is in trouble."

Jack couldn't help chuckling, because when he thought about what he was suggesting—based on Toby's actions—he realized how ridiculous the story could be perceived.

Bryce stood and extended his hand to Jack. "Keep me posted, buddy. In the meantime, go home and get some rest; you look tired."

"Just getting old," Jack smirked. "Me and that old cat of mine."

The friends laughed. Jack took his leave. Bryce returned to his paperwork.

On the way back to his place, Jack drove past Mike's house. He slowed down and then pulled over and stopped. The truck was still in the driveway, but it looked as though it had been moved since he'd been there with Janine to pick up her belongings. It was parked crooked.

Jack gave his head a shake. "You're reading too much into this man," he mumbled. "The guy probably went out drinking and came home a bit drunk ... couldn't park straight." Jack pulled away and drove home.

When Jack arrived home, he found Janine making a phone call in the kitchen.

"Okay, thank you for your time," Janine said and hung up the phone. She picked up her pen and stroked across one of the ads she'd circled in the paper. Looking up at Jack, "That apartment is gone."

"You'll find one ... it takes time. I'm sure Emma won't mind if it takes a couple months." Jack walked over to the fridge and took out some eggs. Turning back to Janine, "Who knows, Emma might even decide you can stay long-term. With her brother being in jail for a long time to come, she might enjoy the company."

Janine's face blanched. "Her brother's in jail? You never mentioned this before." Janine wasn't sure she wanted to make a move to a person whose family member was incarcerated—at least not until she knew what sort of crime they'd committed. "What did he do?" she asked hesitantly.

Jack sat down at the table across from Janine and cleared his throat nervously. Not a subject he really wanted to address; nevertheless, he knew it would be better to be upfront, something he probably should have been when it was first mentioned about the possibility of a room at Emma's place.

Briefly, Jack filled Janine in on the situation: "Emma and her brother, Camden, moved here from British Columbia. Camden had a job at the gym just down the street from our house. He was a shy young man, and it was apparent from the beginning that he was dedicated to his sister, to the point, in my opinion, of being overprotective. Camden and Toby didn't get along, but Toby and Emma became the best of friends.

"Not long after Camden and Emma arrived here, there appeared to be a series of people dying from strange flu-like symptoms. After the first couple of deaths, the police began to get suspicious and, due to a shortage of officers, the captain—the one you met at the station—asked me if I would like to help out by investigating the victims to see if there was some sort of connection between them.

"To make a long story short, the only connection we eventually found was that they all attended the same gym. The one just down the street." Jack paused a moment and smirked. "It was Toby that figured it all out, and he saved the sixth victim from a sure death. Camden was caught, tried, and incarcerated, leaving Emma alone. She knows nobody here except me and Toby, and a couple of my close friends. We look out for her."

Janine was curious as to why Camden had killed people. "Why did he commit these murders?"

The subject was delving further into the story than he really wanted to go; however, Janine deserved to know the whole story, and he also wanted to make sure he assured her that Emma was nothing like her brother.

"Camden's and Emma's childhood was not … how shall I say it … very nice. Their parents abandoned them and they were shuffled from foster home to foster home until one day … I believe Emma was around sixteen at the time … Camden found out she was being raped by the foster father. They made a run for it and never looked back."

"However, due to years of his own abuse from some of the foster parents, topped off by what he learned about his sister's abuse, I guess he snapped. He started poisoning people, so many– –usually six at a time—and then move on to another location…"

"How did he poison them?" Janine intervened.

"Camden worked at gyms and if someone offended him in any way, he would send them an email, which, in short, would ask them to repent of their negative behaviour. The message would threaten if they didn't, they would have to pay the consequences. When they didn't repent to his satisfaction, he spiked their smoothies with ricin, which causes flu-like symptoms, and if it wasn't discovered in time, it would cause death," Jack leaned back, hoping he wouldn't have to say anything more.

"I'm not sure…" Janine began.

Jack quickly cut Janine off: "You have nothing to worry about where Emma is concerned," he said. "She wouldn't hurt a fly."

"She stopped by this morning," Janine informed. "She was on her way out for a run with her dog and just wanted to tell me I could move in this afternoon after lunch."

"Well, now that you know about Emma's brother, it's up to you if you still want to move in," Jack stated, noticing the hesitation in Janine's voice.

The kitchen was quiet. Janine was thinking about her options; Jack was hoping he hadn't scared her away from the room at Emma's. Finally, heaving a deep sigh, "Well, I guess it won't hurt to get to know Emma," Janine expressed.

"Good ... I'll make us up some eggs now ... want some bacon, too?" Jack queried, standing up and heading to the fridge.

"Just eggs would be great," Janine replied.

"Eggs it is, then." Jack pulled a frying pan out of the cupboard and began the lunch-making process.

Toby, who had been lingering in the hallway just outside of the kitchen, wandered into the room. Sitting by his empty dish, he turned and let out a loud meow in Jack's direction.

Janine laughed and got up from the table. "I'll feed Toby for you."

Toby flipped his tail in the air and dug into the kibble. When he finished, he looked back at Jack and Janine, who were just sitting down to eat, and then left through his cat door.

Think I'll check things out at Emma's ... I'm still not comfortable with everything I know ... that Mike was there ... Emma getting Mike's truck and then carrying him out of her house ... her denial about the note ... why did she lie ... things just aren't adding up! How do I get this across to Jack so he can do what needs to be done to save our Emma?

Forty-three

Emma did another quick sweep through the house to assure herself that all evidence of Mike was erased. She took the bottle of Rohypnol up to her room and stuffed it at the back of her top drawer, along with her headache medication. "Can't have Janine finding something like that lying around," she muttered, heading back downstairs.

After having a grilled cheese sandwich, Emma decided to walk over to Jack's and tell Janine she was ready for her. She put Duke out in the back yard before leaving.

Jack and Janine were just finishing their lunch when Emma arrived. She knocked lightly on the back door. "Hello," she called out.

Janine got up from the table: "I'll get it, Jack. Emma must be ready for me." She opened the door with a smile. "Come in, Emma. Jack and I just finished eating, but I have most of my stuff packed and ready to go. Jack has graciously agreed to keep my other stuff here until I find a permanent place."

Emma stepped in the house. "I can help you with anything you need to bring over now then … save Jack the trip over." Emma looked around. "Where's Toby?"

"He took off after he finished his kibble," Jack chuckled. "Probably went over to your place," he added.

"Oh, I didn't see him," Emma said, her heart skipping a beat. *That old cat is trouble … so nosey … I hate it that he's always snooping around … and the note he took home and gave to Jack, bringing Jack back to my place … implying it had something to do with me … I think it's time to cut the apron string from Toby and send him back home every time he comes*

117

over. His nosiness doesn't fit in with my plans—now or anything I might have in the future once I get Janine out of my house!

Jack had said something, but Emma's mind had been elsewhere. When she realized he must have asked her a question, Emma cleared her throat. "Sorry … I was daydreaming … what were you saying, Jack?"

"I was just saying if Toby wasn't at your place, he might have just found a nice cool spot in the shade somewhere … maybe even went hunting, although that's a longshot where Toby's concerned." A hint of humour was sprinkled through Jack's words.

Emma nodded, then turned to Janine who had brought a couple suitcases into the kitchen while Jack and Emma were discussing Toby.

"Ready when you are," Janine said. Turning to Jack, she extended her hand. "I can't thank you enough for all you've done for me. As soon as I get a permanent place, I'll get my stuff out of your way."

"No problem," Jack returned. "Take your time; I'm not going anywhere. Make sure you find the right place."

"Thanks." Janine picked up one of the suitcases, Emma grabbed the other one.

Jack saw them to the door and watched the two young women walk down the sidewalk toward Emma's house. Something was bothering Jack, though. He couldn't put a finger on it, but one thing he did know—Toby had a nose for trouble, and there was something about Emma that was bothering the old cat. Seldom was Toby ever wrong when he had a hunch, and over the past few days, Toby had definitely been trying to tell Jack something. He just had to figure out what it was!

Chapter Forty-four

Emma led Janine up the stairs and showed her into Camden's old room. All traces of her brother had been removed, leaving nothing but a bed and a dresser. The window had a white blind on it, pulled half-way down.

"Sorry, there's only one bathroom in this house," Emma said, pointing to a door at the end of the hall.

"No problem," Janine expressed. "I'm used to sharing a bathroom." She took a deep breath. "I promise not to put you out for any longer than necessary. It must be an imposition for you, taking someone you barely know into your home. I don't expect to stay here for free either, so whatever you think is fair for me to pay, just let me know. I've never not paid my way in life."

"Why don't you get settled in here and then come downstairs. We'll discuss full arrangements then. I am on a limited income, so any little bit helps."

Half an hour later, Janine approached Emma in the living room. Emma was sitting on the couch, writing numbers on a piece of paper.

"Hey there," Emma said, pointing to the spot beside her on the couch. "Have a seat. I've worked out something here," she handed Janine the paper. "How's this?"

Janine glanced at the numbers. "This is more than generous," she whispered emotionally. She was overwhelmed with the kindness of these strangers who had happened into her life.

"We have a deal then," Emma said, standing. She looked at her watch. "I need to take Duke for a run now, if you don't mind," she said. "Make yourself at home. When I return, maybe we can go for some groceries. You'll have to drive; I don't have a licence."

"That'll be no problem. As long as I'm here, I can take you anywhere you need." Janine set the paper on the coffee table and stood. "While you're gone for a run, I'm going to slip out to the bank. It'll save time if I grab some money now."

Emma nodded as she grabbed Duke's leash off its hook. Glancing back for a moment, before heading out to the back yard to get her dog, Emma smirked. *Life is so weird ... so unfair. But she won't be here long, and then, once she leaves, I can get back to my mission!*

Chapter Forty-five

Janine got in her car and drove to the bank. After pulling enough money to cover a week's board, some extra to help with the food, and personal spending money, Janine decided to drive past Mike's house and see if he was home. She had no idea what she was going to do if he was; she didn't really want to see him again. But something was bothering her about how she and Jack had found the house when they'd gone to get her belongings.

Slowing down, then coming to a stop in front of Mike's, Janine sat in the car for a few minutes, staring at the house. The truck was in the driveway. The living room curtains were pulled across. Everything looked okay.

Maybe I should just check on him ... make sure he's okay. Slowly, she turned off the car, got out, and walked up the sidewalk to the front door. Janine rang the doorbell and stood back. *Why aren't you answering the door, Mike?*

Janine shivered again as another eerie feeling crept through her body. She reached in her purse and pulled out her set of house keys. As she put the key into the lock, she discovered the door was already unlocked. Janine turned the knob, and the door swung open. She stepped inside and put her hand over her nose, trying to block out the stench that accosted her.

Another wave of apprehension gushed through her veins as she advanced toward the living room. The smell was more pronounced. Janine gasped when she saw Mike sprawled on the couch. There was an empty glass on the floor—Janine assumed it had been filled with alcohol since there was an open whiskey bottle on the coffee table. A partially eaten T.V. dinner was there, as well.

You aren't interested in changing, are you, Mike? What made me think you might ... that there was even the slimmest chance you would get back on your feet and maybe we could start again.

Janine turned to leave, but something compelled her to turn back and really look at Mike. Staring intensely, she realized there was something not right about the way he looked. His skin was so pale, his cheeks sunken, and dark rings circled his eyes. Janine noticed he'd soiled himself, in more ways than one. He also looked as though he'd been beaten. There were cuts and bruises all over his face and any skin that was exposed.

Pulling out her cell phone, Janine dialled 911.

Twenty minutes later, an ambulance pulled up in front of Mike's house. Janine was glad she'd also called Jack immediately after talking to the 911 dispatcher. He arrived with Toby ten minutes before the paramedics. Janine had busied herself, trying to tidy up some of the mess, embarrassed that anyone would see the house she used to take such pride in so dirty.

Jack walked quickly to her, taking her by the elbow. "Don't touch anything," he warned. "Until we know what happened here, anything could be evidence."

Janine looked up at Jack, the remains of the dinner dish in her hand. Gently, Jack took it from her and set it back on the coffee table. "Come and sit down," he directed. "The ambulance should be here any minute."

Toby sat in the living room doorway, observing the scene. His heart was in his throat. *What have you done, Emma? I saw too much, but how do I tell Jack all I know?*

Jack and Janine were sitting in chairs in the corner of the living room when the ambulance arrived. Jack looked seriously disturbed; Janine stared into space, totally shocked at what was transpiring in front of her.

The paramedics were working furiously on Mike, trying to revive him.

"Got a pulse, but it's weak," one of them commented as they were attempting to hook an IV into Mike's arm.

The other paramedic called to the hospital and let them know they would be bringing in a young man who was comatose and whom they believed had taken a drug overdose, mixed with alcohol. They had no idea what drug or drugs were involved, but there was a glass on the floor, and it still had some liquid in it. They were going to bag it and bring it with them for testing, however, with all the confusion, the glass was forgotten on the floor.

By the time the ambulance was ready to leave, Janine was shaking uncontrollably. Jack put his arm around her shoulders. "It'll be okay," he attempted to comfort her. "He's in good hands now."

Janine swiped a hand across her eyes, catching some of her tears that had sprung forth. "I shouldn't have left him," she said, her words gurgling through the emotion in her throat. "I need to go to the hospital with him. He doesn't have anyone else."

Jack knew better than to argue with the young woman. "I can drive you if you like," he offered. "You're in no condition to drive."

"I'll be fine," Janine said, straightening her shoulders, and digging her car keys from her purse. "I was supposed to go grocery shopping with Emma ... could you please tell her what's happened and that I'm sorry. I'll be home as soon as I know Mike is okay."

Reluctantly, Jack agreed to pass the message on. "Keep me posted, though. You have my cell number?"

"Yes."

Janine made her way out the door, Jack and Toby close on her heels. In her car, Janine's hand shook as she tried to put the key in the ignition. Jack watched, wanting to step in and rescue his new friend, but he knew she didn't want help right now. Instead, he tapped her car door and gave her a reassuring smile. Janine nodded and finally drove off for the hospital.

Jack went straight to Emma's place before going home. He knocked on the door a couple times but got no answer. He looked in the backyard for Duke but didn't see the dog. "I guess they must be out for a run, old man," Jack said to Toby. "We'll have to catch Emma later."

Toby was frustrated. *Oh, Emma. What have you done? I hope you didn't kill this guy ... that would break my heart ...can't wait to see your reaction when Jack tells you where Janine is!*

Jack and Toby settled down in the living room, Jack with his newspaper, Toby with an eye out the window for Emma. To his surprise, Emma and Duke were on their way to Jack's house.

Emma came up the steps, her face red from her run, and knocked lightly on the door. "I saw you at my place," she said when Jack opened the door.

Jack ran a hand through his hair. "Yeah, I have a message for you from Janine. She decided to stop by her boyfriend's place, and a good thing she did, because it looks like he overdosed on some kind of drug. Looked like he was in a fight too. Bruises and cuts all over him. Janine called an ambulance, and he's on his way to the hospital. She went with him."

Emma's insides flipped a dozen times. Toby, who had followed Jack to the door, studied his friend's reaction, knowing why she had turned pale and was shaking.

How are you going to get out of this, Emma? Toby sat behind Jack, not wanting to get confrontational with Duke.

"You okay, Emma?" Jack questioned when he saw how ashen her face had gone the further into his story he'd gotten.

Emma gave her head a shake. *Pull it together, girl ... you need to think about what you're going to do ... maybe Janine will go back to the prick, if he survives, then I won't have to deal with either one of them!* To Jack, "I'm just surprised, Jack. How could Janine even think about going back to that guy?"

"She wasn't going back to him," Jack informed. "She said she just felt something was wrong and wanted to check on him. Good thing she did, too, because if she hadn't, Mike might have died."

"I see. Well, I guess no matter how much of a scumbag the guy is, he deserves to live." Emma grimaced. Just saying that went against the grain of what she had committed herself to do to try and teach abusers a lesson. "Maybe he overdosed because he was truly sorry," she added.

"Maybe." A pause. "Janine's going to give me a call when she's sure Mike is okay."

Emma turned to go down the steps. "Well, I guess I'll head home and have a shower and wait for Janine to call. Keep me posted, Jack."

"Will do." Jack closed the door.

Toby returned to his perch on the back of the couch and watched Emma walk down the sidewalk. She looked back a couple times. He saw the anger on her face. Toby began to fear even more, not just for Emma, but for what she might do to Janine—or Mike—if the guy got out of the hospital in one piece!

Chapter Forty-six

Janine sat in the ER waiting room while the doctors and nurses worked on Mike. Despite everything he'd done to her over the past few months, and having lost their baby, Janine loved Mike. The man he'd been, and could be again if he just started believing in himself.

Reception called her name and Janine made her way up to the desk. The nurse was looking down at some papers. "You called me?" Janine mentioned. "Do you have an update on Mike Sanderson?"

"I'm afraid there isn't much more to tell you. Mr. Sanderson still has not gained consciousness. However, the police have been called, and the officers would like to speak with you." The nurse pointed to a door and pushed a button to open it. "Go through those doors and turn right at the first hallway. The officers are in the nurses' station there."

Janine hurried through the door and to the room she'd been directed to. The police officers, a male and a female, stood as she entered, and introduced themselves.

"Officer MacDonald," the woman informed. Turning to her partner, "Officer Hendricks."

"You're the woman who made the 911 call?" Hendricks asked, not wasting any time.

Janine nodded.

Hendricks motioned to the door. "Let's go somewhere private; we have a few questions for you."

Janine went with the officers, sandwiched between them as they made their way through a maze of hallways until finally settling in a small room on the edge of the ER. Hendricks pointed to a single chair on one side of a small conference table, and he and Officer MacDonald sat opposite her. MacDonald pulled a writing pad and a pen out of her shirt pocket and laid them on the table.

Hendricks took the lead: "We just want to clarify that you are not in trouble. We simply need to get your story on how you came across Mr. Sanderson. Is that okay with you?"

Janine folded her hands in her lap, hiding them under the table so the police officers wouldn't be able to see them shaking. She knew she had nothing to hide, but there was an arrogant air about the officers that troubled her—especially the male.

MacDonald picked up the pen. "State your full name, please, for the record."

"Janine Larsen."

The personal questions kept coming: birthday, parents' names, workplace, current address, etc. Finally, Hendricks took over. "Why were you at Mike Sanderson's house?" he questioned, his eyes piercing Janine's with a no-nonsense stare.

Janine cleared her throat and looked away for a moment, unable to speak. How much about her private life did these officers know? It was enough that she'd bared her soul to Jack in the police parking lot; she didn't want the entire Brantford police force knowing about her private affairs. Looking back at the officers, who were staring impatiently awaiting her answer, Janine decided to give enough information to satisfy them, but no more than that.

"I was worried about him. We had a parting of ways and Mike didn't take my leaving him very well," Janine began. "When I went to get my belongings from the house, I had the feeling something was wrong. Mike's truck was in the driveway, but he wasn't home."

"You went alone to the house?" Hendricks questioned.

127

"Oh no! I was accompanied by a police officer," Janine informed, not telling Hendricks Jack's name.

"Why did you think it was strange Mike wasn't home and his truck was? Maybe you just missed him … maybe he went for a walk," Hendricks suggested.

"Mike is not a walker—any more than necessary," Janine informed.

"Was your parting of ways, as you put it, congenial?" Hendricks changed direction.

Janine twisted her hands in her lap, not wanting to answer truthfully but knowing she must. "Not exactly."

"Explain the circumstances," Hendricks pushed, while MacDonald continued writing on the notepad.

Drawing in a shuddering breath, "Mike had become violent in the past few months since he lost his job. He'd started drinking heavily and doing some drugs…"

"What kind of drugs?"

"I don't know. I was working, and when I'd come home, if Mike wasn't passed out on the couch, he would set into me. I'd finally had enough and asked him to meet me at the park close to our place. I was going to end it with him, and I wanted to do so in a public setting."

"Because you feared for your life?" Hendricks inquired.

"Yes. He'd started out with slaps, which progressed to punches, which progressed to full out beatings. Yes, Officer Hendricks, I definitely feared for my life."

"What happened when you told him you were leaving?"

"He lost it on me … even in a public park. Started pushing me around, then dragged me to his truck and shoved me in. There was no escaping him. He drove back to our place and he dragged me out of the truck, into the house, and beat me within an inch of my life before he finally fell to the floor in a drunken stupor."

"Did you leave then?"

"No, I could barely move. And my car was still at the park. I crawled to the bedroom and managed to get on the bed. I fell asleep. I woke early in the morning and got in the shower and cleaned myself up, hoping I could get out of the house before Mike came to. As I was drying off, I heard him outside the bathroom door."

"What was his mood in the morning?" Hendricks pushed for more information.

"Mike begged me to stay, but there must have been some resolve in my voice that he didn't want to cross, especially when he could see what he'd done to me. Mike is always apologetic after the beatings, promising never to do it again. I told him I just wanted to take a few things and that I would be back with a police escort to get the rest of my belongings."

"How did he take that?"

"Not well, but he finally stepped aside and let me go after I told him we could talk later."

MacDonald set her pen down and tapped her fingers on the table. She looked at Janine and shook her head. "You must have been pretty pissed off with Mike?"

Janine wasn't sure if MacDonald was asking a question or making a statement. So she answered with what she thought would be the safest statement: "I was more upset than pissed, as you put it."

Hendricks turned in another direction now. "So, what did you do when you left the house?"

"Like I already told you, my car was still at the park, so I walked there … it isn't far from where Mike lives. I drove around for a bit, but I wasn't feeling well … I ended up back at the park, left my car parked and went and sat on a swing. I was in severe pain … if you want the entire horrid story, I was having a miscarriage. Mike's last beating made sure I wouldn't be having his baby." Janine's voice lowered to almost a whisper.

"Did he know you were pregnant?" MacDonald asked.

"Yes."

"And he still beat you?"

"Yes."

MacDonald wrote something more on the pad, and Hendricks continued with the questions.

"How did you manage to get to the hospital?" he probed.

Janine smiled. "A good Samaritan happened by. She called the ambulance."

"Okay … so, I take it you did lose your baby?"

"Yes."

"How did that make you feel toward Mike? Were you angry?"

"I was upset." Janine focused her gaze on MacDonald. "Do you have children?"

"One."

"How would you have felt if you never had that child? If you had miscarried it—for any reason? Upset, right? So, like I said, I was upset."

"Upset enough to have returned to the house after leaving the hospital, catch Mike off-guard, and beat him?" Hendricks leaned over the table and fixed Janine with an icy glare.

Janine didn't like the direction the line of questioning was taking. "I think I would like to call a friend before I answer any more of your questions," she specified, a firm set to her lips.

"A friend? Not a lawyer?" Hendricks' eyebrows rose questioningly.

"A friend … Jack Nelson … I believe he's a former police officer with your force, according to Bryce Wagner." Janine figured throwing a couple names from the police force around—especially the captain's—would get Hendricks to back off.

"I know Jack—him and his cat, Toby," Hendricks said. He looked thoughtful for a moment, wondering if Jack was the officer who had helped Janine retrieve her belongings from Mike Sanderson's house. "How do you know Jack?"

"I met him at the police station when I went there to get an officer to help me, and the captain suggested Jack could assist me. He's been helping me ever since … found me a temporary place to live until I find my own apartment." Janine paused, and then with a firm voice, "I'm not going to say anything more until I talk to Jack." She sat back in her chair and folded her arms across her chest. *Jack, I trust … but not these two … especially not Hendricks!*

Half an hour later, Jack entered the room. He nodded to both officers, then took a seat beside Janine. "What's going on here, Hendricks?" Jack asked, turning to the male officer.

"Just routine questions, Jack. Janine was the one who found the guy. You know we have to question her."

Jack's brow furrowed inward as he studied the situation in the room—the two police officers and Janine. He noticed how pale Janine was and the number of notes MacDonald had taken.

"I guess the question I want to ask," Jack finally said, "is why such extensive questioning? Has the patient succumbed to his injuries?"

Hendricks shook his head and scowled. "No."

Jack helped Janine to her feet. "Then we are done here. There's no need to be bothering the young woman who probably saved the man's life. Let's go, Janine."

Janine shook uncontrollably as Jack led her from the room and down the hallway toward the front entrance of the hospital. He stopped at the ER door. "Let's leave a message at the desk for them to call you if there's an update on Mike's condition. I think you need to go home and rest."

"Okay ... I am exhausted," Janine stated tiredly. She stayed close to Jack while he talked to the nurse, keeping her eye out for the two police officers, fearing they might still come after her. *I've nothing to be worried about ... I've done nothing wrong ... I need to stop being so afraid.*

When Jack finished giving reception Janine's information, he took her by the arm again and steered her out of the hospital. "Where's your car parked?" he asked.

"In the main parking lot."

"I'm down at the bottom of the hill," Jack said. He wasn't one to spend a nickel if he didn't have to, and walking up the hill was good exercise. "I'll see you to your car first," he added.

"I'll be fine; I'll meet you back at the house." Janine walked in the direction of the parking lot, not waiting for Jack to insist he accompany her.

Forty-seven

Emma paced around her three-season room, frustrated with the situation. She couldn't have foreseen Janine going to Mike's house and finding him, and she hadn't expected Janine to call an ambulance for the scumbag!

Duke showed up at the backdoor, wagging his tail, whining to be let in. Emma opened the door and Duke charged into the room, pushing his nose at his mistress. Absently, Emma patted her dog on the head and then pushed him away. "Not now, Duke. I need space to think. We … I have a problem … at least I think I do."

Emma continued her pacing while Duke sat patiently, waiting for her to let him into the house. Emma didn't hear Janine come in and jumped when her new tenant opened the door to the three-season room.

"Janine! You startled me!" Emma's hand clapped to her chest.

"I'm sorry. Didn't mean to. I just came from the hospital."

"Yes, Jack informed me that you found your ex passed out on the couch at his place," Emma said, avoiding looking directly at Janine.

"He was more than passed out. He was almost dead. I don't think he would be alive now if I hadn't happened along."

Emma pushed past Janine, who was still standing in the doorway. "Why would you go to the house anyway—after what he did to you?"

Janine turned and followed Emma into the kitchen. "I don't really know why if you want the truth. I just had a gut feeling something was off the day Jack took me over to get my things. Mike's truck was there, but he wasn't, and I've never known him to be one to go for an afternoon walk. Usually, by midmorning, Mike was so inebriated he could barely stand."

Emma walked over to the sink and turned the cold water tap on, letting it run while she reached for a glass. "So, maybe he did go for a walk. After all, you weren't around anymore. Things change."

Janine detected a hint of tension in Emma's voice and wondered why. Instead of questioning Emma about her mood, Janine defended her position. "Well, like I said, it's a good thing I did stop in. Despite what he did to me, I don't want him dead. I should have stayed with him, been more understanding. If I'd encouraged him to get help, maybe we could have worked things out, and he wouldn't be lying in a hospital right now fighting for his life."

Emma leaned against the counter, sipping her water, studying Janine. *Take it easy ... don't blow things now ... no one has any idea what I've done ...there's nothing to tie me to Mike ... let it go ... if Janine wants to play nursemaid to the bastard that beat her, let her ... maybe she'll go back to his house and get out of my life.* Emma finished her water and set her glass in the sink.

"I'm sorry, Janine," she said, trying to sound sincere. "I guess I am just worried about you. After all, I found you in the park and saw first-hand what Mike did to you."

Janine nodded understandingly. "It's okay." Janine didn't want to discuss the issue any further. The last thing she wanted to do was tell Emma that the police had questioned her and had only stopped when she'd called Jack. Janine had met Jack on the sidewalk when they'd returned home and told him she wanted to lie down. He'd said he would call her later. "Do you mind if I go

upstairs and have a rest? This whole ordeal has exhausted me."
Janine walked toward the stairs, not waiting for an answer.

Emma watched her tenant go up the stairs, then grabbed
Duke's leash. "Come on, boy. Let's go for another run. I need to
get out of this house!"

Toby was hiding in the long grass at the side of Emma's house.
He'd watched Emma as she'd paced. He'd heard Emma and
Janine talking. He'd observed how uptight Emma was, and he
was the only one that knew why.

Heading for home after Emma left the house with Duke,
Toby felt his own frustration. *How do I get you to listen to me,
Jack? How am I going to save Emma—if it's not already too
late!*

Forty-eight

The doctor studied Mike's chart, his brow furrowed in frustration. "I don't think this is a clear-cut case of alcohol poisoning," he stated.

The head nurse, Lucy Cameron, came up beside him. "He reeks of booze," she said, pointing to the alcohol level in the blood test that had been taken when he first arrived at the hospital. "And this level—2.5—confirms he was feeling no pain."

The doctor nodded, but still had a puzzled look on his face. "I agree that it is an extremely high level, but he wouldn't be this comatose just on alcohol. I have a feeling he was mixing drugs with the liquor—or someone spiked his drink." The doctor glanced down the list of tests that had been done. "Let me know as soon as any of these tox reports come in, and if he wakes up before then, call me."

Two hours later, Mike opened his eyes. He tried to focus, to figure out where he was. He tried to get up but couldn't seem to move. His limbs felt like lead. His head was pounding. Mike squinted, looking at his hand where a needle and hoses were attached, running up to a bag with a clear liquid that was hanging on a post. He groaned.

"You're awake," a nurse said, entering the room. She did a quick examination of Mike after buzzing for another nurse to join her. Within a minute of the page, Lucy Cameron hurried in.

"He's awake?" she asked, moving straight to Mike's bedside. "Do you know where you are, sir?"

He stared at her blankly.

"Do you know where you are, sir?" Lucy repeated.

Mike shook his head.

"You're in the hospital. You were brought here by ambulance," Lucy continued.

Mike's tongue felt thick as he struggled to speak. "H-h-hos-p-p-pi-t-t-tal?

Lucy nodded. "Yes, you're at the Brantford General Hospital. Your girlfriend, I believe it was, called the ambulance. Apparently, she found you passed out on the couch."

Mike's mind tried to make sense of what the nurse was saying. *Hospital ... girlfriend ... I have a girlfriend ... why do I feel so confused ... why can't I move my legs, my arms ... my head ... oh, God ... it's pounding.* Mike couldn't put enough coherent thoughts together to actually converse, so he said nothing.

Lucy turned to the nurse who had paged her: "Call Doctor Carmichael. I'll stay here with our patient until he gets here."

Ten minutes later, Doctor Carmichael walked into Mike's room. "Has the patient indicated that he knows why he's here?" he directed to Lucy.

"Not really. The only thing Mike said was 'hospital,' and he could barely get that out."

The doctor leaned over Mike and checked his heart rate, then shone a small flashlight into his eyes. Standing and turning to Lucy, "He's definitely on some sort of drug," he said. "Any ideas?"

Lucy had an idea, but what she was thinking of was usually administered to women at a bar, so it didn't fit the profile in front of them. However, anything was possible. "With some of the symptoms the patient is exhibiting, do you think it possible he is on Rohypnol?"

Doctor Carmichael's eyebrows rose as he thought for a moment about what the nurse was suggesting.

"The police were here questioning his girlfriend. I believe they think there might be some foul play." Lucy hesitated, not wanting to accuse the young woman, but there was a possibility she'd done something to the patient. "The girlfriend could have drugged him, and then, having second thoughts about what she'd done, still called the ambulance."

"You think?" Doctor Carmichael picked up Mike's hand and checked his pulse.

Mike moaned, his eyes still open, trying to focus on the man who was standing by his bed. Finally, he managed to speak, his voice raspy: "Who are you?"

Doctor Carmichael glanced at Lucy, then back to Mike. He told Mike who he was, then asked: "Do you know why you are in the hospital?"

Mike shook his head.

The doctor repeated what Lucy had already told Mike. "Your girlfriend called 911. Apparently, she found you comatose on the couch. Do you have any memory of this?"

Mike shook his head again. *What are they talking about ... girlfriend ... passed out on couch...* Mike's eyes rolled around in his head as he tried to figure out what was going on.

Lucy stepped up to the opposite side of the bed from the doctor. "Do you remember anything about how you might have passed out?"

"No ... no, I have no idea what's going on." Mike was starting to put together words without stuttering. "You said my girlfriend called 911 ... is she here? Maybe if I saw this woman, it might jog my memory."

Doctor Carmichael motioned for Lucy to follow him out into the hallway. Out of earshot of Mike, "Is the girlfriend still here?"

"No. I believe she left with an older gentleman. He came to get her when she was being interviewed by the police. I saw them when they left the room where the police had been questioning the girl; the man didn't look impressed."

"Are the police still here?"

"No, they left as well, shortly after the girlfriend. They didn't look impressed either," Lucy told the doctor.

"Do you have the girlfriend's phone number?"

"Yes, it was left at the admittance desk."

"Have them call her and get her back here to the hospital. We need to put her in front of our patient and see if he recognizes her." Doctor Carmichael glanced in Mike's room for a second, then looked at his watch. "Page me when she gets here. I want to be in the room when our patient sees her."

Lucy took a quick look at Mike, and seeing that his eyes were closed again, she hustled off to the admittance desk. After acquiring Janine's number, Lucy went to the nurses' station and picked up the phone. She was about to hang up, having counted out seven rings, when a sleepy voice answered.

"Hello."

"Is this Janine?" Lucy needed to make sure she had the right person.

"Yes."

"I am Nurse Lucy Cameron from the ER. You are the young woman who was with Mike Sanderson?"

Janine sat up in her bed, alert now. "Is he okay? Has he woken up?"

Lucy cleared her throat. "Yes, he's awake. However, he's extremely confused. We'd like you to come back to the hospital and let him see you. It might help him to remember something."

"I can do that," Janine replied. There was a moment of hesitation as Janine breathed heavy into the receiver, fear that the police officers would be there to question her again. "Do you mind if I bring my friend with me?" she asked, feeling safer if she had Jack by her side.

139

"I don't see a problem with that; however, you will have to go into the room by yourself. Your friend will need to wait in the hall. As I said, Mike seems confused and unaware of what has happened to him."

Lucy wasn't sure how much she should tell Janine. She'd witnessed Mike's lack of knowledge of a girlfriend—of her identity. Lucy decided to repeat what the patient had said. "When we told Mike that his girlfriend had called 911 after finding him in his house, he was confused as to if he had a girlfriend, and he asked to see you with the hope it would jog his memory."

Janine got out of bed, the phone still to ear. "I'll be there as soon as possible," she said. "Thank you for calling me." After pushing 'end call,' Janine dialled Jack's number.

"Hello."

"Jack, I am sorry to ask this of you; you've been so good to me. I need you to come to the hospital with me. Apparently, Mike is awake, but he's bewildered. He wants to see me. I'm just afraid those police officers might still be there, and I don't trust them not to start badgering me with questions again." Janine let out a puff of breath.

"Can you give me about ten minutes?" Jack asked.

"No problem. Thank you, Jack. I don't know how I'll ever be able to repay you for all you are doing for me."

"Don't mention it. See you in ten."

Janine hurried to the bathroom and splashed water on her face. Looking in the mirror, she noticed the dark circles around her eyes. A voice at the door startled her.

"Everything okay?" Emma was leaning on the door jam.

"Mike woke up, and he's confused about what happened to him. A nurse from the hospital called and wants me to come up; she thinks Mike seeing me might help jolt his memory."

"I see." Emma swallowed nervously. "Would you like me to come with you?" Emma thought if Mike saw her and didn't recognize her, she would be in the clear.

"Thanks for the offer, but I already called Jack." Janine noticed a hurt look go across Emma's face. "I'm sorry. I just thought if the police were there still…"

"Of course. Jack will keep them away from you." Emma turned to leave. "Take care, Janine. And," pausing in the hallway, "don't let that guy get to you. Keep in mind, he's the one who beat you. He's the one who caused you to lose your baby. Don't let his condition soften your heart and make you decide to run back to him. Abusers never change their ways."

Before Janine could reply, Emma disappeared down the hall, and Janine heard a door open and close. Inside her room, Emma put her hands to her temples and pressed hard. The headache was rearing its ugliness. She slunk down to the floor, her back against the door. She groaned. And prayed.

Chapter forty-nine

Jack directed Janine straight to the ER reception desk and told the receptionist why he and Janine were there. They were buzzed through immediately and told to ask for the head nurse, Lucy Cameron.

"Please, have a seat," Lucy directed. "Doctor Carmichael wants to be in the room when Mr. Sanderson sees you, Janine."

It took the doctor fifteen minutes to get to the ER. "Sorry for the delay," he said, extending his hand first to Jack, and then to Janine. "An emergency I needed to tend to. Shall we?" he said, leading the way to Mike's room.

Lucy entered the room first. Jack remained in the hall but stood in the doorway so he could observe the interaction. The doctor stood at the end of the bed, and Janine stood beside Lucy on the right side of the bed.

Gently shaking Mike's shoulder, Lucy tried to wake him. "Mr. Sanderson, we have your girlfriend here."

Mike groaned. His eyes slit open, squinting against the light in the room.

Janine stepped closer to Mike and reached out, taking hold of his hand. "Mike … it's me … Janine."

Mike turned his focus toward the voice. "Janine?"

"Yes … Janine … I've been your girlfriend for the past year."

Swallowing hard, Mike shook his head. Silence echoed off the walls as the three people in the room waited patiently for a sign that Mike recognized Janine. Suddenly, his lips curled into a half-smile. "Janine," he whispered.

"This is a good sign," Doctor Carmichael stated from the end of the bed. He stepped closer to Mike. "Mr. Sanderson, I take it you recognize this woman?"

Mike slowly turned his head in the direction of the doctor's voice. "Yes ... yes, it's my girlfriend ... but ... but..." Mike was trying to clear his thoughts. *I know there's something more I need to know about this woman ... why can't I remember?*

Doctor Carmichael threw a questioning look at Janine. Then, "Your girlfriend found you at your house, passed out on the couch. Can you tell us anything about what you might have taken? Besides alcohol?" The doctor paused again. He directed his next question to Janine. "Or maybe you can tell us what he was taking ... or what you might have given him?"

Jack, still standing back in the doorway, didn't like the direction the line of questioning was taking. He stepped into the room, and scowling at the doctor, "Janine is separated from Mike, doctor. He was beating the crap out of her, and she just lost their baby. Whatever this guy was doing—or taking—Janine had nothing to do with it!"

Mike reverted his attention back to Janine and waves of memory strained to filter through to his mind. He'd heard what Jack was saying. *OMG! I was beating this beautiful woman ... my girlfriend ... she lost our baby ... I was going to be a father ... but they're saying I am on something ... what did I take ... obviously, I was drinking ... oh, God ... oh, God ... why can't I remember?*

Jack noticed Janine was shaking and he feared she was going to break down. He moved to her side and hooked his hand under her elbow. "We're leaving, Janine."

Hesitating, looking from Jack to Mike and back again, "But..." Janine tried to protest.

"No but ... you asked me to come with you for a reason, and I am telling you we are leaving now. Your *ex-boyfriend* is conscious now, and he's recognized you, which means he's probably going to be okay. The rest now is up to him and the doctors to discover what happened before you found him." Jack glared at the doctor. "Any problem with us leaving, doctor?"

Doctor Carmichael noticed the resolve on Jack's face. He decided not to argue with the man. He would call the police once Jack and Janine left; they would take it from there. Mike wouldn't be able to escape what he'd had done to his girlfriend, nor would whoever had beaten and drugged him escape their part.

"Waiting for your answer, doctor," Jack articulated.

"No problem."

"Good, let's go, Janine."

Before leaving the room, Janine squeezed Mike's hand. "Get better, Mike. We'll talk later. I'm so sorry." Tears streamed down her cheeks as she walked down the hallway with Jack.

Chapter Fifty

mma was sitting in the backyard when Janine arrived back at the house. "How did it go?" Emma asked, standing.

"Emotional. Mike recognized me," Janine replied.

"He did? Did he remember anything else … like how he came to be passed out?" Emma's blood was racing through her body. She felt flushed.

"Not really. Mike seemed confused, and he looked upset when Jack stepped in and said I was beaten and that I'd lost our baby. But he never said anything more. Not while I was still there, anyway."

Emma walked away from Janine, "There's some supper in the oven for you," she called back. "I'm going out for a run. Be back shortly."

When Janine walked into the house and noticed Duke was still there, she was puzzled why Emma hadn't taken her dog with her. Duke's tail thumped on the floor, but he didn't bother to get up. He laid his head back on his front paws and closed his eyes.

Janine took the casserole out of the oven and served herself a plate. She sat at the table, picking at the food, deep in thought.

"Maybe I was too hasty leaving Mike the way I did," she mumbled, looking at Duke. "I should have stayed and helped him work through his job loss." She drew in a shuddering breath. "But I couldn't. I couldn't take the beatings. My father never ever raised a hand to my mother, Duke … he didn't. I remember him and Mom discussing a news article about a man who'd beaten his wife to death, and Dad was so angry … said that no man should hit a woman." Janine was rambling now. "Mike was so

145

wonderful until he got laid off. Why did you change, Mike? Why did you have to ruin such a good thing?" Tears began to flow as Janine pushed away from the table and took her plate to the garbage can, scraping the food into the trash.

Heading upstairs to the room Emma had prepared for her, Janine prayed that she could just lay down on the bed and sleep undisturbed.

Fifty-one

Toby had been watching Emma when she'd been sitting in her yard. He was heartbroken by the sadness that seemed to surround her. He watched when Janine came home, and he should have gone home to Jack then, but something held him back. Toby detected the tightness in Emma's voice during her conversation with Janine.

And then, Emma had left the house—without Duke. Toby decided to follow her once he saw she was just walking. *I hope she's not going too far, I'm a bit tuckered.*

Toby was surprised Emma was going in the direction of the hospital. He could see the building in the near distance when Emma took the route leading under the railroad tracks off of Albion Street, then turned left at the stop sign, and right on the first street.

Look at the size of that hill! Boy, oh boy! This is going to be tough! Why are you going to the hospital, Emma—to visit Mike? But why? I'd think you wouldn't want to remind him about what you did to him.

Figuring Emma was going to the hospital, Toby decided not to climb the hill. He watched until he saw her turn left to the main entrance at the top of the hill. *Can't do anything, anyway ... no cat would be allowed in the hospital. I'll have to think of another way to discover why she's paying Mike a visit! Which is what she's doing, I'd bet my first detective certificate on!* Toby turned and headed for home.

Emma stopped at the information desk and asked what room Mike Sanderson was in. She was informed he was still in the ER;

however, he had been admitted and would be taken up to a room on the fourth floor within the next half hour. No visitors were allowed until he was settled.

"How long do you think that will be?" Emma inquired.

"Most likely about an hour," the volunteer receptionist replied.

Emma was impatient to see if Mike might remember her but knew she was going to have to wait. She went into the Tim Hortons and ordered a sandwich and a large tea, then took a seat by the window. Emma glanced at her watch. She would wait. She needed to be sure Mike couldn't—wouldn't—remember her.

On the way up to the fourth floor, an hour and a half later, Emma felt the tension in her muscles. Another headache was coming on and she cursed at the unfortunate timing of it. The hat, which she'd pushed her long hair under, wasn't helping any; it was too tight. But it was a necessity—a disguise.

Maybe there is another way I can disguise myself ... what if I were to borrow a lab coat, or perhaps I could put on a hospital gown and pretend I'm a patient ... that would bring less attention to me ... I could wander up and down the hall, checking the rooms until I find where he is... Emma was deep in thought as she exited the elevator.

Luck was with her. As she approached the double doors leading to the fourth-floor rooms, she saw a large cart stuffed with hospital gowns. Looking around to ensure she was alone, she grabbed two robes off the cart and, noticing an empty room to her right, Emma slipped in there and gowned up. She removed her runners and hat and hid them behind the couch in the room. She found an elastic band in her pocket and tied her hair back into a ponytail and stuffed it into the back of the gown. Sufficiently disguised now, Emma made her way onto the ward and started searching for Mike's room.

Several nurses passed her, but none paid any attention to the patient wandering down the hallway. Emma was beginning to worry that maybe she had the wrong floor. She was almost to the end of the ward before finally seeing Mike. Carefully, Emma walked past the room, glancing back to look inside from a different angle. Emma couldn't take a chance on bumping into a doctor or nurse who might be tending to their patient.

Once again, luck was with her. Mike was alone. Emma entered his room and closed the door. She stood at his bedside, staring at the man whom she'd tortured and drugged. His eyes were closed, and his breathing sounded shallow and raspy.

Emma reached out and shook his shoulder. Twice, before his eyes opened. He stared blankly at Emma, no recognition whatsoever in his eyes.

"Hello, Mike," Emma didn't use her pet name for him, not wanting to jog his memory too much.

Mike continued looking at her, blankly: "Do I know you?"

Emma backed away from the bed. "Sorry, I must have gotten the wrong room."

As Emma exited Mike's room and returned to where she'd left her shoes and hat, she failed to notice the two police officers who entered the ward from the opposite doors where she'd entered. They were going to Mike's room.

However, the officers saw Emma exiting his room. One of them even followed her, keeping their distance. They observed her go into a room outside the ward dressed as a patient and then leave, fully dressed, no hospital gown, wearing runners and a ball cap.

Emma was also unaware of the photo the officer took of her. A picture that would be shown to Mike. A picture that might just nudge his memory when it was ready to open to the past.

By the time Emma arrived home, her head was pounding. Totally ignoring Duke's request for some affection, she went straight to her room and dug around at the back of the top drawer of her dresser until her fingers closed around her bottle of pills. Popping two tablets into her mouth, Emma rushed to the bathroom, put the container on the counter, then leaned over the sink, turning the tap on and slurping water into her mouth to wash the drugs down. Returning to her room, Emma curled up under her covers and fell off to sleep. Had Emma read the label on the pill bottle, she would have realized she'd grabbed the wrong container.

Fifty-two

Janine woke up in the middle of the night, hungry. She made her way downstairs to the kitchen, where she found a desperate Duke wanting to go out.

"What's the matter, boy? Where's your Emma?" Janine asked on her way to the fridge.

Duke continued to whine at the door.

"Okay, I guess I can let you out. Probably better than having to clean up a mess in the morning." Janine opened the door to the three-season room, and then the outside entrance to the yard. "There you go."

Returning to the kitchen, Janine put a couple pieces of bread in the toaster, then sat at the table and waited. She was still in turmoil about what to do about Mike. *Maybe, I'll go up and see him in the morning, without Jack. He's great and all, trying to protect me, but he doesn't really know everything. Maybe I pushed Mike too far. If I hadn't told him I was leaving him, perhaps he wouldn't have beaten me so badly. I wouldn't have lost our baby...*

The toast popped. Absentmindedly, Janine buttered the bread. She didn't want anything else on it but poured a glass of water to wash it down. By the time she finished her snack, Duke was whining to be allowed back in.

Climbing the stairs back to her room after settling Duke with some fresh water and kibble in his dish, Janine made her way to the bathroom. As she washed her hands, she noticed a bottle of pills sitting on the counter. She picked it up, reading the label.

"Rohypnol? I wonder what this is for." Janine turned the bottle over and read the label on the back. The blood drained from her face as she read the side effects. *Why would Emma have this kind of drug in her house? Is she a drug addict? Is Jack not aware of this? I think I need to get out of here ... hopefully, Jack will take me back for a few days. If not, I'll just go to Mike's place and stay there until he gets out of the hospital. Maybe longer.*

Janine took the bottle of pills back to her room and slipped them into her suitcase. With any luck, she'd be able to make her way back to Jack and Toby's when Emma went for her run in the morning, and she would show Jack what she'd found.

In the morning, Janine went downstairs, expecting to see Emma up and ready to head out for her run. There was no sign of her new landlord and Duke was still lying beside the backdoor. He looked up when Janine entered the kitchen, stood, and walked to the door to be let out. Janine obliged him.

Thinking now would be as good a time as any to slip out to Jack's, Janine returned to her room, grabbed her two suitcases and proceeded back down the stairs. She went quickly to the back door and called Duke into the house, then slipped out the front door and made her way down the sidewalk to Jack's place, going around to the back door.

Janine knocked softly, stood back and waited. Within a couple of minutes, Jack answered. He glanced down at the two suitcases sitting beside his guest.

"What's wrong, Janine? Did something happen between you and Emma?"

"May I come in please, Jack? We need to talk."

Toby, who was just finishing his breakfast, perked up. *Something's not right here.* He went and stood by Jack in the doorway, waiting for his partner to invite Janine into the house.

Jack picked up the suitcases and motioned her in. Toby moved out of the way, making room for the humans to enter.

Jack set the luggage at the entrance to the hallway, then turned to Janine. "Have a seat ... do you want a drink ... some breakfast?"

"No, thanks. I couldn't eat anything right now."

Janine walked over to one of the suitcases and opened a small pocket on the side, pulling out the bottle of pills she'd stashed there the night before. She returned to the table and set them down, pointing to them. "I found these in Emma's bathroom last night."

Jack picked up the bottle and read the label—*Rohypnol*. A long, soft whistle escaped through his lips.

"Do you think Emma has a drug problem?" Janine asked timidly. She pointed to the side effects listed on the bottle. "Haven't you been wondering about her behaviour lately?" she questioned.

Running a hand through his thinning hair, Jack shook his head in bewilderment. "Well, she does seem different, but drugs ... hmmm ... not that I know of. Emma has always been quiet and reserved. She never went anywhere ... well, until recently. But now she just goes for runs with her dog. No friends coming and going. Very much a loner—before her brother was arrested, and since his incarceration." Jack turned the bottle over in his hand. "There has to be a rational explanation for this."

Toby, who was listening intently to the conversation, knew what the explanation was. He had firsthand knowledge of what Emma was up to. *It's not Emma taking the drugs, Jack. She must have been using them on Mike! And it's my guestimate that she overdosed him ... maybe hoping he would die. Must have done it before she transported him back to his place ... perhaps even gave him more once he got there ... maybe put it in the glass with the liquor ... there was an open bottle of booze on the coffee table and a glass on the floor.*

Janine was looking at Jack, tears in her eyes. "You understand that I can't stay with her at the moment until there is an explanation for this. I won't live with someone who is addicted again. I don't know Emma well enough to talk to her, but you do, Jack. You need to ask her about these drugs."

"Touchy subject," Jack commented rationally. "How to bring it up to Emma without insulting her, especially if it isn't her drugs."

"I found it on her bathroom counter, right by the sink, Jack. There is no one else in the house. Just Emma and me. And these drugs are definitely not mine!"

Jack got up from the table and walked over to the coffee maker. He poured himself a coffee and leaned on the counter, mug in hand, a thoughtful look on his face. "You're right, Janine. I'll talk to Emma as soon as I figure out a way of bringing up the subject tactfully. In the meantime, I'll just put your suitcases back in the room you were using."

"Thank you, Jack. I'll get out of your hair as quick as possible, but I think it best I do not stay with Emma. I might even just go back to Mike's and wait for him to get out of the hospital. Maybe we can work things out. Maybe this episode, whatever it is that has done this to him, will make him think about the direction of his life. He really isn't a bad guy. He had a tough upbringing, you know. Brutal parents."

"No excuse for beating you the way he did, Janine. Think twice before you move back with him. If you are serious about working things out with Mike, do it slowly, and from a distance. Go to counselling, if he's willing to go with you. Make sure you are safe. Best advice an old bachelor like me can give you." Jack downed his coffee and set the mug in the sink. "I have a few things to do. Make yourself at home."

After Jack left, Janine headed down the hall to the guestroom. Toby followed close on her heels. As Janine put some of her clothes in the dresser, Toby jumped up on the bed and watched her.

"What am I going to do, Toby?" Janine, having finished unpacking, came and sat down beside Toby. She rubbed behind his ears, and Toby started purring.

Stay here is what you're going to do ... don't go back to Emma's until Jack and I figure out what's going on. And, definitely, don't go back to the scumbag! Jack and I will look after you. We're good at keeping damsels in distress safe!

"Mike recognized me, Toby. I think he's sorry."

Abusers are always sorry.

"But Jack is right. I do need to take it slow. Make sure Mike's going to turn things around. I can't go through another beating like that. Maybe I'll head up to the hospital this morning and pay Mike another visit. Maybe the more he sees me, the more he'll remember. And we can talk."

Toby jumped down from the bed and strolled out to the kitchen. He lapped up a few drops of water before leaving the house. It was time to check on Emma.

Fifty-three

Mike opened his eyes and noticed a tray of food on the hospital table by his bed. A young nurse entered the room and told him she was going to take his vitals and help him try and eat some breakfast. Mike glanced at her nametag. Cindy. He was beginning to feel a bit better physically, but his mind was still not clear.

After taking Mike's blood pressure and temperature, Cindy opened the pudding container. She handed Mike a spoon. "Do you think you can manage to feed yourself?"

Mike grasped the spoon and attempted to dig into the pudding, to no avail. His coordination wasn't there. Cindy took the spoon from him and started to feed him. The first mouthful tasted awful, and Mike had a difficult time swallowing the pudding. He shook his head no as Cindy hovered a second spoonful toward him.

"You need to start eating," Cindy encouraged.

"Tastes horrible. Don't want it," Mike grimaced. Seeing the distraught look on the nurse's face, "Maybe a bit of water or juice."

Cindy opened the apple juice container and held it up to Mike's lips. He swallowed slowly, enjoying the refreshing beverage. "Good," Cindy said, putting the empty juice carton on the table. She picked up the breakfast tray and walked out of the room, stopping just outside the door to talk to the two police officers who were waiting impatiently for her to finish with Mike. "All yours," she said to them.

MacDonald opened her phone and flicked to the pictures she'd taken of Emma. She held the phone out for Mike to see. "Do you recognize this woman?"

Mike focused his eyes on the phone. *She looks familiar ... but ... come on ... get a grip on yourself.* He looked back at MacDonald and shook his head.

"Are you sure, Mr. Sanderson? Take another good look," the officer prodded, pushing the phone closer to Mike's face.

The more Mike stared at the picture, the more his memory seemed to be clearing. Finally, "Yeah, I think that's the woman who came into my room ... not sure when ... but she left ... wasn't here long ... said she had the wrong room ... yeah ... I think she's a patient ... she was in a hospital gown."

Hendricks stepped forward. "She's not a patient," he said. "MacDonald followed her down the hallway. When she left the ward area, she slipped into a room, and when she exited, she was in street clothes. She exited pretty quickly to the elevator." Hendricks paused. "So, let me ask you if this morning was the first time you have seen this woman. Look again. Take your time."

Mike took the phone in his hands and stared at the picture of Emma, long and hard. Something was needling at him, but he couldn't figure out what it was. He handed the phone back to MacDonald. "Sorry ... there's something about her that is familiar, but that's probably because I just saw her in my room not long ago."

"Okay, then." Hendricks swallowed hard. There was something about this case and about Mike that didn't sit well in his craw. Hendricks changed direction. "How did you get all these cuts and bruises, Mike?"

Mike hadn't actually seen himself since being admitted to the hospital. He was puzzled by the question. "What do you mean?"

"Look at your arms, man," Hendricks pointed to Mike's arms. "And your face looks worse!"

Mike took a good look at his arms and his eyes opened wide, shocked at what he saw.

"So, I ask you again ... how did you end up in this condition? Beaten. Drugged. You must have some recollection." Hendricks hesitated, not sure if he should try and put the blame on the girlfriend. *What the heck ... won't hurt. At least I'll get to see his reaction when I accuse her.*

"I think your girlfriend—ex-girlfriend—might have decided to take revenge against you for what you did to her. You beat her. She returned the favour. But the only way she could do it was to drug you. So, somehow, she managed to put something into your alcohol, which she knew you would drink, which in turn incapacitated you. She beat you badly, left, and then having second thoughts about what she did, and probably not on the same day, returned and called 911. She gave us a song and dance about being worried about you, but I don't think that is the case." Hendricks sat on the end of Mike's bed and leaned toward him. "How am I doing, Mr. Sanderson?"

Mike was confused. He was beginning to remember more and more about Janine. There was no way she would do anything like the police officer was suggesting. It wasn't in her. But he couldn't explain the condition he was in either. He couldn't remember how he'd ended in the hospital.

Shaking his head, "I don't think my ex would do something like this to me."

Hendricks was about to say something else when Doctor Carmichael walked into the room. He frowned. "Officers. My patient needs to rest now. You've been here long enough."

Mike heaved a sigh of relief. He was exhausted and would be glad to see the police officers leave.

Hendricks was about to argue with the doctor, but MacDonald grabbed his elbow: "Let's go. I think we should revisit the ex-girlfriend again and finish the conversation we started with her before she clammed up and Jack Nelson happened on the scene."

"Good idea." Taking one last look at Mike, Hendricks added, "We'll be back, Mr. Sanderson."

Mike closed his eyes.

Fifty-four

Janine's heart leapt to her throat when she saw the police cruiser stop in front of Jack's house, and she started to shake when she recognized MacDonald and Hendricks as they walked up the sidewalk to Jack's front door.

"Where's Jack? Why isn't he back yet?" Janine mumbled.

Toby also noticed the visitors. He sat up on the back of the couch and watched their approach. He detected how nervous Janine was. *These cops can't be for real ... why are they coming to see Janine? She's not the one who hurt Mike. Maybe they just want to see Jack. After all, they probably know each other from the force.*

Janine decided not to answer the door. She needed Jack to be with her if those cops were going to question her again. Janine had the feeling they thought she was responsible for Mike's condition. The doorbell rang. Janine remained in her chair, praying the officers wouldn't try and look through the window.

Just as Macdonald and Hendricks were about to leave, Jack's truck pulled into the driveway. He got out of the vehicle and strode over to the constables. "What can I do for you?" he asked, not extending a welcoming hand.

Toby noticed how tense Jack was as he talked to the police. He glanced over to Janine, slunk down in her chair. *Oh no, don't invite those guys in ... Janine's scared of them, Jack! Send them on their way!*

The front door opened and Jack walked in with MacDonald and Hendricks. Janine sat up in the chair, rubbing her eyes, feigning she'd been asleep. "Jack ... you're back. I was just catching a nap … Officers … do you have some news about Mike for me? You could have called." Janine sounded nervous.

"Actually, we have some more questions for you," Hendricks stepped forward. "We'd like to pick up from where we left off in the hospital before you called in your friend here."

Toby swished his tail angrily. His ears flattened. The fur on his neck stood on end. A low growl sounded from his throat. *I don't like these two! Especially the guy!*

Jack stepped between Janine and the officers. "Exactly why are you here?" he asked, a severe edge to his words. "If it weren't for Janine, her ex-boyfriend would probably be dead right now. From what I understand, the line of questions you were asking her at the hospital gave her the impression you were blaming her for Mike Sanderson's condition."

"We're just trying to establish why the man was in the state he was in when he arrived at the hospital, Jack. He was drugged and badly beaten, and we need to find out what happened. Janine," Hendricks stepped to the side and looked directly at Janine while speaking to Jack, "despite having called 911, could have only been doing so because she was the one who administered a drug to him, knocking him out enough that she could beat him, as he'd beaten her. Then, my guess is, she had second thoughts and went back to the house and made the call, ensuring her ex wouldn't die. How does that sound, Janine? Am I on the right track?"

Janine flushed angrily. She stood up abruptly from her chair and waved her finger at Hendricks. "How dare you!" she shouted, bravely stepping closer to him. "Plain and simple, Officer Hendricks, I saved Mike Sanderson's life. I never drugged him. I never beat him. I didn't pour alcohol down his throat. I think instead of trying to discredit me and pin whatever happened to Mike on me, Mike would be better served if you

161

were looking for who really did this to him!" With those words, Janine turned and stomped out of the room.

Good for you, Janine! Toby jumped off the couch, and as he passed the officers, hissed. He followed Janine into the kitchen where he found her sitting at the table, shaking, wringing her hands together. Even though Toby knew he wasn't allowed on tables, he felt this was an exception and that Jack wouldn't get mad at him. He rubbed his head against Janine's hands. She looked at him, tears in her eyes, and reached out and rubbed Toby under the chin.

"Maybe I should have just left Mike there. I shouldn't have gone to the house in the first place, Toby. This is such a nightmare. I don't know how much more I can take."

"They're gone," Jack informed, entering the kitchen. Despite seeing Toby on the table, Jack let it go. "I'll fix you a tea, Janine, and then we can talk."

As MacDonald and Hendricks were getting into their cruiser, Emma was staggering out her back door, into her yard. She stood outside her three-season room, leaning on the wall, trying to catch her breath.

MacDonald pointed in Emma's direction as she and Hendricks drove away. "That woman, Jack's neighbour, looks a lot like the woman who was visiting Mike at the hospital," she commented, taking out her cell phone and pulling up Emma's pictures.

Fifty-five

Emma had woken with a sick feeling. When she tried to get out of bed, her legs felt like rubber, and she'd had to sit on the edge of her bed until she could orient her bearings. Her head was still pounding, which she found strange because her headache pills usually kept the torment at bay.

Finally, Emma managed to get to the bathroom. She splashed some cold water on her face, then made her way down to the main floor, where she was greeted by Duke. She leaned against the kitchen counter.

"I need some air," she slurred.

Duke trotted to the back door and groaned.

"Okay, boy … maybe the fresh air will do us both good."

Emma noticed the police car pull away from Jack's and she got a lump in her throat. A nervous lump. *What are they doing there? Come to think of it, where's Janine? She moved in with me yesterday—I think. I didn't see her when I came downstairs. You're losing it, Emma … pull yourself together!* Emma pressed her hands to her temples. She was so absorbed in trying to figure out what was wrong with her that she didn't hear her yard gate open and close.

Duke started barking as the two police officers approached Emma, and he rushed to his mistress' side. Emma quickly grasped hold of his collar and held him back from fully attacking the unscheduled guests.

"What can I do for you officers?" Emma asked nervously.

MacDonald didn't waste any time. She shoved her phone at Emma. "Is this you?"

Emma was shocked at the intrusion to her personal space. She squinted, studying the picture on the phone screen, and her face drained of any colour that was there. Slowly, she shook her head. "I don't think so."

Hendricks was watching Emma closely. He'd seen how she'd blanched when she saw the picture. He noticed her eyes, glazed and unfocused. "Take a closer look," Hendricks pushed.

"I don't have to. It's not me." Emma started to turn away, "If you don't mind, I was just about to go in for something to eat."

MacDonald followed Emma. "I took this picture yesterday morning."

"Good for you," Emma retorted.

"At the hospital."

"So."

"Were you at the hospital yesterday?"

Emma turned to face MacDonald. "Look, I've been nowhere today. I have a splitting headache and need to get something in my stomach. I've been in bed all day ... *I think* ... so, if you don't mind." Emma hurried into her house, making her way through the three-season room and into her kitchen. She closed and locked her door. Gasping for breath, Emma staggered to her sink and splashed cold water on her face.

Outside, Hendricks attempted to follow Emma into her house, but Macdonald stopped him. "Let her go. Our gut feelings are telling us she's got something to hide, but we're not getting any more out of her today. She looked pretty rough."

From her kitchen window, Emma watched the police leave her backyard. She breathed a sigh of relief; however, it was short-lived as she realized the police might return.

"I need to get out of here quickly." Emma turned to Duke. "Sorry, boy. We're going to have to move. I can't stay here any longer. Those cops might be on to me. I can pick up from where I left off here somewhere else. There's scum wherever you go in this world!"

Forgetting all about how hungry she was, Emma darted to her room to pack some basic necessities. She'd wait until dark before calling a cab to take her to the train station. From there, she'd decide where to go.

"She's lying," Hendricks said as they pulled away from Emma's house.

"Of course she is, but now is not the time to push the issue. If my guess is right, and if she is the woman in the picture, she knows something about what happened to our victim. She might even be the one responsible for what happened." MacDonald paused. "It might be a good idea to have her watched."

"Good idea, MacDonald ... I think you're spot on." Hendricks pulled to a crawling stop at the intersection.

Fifty-six

Toby decided it was time to pay Emma a visit. Jack could hold down the fort with Janine. Making his way over to Emma's, Toby wondered at the silence in the house. He jumped up on the living room window sill to look inside. The curtains blocked his view.

Strange. The curtains shouldn't be closed yet. It's too early.

Toby pawed at the window and meowed as loudly as he could. Still nothing. He jumped down from the sill and made his way around to the back of the house to the three-season room door. He noticed a light on in the kitchen but couldn't see anyone moving about. Toby glanced up to the second floor. There was a light on in Emma's room. He wondered what she was doing. She hadn't been out at all—that he'd noticed—since she'd returned from the hospital. Toby turned to leave, thinking there was nothing he could do at the moment to reach Emma.

A sharp yelp sounded from inside the house. Toby gazed back up toward the bark. Duke was at Emma's bedroom window, his paws on the sill. The dog left the window, and Toby heard the clipping of his feet as he raced down the stairs and into the kitchen. He stood at the kitchen door, looking into the three-season room, and started barking.

"Duke, what is it, boy? Are those cops back?" Emma's voice followed Duke into the room.

The cops were here? Emma must be panicking.

Duke continued barking, letting out several low growls in between. He anxiously pawed at the door, demanding to be let out.

166

He knows I'm here. Need to get out of here. Toby looked around for the shortest exit from the yard. Finding it, he watched from under a tree on the other side of the fence as Duke ran around the yard, sniffing. Emma came to the door, leaning against the doorjamb. She scrutinized the yard.

"Come on, Duke. There's no one out here. Finish your business and get in here. We need to leave as soon as possible."

You're leaving, Emma? This isn't good. You can't run away, Emma. I know you're hurting. I know your past was not the best. But you can't run from this, Emma. I won't let you. I have to stop you from ruining your life!

Toby darted home, hoping Jack would be willing to follow him back to Emma's.

Emma raced back upstairs and grabbed the suitcase she'd packed. As she was about to leave her room, she remembered her headache pills; she turned around and ran to her dresser. Opening the top drawer, Emma dug into the back and took out the bottle of pills.

"Christ! I can't leave the Rohypnol behind either." Emma dug further into the drawer, her fingers searching for the incriminating bottle of pills. "What the—?" She pulled all the clothes out of the drawer, throwing them onto the floor. Nothing.

Emma put a hand to her head. "Think. I woke up with a headache, which meant I must have had one before I laid down for a nap. So I would have taken a pill before lying down. And I would have needed water to wash it down."

Emma walked down the hallway to the bathroom. Her eyes scanned over the contents of the counter. No bottle of pills. "Did I take the wrong pills? ... I was pretty out of it when I returned from the hospital ... where's the bottle ... did I leave it here and maybe Janine found it? Oh, my God! What if she took it? And she's gone. Probably to Jack's. What if she shows it to him? Why would she leave here just after getting here? What to do … what to do!" Emma scurried back to her room, shut her suitcase, and charged downstairs. She knelt beside Duke, who was waiting patiently for her return. There were tears in her eyes as she spoke: "I can't take you with me right now, Duke. People will notice me if I have you with me. I'll leave a note on Jack's truck for him to make sure you're looked after. Tell him I decided to go and see Camden—that I needed to see my brother."

Quickly, Emma scribbled the note for Jack, pushed Duke into the backyard, then left through the front door, suitcase and note in hand. As she made her way to Jack's truck, Emma was totally unaware of the number of eyes following her movements.

Fifty-seven

Toby burst through his door, racing through the kitchen and into the living room where he assumed Jack would be comfortably resting in his chair, watching television. He couldn't have made a better guess. Toby jumped onto Jack's lap and began circling around, meowing.

"Toby! What's going on, old man?" Jack asked, startled from his almost nap.

Toby jumped down and raced to the front door, circling again, scratching at the door, meowing loudly.

"Okay ... okay. You want me to follow you somewhere again." Jack got up from his chair, shoved his feet into his slippers, and made his way to the door. As soon as he opened it, Toby darted out and down to the sidewalk, where he turned to make sure Jack was still following.

Come on, Jack. There's no time to waste.

Toby raced to Emma's, Jack close on his heels. As he passed by his truck, Jack noticed a figure trying to place something on his windshield. He stopped and stared.

"Emma!"

Emma turned, panicked. There was no way she could run now. She'd have to just tell Jack she was going to see her brother for a few days. "Jack! I was coming over to give you a key to my house and ask if you would look after Duke for me until I return from seeing Camden."

"Were you just going to put a note on my truck and then sneak away?" Jack asked.

"No! No! I thought I saw something on the windshield. I was going to your back door," Emma said quickly.

"How were you going to get to the jail? Tessa said she would take you. Can't you wait until tomorrow?"

Jack had her there. She couldn't refute that Tessa had made the offer, and now she had to talk herself out of this predicament. However, before she had a chance to say anything, a police siren sounded, and a cruiser pulled up in front of Jack's house. MacDonald and Hendricks exited.

"Going somewhere, miss?" Hendricks asked, striding straight to Emma.

Jack stepped between Hendricks and Emma, but the police officer put his hand up. "Don't interfere, Nelson. This is police business. We believe this woman has something to do with Mike Sanderson's circumstance, and we need to bring her in for questioning. Good thing we kept a watch on her place, or we might have missed her." Hendricks' lips curled sarcastically.

Looking from Hendricks to Emma and back again, Jack motioned Hendricks to the side. "A moment, please."

Emma watched nervously. Toby came and sat down beside her, as though he was going to protect her. Stop the cops from taking her away. He looked up at his friend. *I know what you've done, Emma. But the scumbag isn't dead. You didn't cross the line, and I don't think you wanted to. That's why you took him back to his place. Problem is, these cops must have something on you, or they wouldn't have staked out your home, waiting for you to make a move.*

Toby saw Hendricks reach for the phone MacDonald was handing to him. He was showing Jack something on the screen. "What do you think? Is this Emma?"

Jack couldn't deny the resemblance. "Certainly looks like it could be. Looks like this picture was taken at the hospital, though. Is that correct?"

"That's correct," Hendricks responded. "We saw this woman coming out of Mr. Sanderson's room."

"I see," said Jack, stroking his chin. After a few moments of silence, "Do me a favour, Hendricks. I know you're anxious to talk to Emma, but I'd like you to give me the chance to speak with her first. I know her. She's been through a lot over the past year, with her brother being charged and convicted of several murders. It hasn't been easy for her. She trusts me.

"Toby has been sensing something going on with her over the past week or so, and has dragged me to her house on more than one occasion." Jack was thinking about the note that Toby seemed to insist came from Emma. He noticed the hesitation in Hendricks' eyes. "Come on, man. Just this one favour. I'll deliver her to the station myself, and you can ask all the questions you want then."

Hendricks glanced over to MacDonald. She nodded. "Can't hurt. Maybe he can get her to talk." He turned to Jack. "By the way, we have already shown this picture to Emma, and she basically ordered us off her property by rushing into her house and locking the door. That's when we decided she might be a flight risk and set up to watch her house. Guess we were right, eh? You've got two hours, Jack; then we expect her at the station." Hendricks spun around and walked to the cruiser. "Coming, MacDonald?" he called back.

After the police left, Jack turned to Emma, who was standing still as a statue. If Jack could have read her mind, the story she was telling herself would not have pleased him.

"Shall we?" he pointed to the house. "We don't have much time."

Emma picked up her suitcase and meekly followed Jack into the house, Toby trotting along behind her.

When the trio walked in the house, Janine was waiting in the living room. She'd been watching what was going on from the window. She blushed when she saw Emma. Emma glared at Janine. Jack noticed the silent interaction. As did Toby.

This should be interesting. I wonder how Jack is going to deal with this kettle of fish. Speaking of fish, I hope he takes the talk to the kitchen so I won't miss anything while I grab a few kibbles to hold me over till morning.

Toby was in luck as Jack ushered the two women toward the kitchen. "Best we talk in here," he suggested, heading to the coffee machine. "I'll make us some coffee."

Emma and Janine sat on opposite sides of the table, neither one looking at the other. Janine's hands were on her lap, tightly clasped. Emma's were folded on the table, her knuckles white from the pressure. Jack placed some cream and sugar on the table, then took a chair at the end of the table so he could watch the reactions of both women. Once Toby finished his snack, he jumped up on the chair across from Jack, which also allowed him to observe what was about to take place.

The final gurgle of the coffee machine sounded, and Jack got up and poured three cups. "Okay," he began after everyone had fixed their coffee to taste. "Where shall we begin?"

Emma scowled at Janine. "Why don't we start with why Janine left my house like a thief in the night?"

To Emma's surprise, Jack agreed with the starting point. He reached into his pocket and took out a bottle of pills. Setting it on the table in front of Emma, "Janine found these on your bathroom counter, and she panicked after reading the label of what they were for."

Emma leaned back in her chair. Toby could almost see the wheels turning in her head as she tried to think of a reasonable answer to give Jack. When it came, the old cat was shocked!

"I researched this drug online ... actually, more than this one. I have terrible nightmares sometimes ... about what

172

happened to me when Camden and I were in foster care. I read that Rohypnol might be able to erase unpleasant memories, so I ordered a bottle." Emma reached over and picked up the pill bottle and opened it. Holding it out, "As you can see, I haven't used very many of them. I am careful. After Camden went to prison, my nightmares increased … I guess because it was the first time I was really alone." Emma looked at Janine. "If you'd just asked me about this, I would have explained."

Oh, Emma. You are such a convincing liar. Have I been so wrong about you? Are you more like your brother than I thought? Or, are you worse? More calculating? Camden was mentally ill because of what he'd witnessed. He murdered those people because they all represented someone from his past that had abused you and him.

Janine didn't miss a beat as she replied to Emma: "I know all about this drug, Rohypnol. My best friend, from my hometown, was raped after being given this drug. The guys got off because she couldn't remember exactly what happened to her." Janine took in a breath. This was something she'd never talked about to anyone and had totally forgotten the incident when she'd previously spoken to Jack. "So, you're right. It does erase or cloud memories. When I saw this on your bathroom counter, it brought back some horrible memories, and I needed to get as far away from your house as possible, not wanting to be anywhere near another person dependant on drugs."

Jack decided it was time to address the issue touched on by the police. "Emma, I think you need to explain, truthfully, about the picture the police showed me."

"Picture?" Janine cut in.

"Yes," Jack resumed. "The officers who were just here showed me a picture they took of a young woman at the hospital this yesterday. Could pass as a twin for our Emma here. They said the woman in the picture was in Mike's room." Jack fixed

Emma with a knowing stare, not that he wanted to believe the police, but... "Care to explain, Emma? Were you at the hospital yesterday?"

Emma looked down at her hands. She took them from the table and placed them on her lap so Jack and Janine wouldn't be able to see her shake. Her voice was small as she answered. "I can't explain the picture. I know what it looks like, but Jack, come on, you know me. I'm not lying. I was not at the hospital yesterday this morning. I was not in Mike's room. Why would I be? I don't know him, other than what Janine has told me about him. It wasn't me.

"As for the police thinking I didn't want to talk to them, well, I admit, I didn't. I was still suffering from one of my headaches, and from the looks of it, I grabbed the wrong pill bottle, and instead of taking two Tylenol threes, I took two Rohypnol! Camden and I suffered a lot at the hands of law enforcement officers in the past. I know what they are like when they think they have a lead. They can be ruthless. I needed to get away. That's why I was leaving. The only reason. Believe me, Jack. Please." Emma managed to squeeze out a few tears for good measure. "Besides, I never even left the house yesterday," she added another lie to her speech.

Wow! Why are you lying, Emma? Toby was distraught at what he was hearing come out of his friend's mouth.

Janine had a puzzled look on her face at Emma's last statement. Finally, she spoke up: "I thought you went for a run," she alleged. "I thought it strange you left Duke home, at the time."

Emma was quick to offer an option for Janine's disclosure. "Actually, after I left you, I went up to my room to change, and because I wasn't feeling well, I just laid down instead of going out."

Emma ... Emma ... Emma! You just keep building lie upon lie. Your deceit is going to come back and bite you if you're not careful. How are you going to be able to keep all your lies straight?

Jack was puzzled by the conversation. *I want to believe you, Emma, but the picture is pretty convincing. Why would you go to the hospital and seek out Janine's ex-boyfriend? Unless you decided to take matters into your own hands ... is that possible, Emma? Are you really as innocent as what you portray? Is what happened to you in the past dictating unsavoury actions now? Revenge for what was done to you meted out on like-minded individuals. On abusers. And, were you really in your room all day, as you say? Janine seems confident you went out ... then again, you never do go out without Duke...*

"Jack?" Emma's voice was filled with emotion. "You believe me, don't you? I was just leaving to get away for a few days. I was coming back. I could never leave Duke behind. I wouldn't do that." Emma dug into her pocket and pulled out the note and the key to her house and laid them on the table.

"I want to believe you, Emma. But that picture..."

"It wasn't me, Jack. Like I said, I never left the house because of my headache." Emma turned her attention to Janine. "Mike had a lot of girlfriends before you, didn't he? Maybe it was one of them. Maybe he called an old ex, and she did this to him, for revenge. If he treated them like he treated you, Janine, it is a possibility, isn't it?" Emma laid out another option for what had happened to Mike.

Janine studied Emma. There was something about her that was beginning to bother Janine. Was it the harsh look in her eyes that Emma was unable to erase with her tears? Whatever it was, it didn't seem to be remorse for all the trouble Emma was causing at the moment.

175

"Yes, Mike had a few girlfriends in the past, but none that I know of who would take this sort of revenge on him." Janine pushed her chair back from the table and stood. "I think I've heard enough for now. I don't know what happened to Mike, but he didn't deserve to be hurt this badly, regardless of what he did to me. I hope the police find out who did this to him and put them in jail for attempted murder. Whoever it was, they can thank me they won't be being charged with murder!" Janine stared directly at Emma as she spoke, then turned and left the room.

Emma cringed under Janine's scrutinizing eyes. *Does she know something? Oh, my God ... did I miss something when I cleaned up? Was she snooping in my basement?*

After Janine left the room, Jack and Emma made some small talk. Jack finally looked at his watch. "I guess we better go," he said. "I promised the officers I'd have you to the station within two hours."

Toby decided to stay home. There was no need for him to go along for this ride. Besides, he had a lot of thinking to do, and he couldn't do that with Emma right in front of him. Somehow, Toby needed to get Jack over to Emma's to check out the basement. Now that they had a key, and she was not home, it was going to make getting into the house more manageable.

Hopefully, there was still some evidence of the crime there that Toby knew Emma had committed.

Fifty-eight

More of Mike's test results came back the next morning. Doctor Carmichael had put a rush on them, and he frowned as he read them. "Rohypnol!" he exclaimed to no one in particular. He picked up the phone on his desk and dialled the police station.

"Officer Hendricks, please," he requested of the switchboard operator.

"Officer Hendricks is interviewing someone at the moment. Could I have him get back to you?"

"This is Doctor Carmichael from the ER at the Brantford General Hospital. I just received some test results for a patient that was brought in here a couple days ago under some strange circumstances. I believe the officer will want this information sooner rather than later."

"One moment." The attendant put the doctor on hold.

Several minutes passed. Doctor Carmichael was getting impatient; he had patients to attend to. Finally, "Hendricks, here. What do you have for me, doctor?"

"The urine sample results from Mike Sanderson came back this morning. Rohypnol was found. I thought you might like to know and possibly get someone over to his house and see if there is any evidence there that he was using this drug."

Hendricks smiled. This was a good break for the case. He and MacDonald hadn't gotten too far with Emma. She'd started to fall asleep while they were trying to question her, so they put her in lockup for the rest of the night and had just sat down to begin again when the call came through from switchboard.

"We'll get someone over there right away ... thanks, doc." Hendricks hung up the phone and went directly to Captain Bryce Wagner's office. "Need a favour, cap. Could you send a couple officers over to Mike Sanderson's place ... you know the guy who was found comatose in his house by his ex-girlfriend ... a doctor from the hospital just called and informed me that Sanderson had Rohypnol in his system. We need to check his place and see if he was using. If we don't find anything there, that means someone else administered it to the guy."

The captain nodded and said he would dispatch someone immediately. Hendricks returned to the interrogation room where his partner and Emma were waiting.

"Everything okay?" MacDonald inquired.

"Actually, I think we should talk privately before we question Emma further." Hendricks nodded to the door, and the two officers stepped out of the room.

"Wow! Good break," MacDonald said after Hendricks filled her in. "Do you think we'll find that drug in the house?"

"Something in my gut tells me we won't," Hendricks replied before re-entering the room where Emma sat waiting.

Fifty-nine

By the time Jack arrived back from taking Emma to the police station, both Janine and Toby were sound asleep. Jack popped in quickly to check on Duke, but he was sleeping as well, and when he realized it was a friend, the dog didn't bother to make a fuss. The police had said they would probably have to keep Emma overnight and not to expect her until morning. They would call when they were finished questioning her. Jack ambled off to bed; he was bushed!

Toby woke early in the morning, anxious to get Jack over to Emma's before she returned from the police station. He wandered into Jack's bedroom and jumped up on the bed. Jack groaned, not wanting to get up so early.

"Toby, I need another hour," Jack grumbled.

Toby refused to take no for an answer. *Not this morning, buddy. We have work to do, and we've gotta do it now before our Emma is released. Get your lazy ass out of bed!* Toby began meowing and circling around on the pillow.

Jack finally gave up and staggered out of bed. Toby scurried from the room and ran to the kitchen, where he noticed the key to Emma's house still sitting on the table. He jumped on the table, sat down beside the key, and waited for Jack.

"What are you doing on the table, old man?" Jack admonished when he entered the kitchen.

Toby's ears flattened back, and his tail swished across the table. He tapped the key with his paw and meowed.

Jack laughed. "You anxious to go over and see your buddy, Duke? Give me time to grab a coffee and a piece of toast. I'm sure the dog will survive for another twenty minutes."

Toby didn't move from his spot on the table, guarding the key with a cat's eye, not allowing Jack to rethink the objective of getting over to Emma's sooner than later. *You have no idea what we are dealing with here, Jack. Emma has been up to no good, and I need to get in her house and down to the basement to see if there is any proof left of Mike having been Emma's prisoner. So, hurry up and finish that toast and coffee! We have a job to do.*

As Jack sat down to eat his toast, Toby moved the key a little closer to his partner.

Half an hour later, Jack and Toby made their way over to Emma's. Janine, who had gotten up and joined Jack for a coffee, asked if he minded if she came along. As the key turned in the lock, the trio heard Duke approach the door.

Jack looked down at Toby. "Wait here a minute while I put your nemesis in the back yard."

Janine reached down and scooped Toby up in her arms. "I got you, Toby. That big old dog won't hurt you," she smiled, stepping into the house behind Jack.

Duke growled. Toby hissed. Jack and Janine chuckled. Jack took Duke by the collar and led him to the back door, letting him out in the yard. Janine put Toby down, and he made straight for the basement door, which was ajar. He stuck his paw in the opening, and the door creaked open. Toby meowed loudly.

"We aren't here to go through Emma's house, Toby," Jack scowled at the old cat.

Toby meowed again, louder and more insistent. He circled around and then stepped through the doorway, looked back, and meowed again.

"Looks like he wants us to follow him," Janine noted, smiling.

"And if we don't, he won't let it go," Jack smirked. "So, let's see what it is Toby wants us to have a look at."

Finally ... come on you two ... I need to show you the room Emma has down here ... the place where she tortured a man ... where she drugged him ... where she beat him.

"Wow!" Janine exclaimed. "Emma has quite the setup here. I had no idea she worked out."

"Yeah, I didn't either," Jack said. "She actually just mentioned it to me the other night."

Toby paused and looked back at the two stragglers. He meowed, then growled as he proceeded to the room at the end of the basement.

Jack and Janine caught up to Toby and when they reached the room in question: "So what is it, old man?" Jack asked, looking through the doorway. "Looks like a storage room to me. Probably most of these boxes contain Camden's belongings." Jack pointed to the writing on a couple containers. "See? Camden's books. Camden's clothes."

Toby was frustrated. *This certainly isn't what this room looked like a few days ago! All these boxes were piled randomly in the basement. I wonder if there's some evidence under the boxes ... like some of Mike's blood. But how do I convince Jack to move them so I can take a look?*

"Come on, Toby," Jack ordered as he left the room and headed back to the stairway. "I want to get the dog fed and then head over to the police station and check on what's going on with Emma. Hendricks should have been able to finish up with his questions by now and either charged her or realized he was barking up the wrong tree!"

Toby began to follow, reluctantly. *There has to be something down here ... there just has to be.* Toby wracked his

181

brain to try and figure out where there might be some other evidence. His eyes scanned the basement, but the closer he got to the stairs, the more desolate he began to feel.

Jack and Janine were almost to the top of the stairs before Toby began his ascent, peering through the stair openings as he climbed. Suddenly, his eyes caught sight of something shiny on the floor under the flight of stairs. He turned around and returned back the way he'd come, circling around until he arrived at the spot where he noticed the item.

It was a ring! *Could this be Mike's ring?* Toby tapped it over to the bottom of the stairs with his paw, then sat down and meowed loudly.

Janine, realizing Toby hadn't followed her and Jack up to the kitchen, went back to the doorway. Seeing Toby sitting at the base of the steps, she started down to get him. "What's the matter, Toby? You need a lift?" Janine giggled as she made her way down to him.

Leaning over to scoop Toby up in her arms, Janine noticed what the old cat had his paw on. "What's this?" she asked, picking up the ring. "Jack!" Janine screamed.

Jack came running to the top of the steps. "What's wrong?" he called down.

Janine held up the ring. "This is the ring I gave Mike on our first anniversary." She raced upstairs and showed Jack the inscription on the inside of the ring— *'MS & JL Forever'*—Mike was here, Jack! He was here. Emma did something with him! We need to tell the police!"

Jack shook his head in disbelief but knew what had to be done. This evidence was too damaging to ignore.

Toby waddled up the steps. Once in the kitchen, Toby sat down beside Jack as he made a call to Hendricks.

"How'd you find it?" Hendricks asked after Jack filled him in on the ring.

"Toby found it. Believe it or not, he insisted I go down into the basement. If I were a betting man, I'd say Toby already knew what was going on over here and was trying to figure out how to tell me. Do you know how many times he tried to get me over to Emma's over the past week?"

"Should be interesting to hear Emma's explanation for how Mike Sanderson's ring got in her basement," Hendricks commented. "She's quite the storyteller," he supplemented, indicating to Jack that he'd not gotten much satisfaction out of his interrogation of Emma.

Jack was debating telling Hendricks about the Rohypnol Janine had found in Emma's bathroom. However, holding the ring in his hand, he knew he had no other choice but to come clean. He filled Hendricks in.

"I see." Hendricks' voice was tense. "Well, Jack, I suggest you bring me both the bottle of pills and the ring. Now!"

"Okay ... no problem ... I'll be there shortly."

Sixty

Hendricks decided to go for Emma's jugular. The pills could wait; they were secondary to the trump card he held. He set the ring on the table between him and Emma. Her face remained blank, having no idea what the ring had to do with her.

"Guess where this ring was found?" he probed, not having gotten the reaction he'd wanted.

Emma remained silent, despite the butterflies that were beginning to escape their cocoons in her stomach.

"In your basement," Hendricks continued.

Still no comment from Emma. She didn't trust herself to speak, fearing what might be coming.

"Guess who the ring belongs to?"

Emma finally spoke: "No idea."

"Mike Sanderson." Hendricks leaned over the table, his coffee-infused breath blowing into Emma's face. She cringed. "Any idea how Mike Sanderson's ring got in your basement?"

"I want to talk to Jack Nelson," Emma said.

Hendricks laughed. "Jack's pretty popular with you young ladies, isn't he?" Hendricks leaned back in his chair and clasped his hands behind his head. "Jack's the one who found the ring … let me rephrase that … the cat, Toby, found the ring; Jack just brought it to me." A long pause. "Guess what else he brought me?"

Not waiting for Emma to answer, "A bottle of Rohypnol, which he claims Janine, Mike Sanderson's girlfriend, found in your bathroom."

"I explained to Jack about the Rohypnol," Emma muttered. "I take it to forget all the crap that happened to me a

184

long time ago. I have nightmares about it. Rohypnol is supposed to help a person forget things." Emma was hoping she could play on Hendricks sympathy, if he were capable of such emotion.

Hendricks' eyebrows rose in disgust. He didn't believe a word that had just come out of her mouth. He tapped his pencil on the table. "Thing is, Emma, the hospital ran some tests on Mr. Sanderson, and guess what they found?"

Emma opened her mouth to reply, but Hendricks raised his hand. "Let me cut to the chase … they found Rohypnol in his urine sample. And now, we have a ring, which belonged to Sanderson, found in your basement. I think there is more to your story—a more truthful version. Want to enlighten me?"

The door to the interrogation room opened, and MacDonald walked in with two coffees. She set one in front of Hendricks, then sat beside him with the other. She'd been watching through a two-way mirror, so was up to speed on what was going on.

Emma's eyes roved from one cop to the other, and her heart started pumping overtime. She knew if Jack found the ring, she was doomed. He was her only friend besides Toby. But Toby was a cat; he wouldn't be any help. Heaving a big sigh, "I want to talk to Jack," she repeated for the second time.

"I think that can be arranged," MacDonald said. "He's waiting with the captain. Hung around figuring you'd want to see him."

Hendricks pushed back from the table. "I'll get Jack," he said.

Emma started sweating as she sat there with Officer MacDonald, just staring at her and rolling her fingers on the table. *Damn! How did that ring get in my basement?* Emma wracked her brains on how that could have happened. *It must have slipped off his finger when I carried him up the stairs. He had lost some weight. How do I explain this? How the ring was in my house ... they can't prove I am the one who drugged Mike ... I clarified why the Rohypnol was in my house ... think ... think.*

MacDonald stopped drum-rolling her fingers and leaned back in her chair. "My advice to you, Emma, is that you start coming clean with what you've done here."

"I haven't done anything," Emma spit angrily. "You have nothing on me that will stick. You have a drunken druggy in the hospital and want to make a case of it."

"If you say so," MacDonald smiled knowingly.

Emma's wheels were turning. *I can say I found the ring at the park when I was out for one of my runs ... that will work ... and I'll say it must have fallen out of my pocket when I went downstairs to work out. It will be believable because the park where I found the ring is where Mike accosted Janine, and where I helped Janine when she was miscarrying! That will work!* Emma looked MacDonald in the eyes and smiled.

MacDonald's blood ran cold.

"Jack, thank God you came for me," Emma cried when Jack walked into the room with Hendricks. "Please get me out of here. These police officers are trying to say I had something to do with what happened to Janine's boyfriend—ex-boyfriend. I didn't, Jack. I found that ring in the park, the one where he accosted her. You know I go for runs all the time, and that park is on one of my regular routes." Emma saw the doubt in Jack's eyes. "Please, Jack, believe me. You know me, Jack. Haven't I been through enough?" Emma started crying for added effect.

Hendricks was watching her closely. *Damn, she's good. Wonder how long it took for her to think up that story? It's one that could be believable, could easily sway a jury. Both her stories, the one about the drugs, and this, are swayable.* Hendricks glimpsed at Jack. *He's caving. He's too emotionally involved with this young woman. She's too convincing.*

Pulling a chair up beside Emma, Hendricks leaned in close to Emma. "You're a good storyteller, Emma. But, you know, that's what I think you are telling us here—stories. I think it's time you cut the crap and spoke the truth. If not to us, then to a judge.

"I am arresting you for the attempted murder of Mike Sanderson; and, from everything I know, you're a lucky lady that it is only attempted!" Hendricks motioned to MacDonald. "Take Emma back to a holding cell. She can stay there until we get in front of a judge."

Jack stepped forward. "Hendricks, let me take her home. Look at her. She doesn't belong in jail. I'll make sure she shows up to court."

"I have looked at her, Jack. I've listened to her, too. Her stories. Her lies." Hendricks wagged a finger at Jack. "She's not going anywhere but a jail cell. Emma's a flight risk, or have you forgotten, Jack? She was leaving, wasn't she? My advice, Jack: spend your time getting her a good lawyer. My gut tells me she's going to need one."

Sixty-one

Emma lay on the cot in the holding cell. She reopened in her mind her visit with her brother in the same cell. How cold she'd been to him. How she'd thought he was so weak to have gotten caught. And now, here she was, in a similar circumstance. The difference was the cops had no tangible proof she'd done anything. All the evidence they had was circumstantial and could be explained. No jury would convict her. Hell, it might not even make it to trial. If the Rohypnol did its job, Mike would never recognize her. She'd make sure of it, too. She knew how to change her looks.

Jack called his good lawyer friend, Jeremy Davies. "Jeremy, how's life treating you?"

"Jack, old buddy. What's up? Been a long time."

"I need a favour if you're not too busy."

"What do you need?"

"A friend of mine is in some trouble, and she needs a lawyer," Jack said. "You available?"

For the next twenty minutes, Jack filled Jeremy in on the case. He agreed to talk to Emma and be at the court hearing when it was scheduled. Jack thanked him and hung up the phone, then left to go pay Emma a visit in jail. He needed to assure her she had legal representation.

Toby watched Jack leave. He could have gone with him, but his heart wasn't ready to see Emma just yet. He decided to leave her fate in Jack's hands for now. Toby knew how much Emma had suffered over the years, but she was not being truthful right now, and she'd done something awful. Something against the law. Toby wasn't sure if he could overlook that.

Janine had been in shock since discovering Mike's ring in Emma's basement. Even after Jack filled her in briefly about Emma's past, Janine couldn't bring herself to forgive the woman.

"Do you want to come to court this morning with me?" Jack asked. "Emma's hearing is at ten."

At first, Janine was going to say no, however, "You know, I think I will," she answered slowly. "I want to hear what Emma has to say for herself."

"Emma won't have much to say this morning—if anything. This is more of a bail hearing. Hendricks is going after her for attempted murder," Jack enlightened Janine about the morning proceedings.

"Do you think she's guilty?" Janine couldn't look Jack in the eyes when she asked her question, knowing how close he was to Emma, and how much sympathy he had for her.

"A lot of the evidence points in that direction, but truthfully, I just can't see her doing such a thing."

Toby was listening intently to the conversation. *Oh, Jack. She did. But, if I am to be truthful to myself, I don't want to see my Emma go to jail. Does she need help? Yes. But not from a jail cell. She'll die there. My beautiful Emma. You have to think of a way to help her, Jack.*

Jack and Janine arrived at the courthouse at quarter to ten. They sat in the back row. Jeremy Davies entered shortly afterwards and stopped to chat with Jack for a moment.

"Since Emma is your friend," he began, "are you willing to put up bail for her?" Davies paused. "Do you trust this young woman enough that she won't flee?"

Jack was tortured inside. Emma had become a big part of his and Toby's lives, but lately, as Toby had tried to point out several times, she was not the Emma they knew. However, what she needed was help, maybe even counselling. She wasn't a cold-blooded murderer like her brother. Finally, Jack nodded. "Yeah, I'm willing to put up the bail and go one further if you need it. I'll guarantee she won't run."

"Okay. You're sure?"

Jack wasn't as confident as his words but he nodded affirmation.

Davies patted his friend on the shoulder before making his way to the front of the courtroom.

A few minutes later, MacDonald escorted Emma into the room and sat her down beside Davies. She glanced around the courtroom and her eyes landed on Jack and Janine. She gave a half-smile, directed to Jack, then turned back and faced the front. Davies leaned toward Emma and whispered something in her ear. She nodded.

Hendricks, to Jack's surprise, came in through the main door and when he noticed Jack, he approached.

"She's guilty, you know, Jack. Guilty as hell! Don't let her innocent looks and her tears fool you."

Jack pursed his lips. "Everyone is supposed to be presumed innocent until found otherwise, Hendricks. We need to remember that."

"You the one who lawyered her up with Jeremy Davies?"

"Yeah. He's an old friend. Owes me a few favours."

"Well, good luck. To you both." Hendricks walked off with a smirk on his face.

The judge was running late, but soon the court was called into session. Emma's case was up first. "What's the charge?" the judge inquired.

The Crown Attorney, Brian Gregory stood. "Attempted murder, Your Honour."

The judge scowled down at Emma. "How does the defendant plead?"

Davies nodded to Emma to reply. "Not guilty, Your Honour."

"I assume, councillor, you're going to be asking for bail?" the judge directed to Davies.

"I am, Your Honour. And I have already established not only bail but a guarantor that my client will show up for court when required."

"Your Honour," Gregory jumped to his feet. "It is my understanding that the defendant has already attempted to flee, and the Crown requests that she be kept incarcerated until her trial."

Davies was just as quick on his feet: "The defendant was not trying to flee from anything, Your Honour. She was simply leaving to go and visit her brother when two police officers swooped in to question her. A former police officer, Jack Nelson, who is also my client's neighbour, has agreed to put up her bail and to ensure she does not flee the city. I believe that alone should be enough of a guarantee." Davies waited for the judge to make his decision.

The judge perused the police file on his desk. He frowned a few times, but finally, setting it aside, "Bail is set at $100,000. We will set a hearing three weeks from now to establish if this case needs to go to trial." Banging his gavel on the desk, "Next."

Outside the courthouse, Emma threw her arms around Jack. "I can't thank you enough, Jack," she murmured into his jacket.

Jack pushed her gently away, holding onto her shoulders. "Just don't let me down, Emma," he said softly but firmly. Turning to Jeremy Davies, "Thanks, buddy. I hope you'll take on her case. Hendricks," Jack motioned to the police officer that was standing not far away, staring at him, "is totally convinced Emma is guilty, and he's going to do anything to prove it. I want to make sure she has a fair trial..." Jack hesitated, and looking directly in Emma's eyes, "either way."

Sixty-two

Emma was silent on the drive home. She'd chosen to sit in the backseat of Jack's truck, leaving the front to Janine. Emma's mind was spinning, trying to establish firm alternatives for all the allegations that were being thrown at her. She assumed the main ones were already covered, but seeing how adamant the cops—especially Hendricks—were, Emma knew she had to be on her game.

"Come in for a bite to eat before you go home," Jack offered. Before Emma could refuse, he added, "and we can have a talk."

Toby was waiting by the door when the trio entered the house. *Thank goodness. My Emma isn't stuck in jail. It must have been horrible for her.* Toby meowed a friendly greeting to his friend, despite what he knew about her recent actions.

Emma knelt down and scratched behind Toby's ears, but said nothing. Standing, she followed Jack to the kitchen; Janine made her way to her room down the hall.

Jack went about making a pot of coffee, pulled some eggs and bacon out of the fridge, and began putting some lunch together. Silence, other than the water dripping into the coffeepot, soaked the kitchen with a depressing mood. Emma watched Jack closely from her chair, not offering any help. Toby sat at Emma's feet, staring up at her, trying to get a read on her.

The coffee machine gurgled its final drip. The smell and sound of sizzling bacon inched its way into the silence. Jack whipped up the eggs and set them aside until the bacon was almost done. He opened a loaf of bread, ready for the toaster, then poured himself a cup of coffee, offering Emma one, as well.

She shook her head, thinking she couldn't stomach coffee at the moment. She wasn't even sure if she could eat the meal Jack was preparing. Her stomach was churning.

Janine entered the kitchen and went directly to the coffee, pouring a cup, then taking a seat at the table with Emma. An oppressive quiet hung over the table.

"Anything I can do to help, Jack?" Janine asked.

"No ... I got this ... thanks." Jack's voice sounded strained to Toby. The old cat knew what evidence the police had against Emma, and he knew Jack was aware of the same. Toby knew Jack was in turmoil about which side of the story to believe.

Ten minutes later, Jack set a platter of eggs, bacon, and toast on the table. Janine got up and fetched some plates and cutlery. Toby meowed and made his way to his dish, looking back at Jack.

The first laugh since the return home echoed warmly in the kitchen. "Okay, old man. How could I forget to feed you?"

Once lunch was finished, the group retired to the living room. "Just leave the dishes; I'll get to them later," Jack stated.

"I'll let you two chat," Janine suggested, standing in the doorway.

"No, I think you should be in on this conversation," Jack said and motioned her to sit down.

Toby, having finished his kibble, padded into the living room and took up his usual spot on the back of the couch, where he had a cats-eye view of the room. Emma, feeling more secure close to her furry friend, sat on the sofa as near to Toby as she could.

Once Jack was settled in his chair, he turned directly to Emma. "I hope you understand the severity of your situation," he began, "and also the position you have placed me in."

Emma nodded.

"I have hired you one of the best criminal law lawyers in Brantford, and I want to stress to you, Emma, the importance of being totally open and honest with him. If Jeremy has any inkling that you aren't honest with him, he'll drop you like hotcakes. Do you understand this?" Jack leaned forward. "Not to mention the added fact that I have put everything I have on the line for you by putting up your bail money. I need your guarantee that you won't go anywhere until this nightmare is over."

A hint of the old Emma that Toby knew began to creep into her countenance. She hung her head. Her lips trembled with emotion. Her hands shook. Clearing her throat, "I would never do anything to hurt you, Jack." However, it was Emma's next statement that caused Toby to fear what her plan was. "As God is my witness, I have not done what they are accusing me of."

Jack noted, despite Emma's emotional display, she didn't look at him when she spoke. Toby's heart fell apart because he knew now Emma was going to stick to her story—which he knew wasn't the truth.

Do I let it go and hope Jack's friend gets her off? But, if I do that, Emma won't get the help she needs now, and down the road, if she gets away with what she's done, after everything settles down, she may do this again. Only next time, I am sure Emma will be more careful. She might even move away ... maybe closer to the prison where her brother is ... apart from us.

Janine stood up, not wanting to be a part of the conversation. "I really don't want to be here, Jack. I'm going for a walk."

Jack didn't stop her.

After Janine was out the door, Emma turned to Jack. "She doesn't like me. I don't think she believes me, either," she said.

Jack cleared his throat. "Your explanations are pretty hard to accept as true."

195

"Jack…"

"No, Emma. I am having a difficult enough time with your stories right now. There's one more thing I need you to do."

"What's that?"

"I need you to see a counsellor … someone to help you deal with your past. Are you willing to do that?" Jack watched Emma closely, studying her body language.

A counsellor was the last person Emma really wanted to talk to. She'd been down that road and didn't like the way they pried. However, knowing she had no choice, Emma nodded. "No problem. Whatever you want, Jack."

"Good, I'll set it up for you."

If anyone had looked at the old cat, they would have seen him smiling from ear to ear. *Good man, Jack. Glad we're on the same page. Emma definitely needs help.* Toby jumped down on the couch and pushed his way onto Emma's lap. He felt he needed to show her she was still loved.

"Hey there, Toby. Need a backrub?" she asked, running her hand up and down his back. He arched up, absorbing the love. Emma turned to Jack. "Do you mind if I go home now? I'd like to lie down, and I want to see Duke, too."

"Of course, Emma. I'll let you know as soon as I get your appointment with the counsellor set up. In the meantime, if you need anything, let me know." Jack stood up. "Also, Jeremy will be contacting you about setting up some meetings to go over your case, so be prepared for that. I want you to touch base with me at least once a day, as well—okay?"

Emma gently pushed Toby off her lap. *Feels like I'm already in prison. But, I guess if I am going to continue my mission in the future, I'm going to have to play this game out!* "No problem, Jack. I can't tell you enough how much it means to me that you are helping me." Emma turned when she reached the door and looked at Toby. "You too, my friend. Make sure you come over any time you like. I'm sorry for being so unaccommodating lately."

Toby, despite his love for Emma, wasn't sure if she was sincere—especially with what he knew about what she'd done.

Sixty-three

The three weeks to trial date sped by. Emma kept a low profile, playing the meek young woman that had first moved next door to Jack and Toby. She attended two sessions with the counsellor Jack found for her and met with Jeremy Davies once to go over her story for the hearing. She was scheduled to meet with him again today, the day before the hearing.

Emma smiled as she recollected her last meeting with the counsellor, Sandra Winters. Duke was sitting by her chair in the kitchen, hoping she would give him a bit of something from her plate. "She thinks she knows who I am, Duke," Emma said to her dog. "She thinks she has me all figured out already, after meeting with me twice. What a fool! It's so much fun playing with these so-called professionals. They are so easy to manipulate when one knows how," Emma rambled. She glanced at her watch. There was time for a workout before Jack would be over to take her to the lawyer's office.

Jeremy Davies was having a tough time believing all of Emma's stories. However, he had not been able to break her. She stayed true to her rendition of how she came into possession of the ring, and what the Rohypnol was for. She still had no explanation for the pictures taken in the hospital, sticking to the fact that she had not been there. When Jeremy looked at the photographs the police took, he figured he could get away with saying it was not really her; the images were fuzzy, to say the least.

Jack and Emma arrived at Jeremy's office a few minutes early and waited in the reception area for him to call them in.

"Tomorrow's the big day," Jack stated, more for something to say than any real start to a big conversation.

Emma sighed and looked out the window.

"Nervous?"

"Not really ... well, a little. But my truth will prevail." Emma continued looking away from Jack.

"Jack ... Emma," Jeremy entered the waiting room. "Follow me. We're going to meet in one of the conference rooms."

After sitting, Jeremy took out a pad of paper that already had several notes on it. "Let's just go over everything we've talked about, Emma. I asked Jack to sit in with us this time as a second set of ears for me."

Emma wondered why her lawyer would need a second set of ears, assuming that he possibly was trying to catch her up in a lie. *I better be careful ... can't have my lawyer thinking I'm lying if he might already not trust my story.*

For the next half hour, Jeremy went over all his notes. Emma answered as she had before, sticking one hundred percent to her story. Jack watched her body language and listened carefully for any deviation. He was impressed with how solidly Emma stuck to her story.

Jeremy set his pen down and leaned back in his chair. "I think you're ready, Emma. I'll see you in court tomorrow morning. We'll meet in the lobby downstairs at 9:30." Gathering his papers, Jeremy left the room, Jack and Emma right behind him.

Sixty-four

Emma put a cute dress on for court. She braided her long hair and wound it into a bun at the nape of her neck. She applied some makeup, unusual for her, and dug in her drawer for the pair of glasses she sometimes used. The lenses were plain glass, but they were a good disguise for her when she needed one. If Mike were in the courtroom today, he would never recognize her. Emma looked in the mirror one last time before heading downstairs.

"See you later, Duke," she said, patting her dog on the head. "Wish me luck," she added. Duke's tail thumped excitedly on the floor. "Do you want to go out for a few minutes?" Duke moved to the door and waited.

Ten minutes later, Emma walked over to Jack's. Toby was sitting on the front step, devastated he wasn't able to attend court—some rule about no animals allowed unless they were a service animal. *I guess they don't realize who I am ... the service I provide the police force ... oh well, Jack will fill me in on what happens. I'll have to trust that he gets all the details right.*

Jeremy Davies met Emma and Jack in the lobby, as pre-arranged. Davies said a few words of encouragement to his client before leading the way up the stairs to the courtroom. Jack took a seat in the viewing area; Emma followed her lawyer to the defendant's table. She glanced over at the Crown Attorney.

He looks like a cat that just ate a big mouse ... well, my lawyer and I are going to tear his case apart. Hopefully, this won't go to trial with a jury ... could get dicey for me if it does.

Emma sat down and demurely folded her hands on the table and waited for the judge, who entered the court a few minutes later.

The clerk stood: "All rise for the Honourable Frank McKinnon."

The judge shuffled through the files on his desk, then selected the one for the case first on the docket. He glanced over the top of his glasses. "The reason for this hearing is for me to decide if this case should go to trial. Reading through the evidence, I am inclined to think it may be moving in that direction. However, I like to save the taxpayer's money, so if we can come to some sort of agreement here, let us do so." The Honourable Frank McKinnon hit his gavel on the podium. "I'll hear from the Crown first."

Brian Gregory stood: "Thank you, Your Honour. This case is strange, to say the least. The victim spent two weeks in the hospital but is still in no shape to present in court. Based on the evidence the Crown has gathered, we feel the defendant was involved in his beating and his drugging. It was confirmed by the hospital that Mike Sanderson was drugged with Rohypnol. The defendant was found to be in possession of the same drug. Mike Sanderson's ring, given to him by his fiancée, was found under the stairs in the defendant's house.

"Two police officers saw the defendant exiting Mike Sanderson's room at the hospital and took pictures of her changing out of a hospital gown and leaving the floor. When the police paid a visit to the home where Mike Sanderson's girlfriend was staying, as they were leaving, one of the officers noticed the defendant in the backyard of the house next door. When they approached her, questioned her and showed her the picture, the defendant was evasive and said it was not her, then ran into the house and locked the door. The officers thought they should watch her, fearing she might flee. They were right. Later that same night, the defendant was leaving, with a suitcase, under the pretence of paying her brother, who is in prison, a visit.

"With all this evidence, we believe the defendant is definitely involved with what happened to Mike Sanderson. If it were not for a timely visit to Sanderson's house by his girlfriend, we would be charging the defendant with murder today, not attempted murder. The Crown is willing to accept a deal of some sort if the defendant will admit what she has done and plead guilty. If she doesn't wish to do that, we are willing to go to trial." Gregory sat down, satisfied he had made a good case.

The judge nodded to Jeremy Davies, who was already getting to his feet. Emma was about to stand as well, but he motioned for her to remain seated.

"Your Honour," Davies began, "My client is innocent of these accusations. Before I start to refute the allegations against her, I would like to point out that she does not even know Mike Sanderson, never having met him. Miss Gale came upon Mr. Sanderson's girlfriend in a park and assisted the young woman, who at the time was having a miscarriage. It was at that same park, which happens to be on my client's running route, she came upon the ring in question. According to Mr. Sanderson's girlfriend, it was at that park that he accosted her. We can assume that during the altercation, his ring slipped from his finger.

"Moving on to the drug, Rohypnol, found in Mr. Sanderson's test at the Brantford General Hospital, my client admits to taking this drug herself on occasion. She has suffered a great deal in her past and has nightmares. When she read about this drug being able to erase memories, she thought to give it a try. There is no way she administered it to Mr. Sanderson, because, as I have already pointed out, she does not know him— never met him.

"The police officers claim it was my client in the hospital that morning, and that she is the individual in the pictures they took. She claimed, when they confronted her with the photos, it was not her. She was not at the hospital that day, but home nursing a bad headache. The pictures themselves are so fuzzy one cannot say for sure who it is. My client says she was still suffering from her migraine when the police were, in her words, harassing her in her backyard, which is why she fled into her home and locked the doors.

"My client says she had been planning for some time to go and see her brother but had also been procrastinating doing so. Her friend, Tessa, who is a police profiler, offered to take her, but my client did not wish to bother her. It was a last-minute decision to go see her brother. She was not fleeing the city because of some crime she allegedly committed. If she were, she would have been taking her faithful pet with her. But she wasn't leaving her dog without care. She was taking a key to her house to her neighbour, a retired police officer, and the individual who put up her bail, to look after her dog. That is when the police swooped in assuming she was fleeing because she'd committed a crime.

"I suggest, based on my client's side of the story, the Crown has no substantial case against her, and there would be no need for a trial by a jury here. I suggest that Mike Sanderson, who has a history of hard-drinking, drug consumption, and, if I might be permitted to add, beating his girlfriends, is the one who administered the drug to himself. Only Mr. Sanderson took more than planned, trying to forget his breakup with his girlfriend—and he mixed it with alcohol.

"I put my client's fate in your hands, Your Honour, to make the right decision and rule on this case as one of total misunderstanding and over-zealous police officers attempting to close a case that isn't an actual case at all. My client is not guilty of any of this, and a trial would only waste time and money. There are no deals to be made here, only the release of an innocent woman." Jeremy Davies nodded to the judge and sat down.

Gregory glared at Davies. He was pissed the lawyer had brought up Mike Sanderson's drug and alcohol abuse, as well as his mistreatment of women. That didn't bode well at all and could sway the judge to consider letting the defendant go free. He firmly believed she was guilty and a terrific liar.

Judge McKinnon shuffled the notes he'd been taking while the lawyers delivered their cases. He was disinclined to make a decision immediately. "This court will take a two-hour recess and return at two o'clock for my verdict. Court dismissed." He banged his gavel, stood, and left the room.

Emma felt butterflies in her stomach as she exited the courthouse with Jack and Jeremy. She felt Jeremy had presented a good enough case to refute everything the prosecution had against her, and the addition of the kind of man Mike was, was a genius move. But, the judge might decide it was worth it to have a trial by jury, and anything could happen there. Especially if Mike showed up. Especially if anything was brought up about her past abuses and the possibility of her taking revenge on men who battered women. Especially, because Janine had confided what Mike had done to her and Emma had taken the real victim under her wing.

Yes, anything could happen. Emma realized how much her future was being held in the hands of a pompous old man with the power to set her free now—or not.

Two hours later, Emma was back in court. She and Jeremy Davies, and the Crown Attorney took their places at their respective tables.

Once Judge McKinnon was settled into his chair, he looked down at the two parties before him. He cleared his throat. "I have decided that this case should go to a juried trial. I would like to hear more evidence from the police officers, the ex-girlfriend—as I understand she now is—from the doctors, from the victim, and from the defendant. I am setting a trial date for two weeks from today, at which time a jury will be selected. Is this date satisfactory to the Crown and the Defense?"

Both attorneys checked their calendars and nodded in the affirmative. The judge banged his gavel, stood, and left.

"What does this mean?" Emma turned to her lawyer.

"It means the judge is undecided about your innocence, or your guilt," he replied.

"Is this good for us?" Emma was nervous to even hear Jeremy's reply to this question.

"I'm not sure. Obviously, the judge is uncertain of the evidence in front of him and wants to hear directly from all parties involved. We have to trust that your explanations for the evidence against you will win out." Jeremy Davies didn't feel as confident as he was portraying to his client.

Sixty-five

The two weeks leading up to the trial seemed to drag for everyone involved. Emma was wound tighter than a drum, worried the more time that passed, Mike would start remembering what happened to him and who did it to him.

Jack was concerned for Emma, having talked privately to Jeremy, who was troubled about the judge's decision to go to trial.

Janine was nervous. She would have to testify in court this time; the prosecution had approached her. The police had also considered her as a possible suspect for what happened to Mike. She wasn't looking forward to the court date.

Jeremy was bothered by Emma's stories. They refuted the evidence against her well enough. However, that's what he was beginning to think they were—made up stories. He'd noticed her control of body and words. Emma calculated everything she said, ensuring she didn't deter from what she'd said before. It bordered on over-control. Under normal circumstances, Jeremy wouldn't have taken Emma's case on if it weren't for his friend, Jack, asking him to.

Mike had been contacted by the Crown Attorney about the case and the fact it was going to trial. He was unsure how he felt about that; he was still unclear as to what had happened to him. In truth, Mike just wanted to forget the past and start over. He hadn't had a drink since the hospital and was trying desperately to stay on the wagon. His boss had phoned and said he was being called back to work within a couple weeks. The last thing Mike needed was to not be able to work because of a trial for something he just wanted to forget.

Officer Hendricks was pleased with the judge's decision. He wanted the case to go to trial. He was a great observer of human behaviour, and in his professional opinion, Emma was the perpetrator. Hendricks just had to figure out the main missing link—how she knew Mike beyond what she'd been told by Janine.

MacDonald, a less-seasoned officer than Hendricks, wasn't sure a trial was worth the taxpayer dollars it was going to take. She had apprehensions about Emma, but from what she now knew about Mike Sanderson, the victim, in her opinion he was a scumbag, and if someone did this to him, he probably deserved it. MacDonald even considered, as Jeremy Davies had pointed out at the hearing, Sanderson overdosed himself and had Janine, his ex-girlfriend, whom he'd brutalized, to thank for still being alive.

Toby was nervous for Emma now that the judge had determined a trial was necessary. In many ways, he was glad he was a cat because he wouldn't have to testify. He was the only one besides Emma who knew the truth.

On the morning of the trial, Emma once again dressed to disguise her looks. Today, more so than the last time, would be the moment of truth of whether Mike recognized her or not.

Jack and Janine were waiting in the truck for Emma when she left the house. Sitting in the backseat, Emma felt a chill when Janine, despite saying good morning to her, sounded artificially warm. Jack was his usual composed self.

"You ready for this?" Jack asked, turning to look at Emma.

"As ready as anyone can be when their life is on the line," Emma replied reservedly.

Jeremy Davies met Jack, Janine, and Emma on the courthouse steps. He directed them inside and up to the courtroom. Jack and

Janine sat in the front row of the visitor's galley; Emma took her place beside Jeremy.

Once Judge McKinnon showed up, the proceedings to choose a jury began. Several people were sitting in the galley, each holding the letter they'd received, calling them for possible jury duty. A large wire cage was brought out, filled with matching numbers to the letters, and the clerk began drawing from it. The first twelve potentials took their places in the jury box.

"Are there any amongst you," Judge McKinnon began, "who have a valid reason why they are unable to serve on the jury?"

Four individuals raised their hands and voiced their reasons. They were dismissed. Only five of the remaining twelve were accepted by both Crown and Defense. The process continued until twelve jurors and three alternates were chosen. The balance of the potential jurors was dismissed from the courtroom.

Judge McKinnon turned to address the jury. "You will now be taken to a room and receive instructions as to what will be expected of you over this trial. Before following the clerks, I must instruct you that whatever you hear in this courtroom, stays in this room. You are not to discuss this case with anyone during the trial. We'll meet back here in one hour and begin opening arguments." The gavel reverberated through the room and the judge left through the door leading to his private chambers.

An hour later, everyone was back in court. Jeremy had taken Jack, Janine, and Emma out for a quick lunch during the recess. The clerk called the Crown Attorney to begin his opening statements.

Gregory stood and ambled slowly over to the jury box, which contained seven women and five men. "Ladies and gentlemen of the jury, you are being charged with hearing the evidence about to be presented in this court. The Defense will try and convince you that the stories the defendant, Emma Gale, tell you are true..." Gregory went on for another ten minutes before concluding his précis.

Jeremy Davis took his time walking to the jurors. He walked along the railing, looking at each individual who was sitting there, waiting for him to begin. Finally, "Just look at her, ladies and gentlemen," Davis began. "The Crown would have you believe that Emma Gale is cold-blooded enough to have beaten and drugged a man she doesn't even know—has never met. They will present circumstantial evidence, which Miss Gale has explained over and over why she possessed such items. Her only connection to this man is that she helped his ex-girlfriend, who was miscarrying his baby in a park after he had brutally beaten her the day before." Davis paused and again looked at each of the jurors, then back to Emma, a perplexed look on his face.

"I trust you will come to the right and just conclusion once you've heard all the evidence, and you will set this young woman free. Look again, ladies and gentlemen. See Miss Gale for who she is—an innocent bystander that happened by another young woman in despair and helped her. That's it. Thank you." Davis strolled back to the table where Emma was sitting, ensuring that the jurors still had a clear view of her.

Emma played her part well, too, allowing a few tears to drip down her cheeks. Hendricks, watching from the front row of the courtroom, couldn't believe what a good actor she was. He realized the Crown was up against a superior lawyer and that a potential killer might get off scot-free if she couldn't be proven guilty beyond a reasonable doubt. The one link that was missing in the Crown's case was an actual witness to prove Emma had met Sanderson, so they didn't have to depend on a few fuzzy pictures taken in the hospital! The woman in those pictures looked nothing like the one sitting beside her defence attorney!

Judge McKinnon decided to delay calling the first witnesses and adjourned the trial till the next day. He thanked the jury and reminded them that they were to speak to no one about anything that had gone on in the court.

Sixty-six

The next morning court got underway at ten o'clock. The prosecution called their first witness—Janine. She made her way to the witness box and was sworn in. She was nervous, not knowing what to expect, still unsure of which side of the case she was going to benefit—if either.

Brian Gregory approached her. "Good morning, Miss Larson."

"Good morning."

After the greeting was over, the prosecution didn't waste any time getting to his questions. "I understand you are in a relationship with Mr. Sanderson."

"I was."

"Right ... what happened?"

"We had a parting of ways," Janine wrung her hands nervously. Gregory was treading on ground she didn't want to step on.

"I see." A pause. "Well, despite your parting of ways, you still had enough feelings for Mr. Sanderson to check up on him ... is this true?"

"I was worried there might be something wrong. When I went to get my belongings with a police officer, Mike was not in the house but his truck was in the driveway."

"Why did that concern you, Miss Larson? Is it not possible, Mr. Sanderson just went for a walk?"

"Not likely. Mike didn't walk anywhere he didn't have to."

"I see." A pause. "So, you decided to stop in and check on him ... make sure he was okay?"

211

"Yes."

"When you got to the house, what did you find?"

"I saw what a mess the house was and Mike passed out on the couch."

"What was your initial thought?"

"Well, at first, I thought he was just passed out drunk," Janine replied. "He'd been drinking a lot since getting laid off from his job. But, there was something different about the way he was laying on the couch. I decided to call 911. I'm glad I did."

"You said he looked different ... how so?"

"He had cuts and bruises on his face and arms."

"So, to reaffirm, you just went to the house because you were worried about him and your fears proved to be right. Essentially, you saved his life."

"Yes."

Gregory changed direction with his questioning: "I understand detectives MacDonald and Hendricks questioned you extensively in the hospital. They were under the impression that you might have had something to do with what happened to Mr. Sanderson, were they not?"

"Yes."

"Did you?"

"No. I could never hurt anyone. If I wanted Mike dead, why would I have called 911?"

"Thank you, Miss Larson." Gregory turned to Jeremy. "Your witness."

Jeremy hated what he was about to do. Janine was a sweetheart, in his opinion, compared to what he actually thought of Emma. But, he had a client to defend, so he had no choice. "Miss Larson ... you have painted a pretty picture of how compassionate you are ... how concerned you were for Mr. Sanderson ... the same man that beat you within an inch of your life and caused you to miscarry." Jeremy took a moment and looked at the jury, allowing time for his words to sink in.

"Do you want us to believe you didn't wish any harm to Mr. Sanderson for what he'd done to you?"

"Yes ... I want you to believe me. I just wanted out of the relationship, and I'd finally managed to leave him."

"So, you want us to believe you had no desire for revenge?"

"That's right. I'd ended it with Mike, as difficult as that was to do."

"Too bad it was too late for your child." Jeremy kept driving in the nails, hoping to break Janine's testimony. He continued: "I suggest that you went back to Mike Sanderson's house intent on teaching him a lesson ... you'd lost your baby because of him ... he'd beaten you ... he'd destroyed your life ... your dreams. My client, Emma Gale, found you in the park, curled up in pain, losing your baby. She is the kind of person to help a complete stranger, as she helped you. She is not the kind of person who would break into someone's house to drug and beat them..."

"Objection!" the Crown Attorney jumped to his feet. "The councillor is badgering this witness ... she's not the one on trial here!"

"No, but maybe she should be," Jeremy managed to get in, with a pleasant glance toward the jurors, before the judge intervened.

"Sustained," Judge McKinnon said. "Mr. Davies, if you have a question to ask of Miss Larson, ask it."

Davies nodded, a slight smile curling his lips. Turning back to Janine. "Miss Larson, did you return to Mr. Sanderson's home—the home of the man who had just beaten you within an inch of your life—with the full intention of teaching him a lesson?"

"No, I did not."

"Then why?" Jeremy figured the longer he dragged out this line of questioning, the more doubt would be in the jurors' minds about who had committed the crime.

"As I've already said, I was worried..." Janine began before being cut off by Jeremy.

"Why would you worry about a man who had just beaten you ... who had caused you to lose your baby?"

Gregory jumped to his feet again, irate. "Your Honour, objection! I believe we've already established that Mr. Sanderson beat his girlfriend, but he is not on trial here for that ... he's the victim."

"Maybe, he should be," Jeremy commented, throwing another look over to the jurors, especially the women sitting in the front row.

Judge McKinnon was no fool. He knew precisely what Jeremy Davies was doing. Nevertheless, deep inside, the judge had no use for men like Mike Sanderson, and he was willing to allow a bit of colouring outside the lines. "Mr. Davies, please keep your questions..."

"Your Honour," Jeremy interrupted, "I simply asked Miss Larson why she would worry about a man who had beaten her. Why she would return to his house, and alone. I believe that is a pertinent question to this case." Jeremy got in another reasonable doubt statement.

The judge looked at Gregory: "Objection overruled. The witness will answer the question."

"Shall I repeat the question for you, Miss Larson?"

Janine shook her head. "I went to his house because I was worried—like I said. For no other reason."

Jeremy figured he'd given the jurors enough to think about. It was time to end it with Janine. "If you say so ... I have

214

no further questions, at this time, for this witness." Jeremy turned and walked to his table and sat down beside Emma.

Janine stepped out of the witness box and made her way back to her seat beside Jack. She leaned over and whispered to him: "Why did Mr. Davies try and make me look to be the one who did this to Mike?" she asked, tears brimming in her eyes.

"I don't think it's anything personal, Janine. Jeremy is just trying to put doubt in the jurors' minds, presenting possible scenarios other than Emma."

"But I didn't do anything to Mike. You know that, don't you, Jack?"

Jack patted Janine on the knee. "Yes, I know you didn't do this." *Jeremy, I hope you know what you're doing ... trying to paint Janine as a possible for this crime might get Emma off but it also might get Janine arrested! And she, for sure, is totally innocent.*

Gregory called his next witness. "I call Martin Harper."

Martin Harper was one of the paramedics to answer the call to Mike's house. He took the stand and was sworn in. Jeremy knew his testimony was reasonably harmless to his client, so he sat back in his chair, feigning a disinterested look.

Gregory went through a list of general questions for Martin and established the condition Mike was in when the paramedics showed up on the scene.

"Mr. Sanderson was barely alive when we arrived," Martin informed. "If Miss Larson hadn't called when she did, Mike Sanderson might not be here today."

"I see. And what was Miss Larson doing when you arrived at Mike Sanderson's house?"

"She was sitting in the living room with another gentleman and a big orange cat. I believe the man is the retired police officer who had gone to the house with Miss Larson previously—so she informed me when she made introductions."

215

"Did Miss Larson appear to you like someone who would be capable of beating a man and drugging him?" Gregory was attempting to discredit what Jeremy had presented when cross-examining Janine.

Jeremy was on his feet in an instant. "Objection! This man is not qualified to give an opinion on whether Miss Larson is capable or not of committing such an offence."

"Objection sustained," Judge McKinnon said.

"Withdrawn." Gregory walked over to his table, shuffled a few papers; he asked his next question from there. "Did Miss Larson accompany Mr. Sanderson to the hospital?"

"She followed the ambulance."

"In your opinion, is that the action of someone who had…"

"Objection! Once again, this witness is not qualified to give an opinion on this, Your Honour. I thought we already clarified this!" Jeremy gave a look of indignation, directing it more to the jury than to the judge.

Judge McKinnon glared at the Crown Prosecutor. "You have been warned about this line of questioning. Please stick to the facts this witness is qualified to answer."

Gregory shook his head and raised his hands in frustration. "No further questions." He walked to his seat and scribbled something on a pad of paper. It was nothing of any importance, just to make it look as though it might be.

Jeremy really had nothing much to ask the paramedic. He was of no vital importance to Emma's case, not having had any interaction with her. "No questions at this time for this witness."

The judge checked his watch and ordered a two-hour recess. Court would reconvene at two o'clock.

Sixty-seven

Two o'clock saw all the parties back in the courtroom. The Crown called their next witness, Doctor Carmichael. "It is my understanding that you were the doctor who oversaw the care of Mike Sanderson?" Gregory opened with.

"I am."

"What was Mr. Sanderson's condition when he arrived at the hospital?"

Doctor Carmichael cleared his throat. "Mr. Sanderson was unconscious and close to death. We hooked him immediately to an IV and drew several vials of blood to be tested. We also managed to get a sample of urine from him." The doctor hesitated, his mouth partially open as though debating if he should carry on. He decided to continue. "It was also obvious the patient had been drinking; he reeked of alcohol ... and excrement.

"Besides the high level of alcohol we found in his blood, I believe the test result showed a level of 2.5 when Mr. Sanderson's urine test came back, it showed high levels of Rohypnol." The doctor sat back in his chair and gazed over at the jurors.

Gregory scratched his head. "Rohypnol? Is that a dangerous drug?"

"Extremely dangerous. In fact," Doctor Carmichael began, "Rohypnol can paralyze an individual within a half-hour or less, reaching its peak within two hours of consumption. Its effects can last for eight to twelve hours. With the alcohol level we found in Mr. Sanderson's blood, the effect would be escalated. Typically, if taken in small doses, it will pass from the system within twenty-four hours."

"And if it were taken in large doses?" Gregory pushed on.

"It would take a lot longer to leave the system."

"You mentioned that Rohypnol can paralyze someone … what other side effects are there to this—what sounds like to me--a hazardous drug?" Gregory inquired.

The doctor cleared his throat again. "This drug has been nicknamed the *date rape drug*, the reason being that it can cause a person to become drowsy and lose control of their limbs. They will be confused, their speech will be slurred, and they will be extremely confused. Loss of memory of what might be done to an individual while under the influence of Rohypnol is one of the main reasons it is used amongst a lot of people who want to take advantage of a person—usually, a female—and the person won't remember what happened to them, or who the perpetrators were."

"Is Rohypnol addictive, doctor?"

"It can be if it is used excessively."

"In your professional opinion, was Mr. Sanderson addicted to Rohypnol?"

"Personally, I don't think so. I believe his use of this drug was fairly recent. He's probably more of an alcoholic than a user of Rohypnol."

"How can you tell?"

"Well, his withdrawal symptoms were not as severe as they would have been with a long-term user. Mr. Sanderson did have a great deal of anxiety, and once he woke up, it was difficult for him to fall back to sleep. If he'd been a long-time user, he most likely would have suffered seizures and drastic behavioural changes."

"How was Mr. Sanderson when he left the hospital?"

"I released him after two weeks, making sure he was well enough to go home on his own. He seemed okay but still had a lot of confusion about what had happened to him. The one thing that could not be explained was the severe beating Mr. Sanderson had endured. When he left the hospital, he was drug and alcohol-free and had agreed to go to AA for his alcohol problems."

"Thank you, doctor." Gregory looked at Jeremy: "Your witness."

Jeremy stood, staying behind his table. There wasn't a lot he wanted from the doctor—not a lot the doctor could say to help Emma's case. "You have said, Doctor Carmichael, Mr. Sanderson was drunk, and on some sort of drug when he was brought to the ER via ambulance, which you later learned was Rohypnol. Correct?"

"Correct."

"But you don't know if Mr. Sanderson administered the drug to himself or if someone else slipped it to him … maybe even into his alcohol, knowing he was a heavy drinker."

Doctor Carmichael shook his head. "No, I have no idea how the drug got in his system. Mr. Sanderson had no idea. Like I said, he was confused about what happened to him. Didn't even know how he'd gotten beaten."

"Is this drug legal in Canada?"

"No, not in Canada or the United States. It's been banned."

"How does one obtain it then?"

"It can be purchased on the internet from countries in Europe and Latin America. Easily accessible."

"Anyone can purchase it?"

"Yes."

"Even Mr. Sanderson?"

"I suppose."

"Thank you, doctor. That will be all."

As Jeremy sat down, Emma breathed a sigh of relief to hear that Mike didn't remember anything about his ordeal.

Judge McKinnon was looking at his watch. He glanced at the witness list, debating on whether to call it a day or have one more witness take the stand. Thinking it over, the judge realized that if he moved the trial along, they could wrap the trial up and everyone could go home before the weekend, having solved the mystery of who did what to Mr. Sanderson, if indeed there was a crime beyond him abusing himself with alcohol and drugs. "Call your next witness," he directed to Brian Gregory.

Gregory stood. "I call Officer Hendricks."

Emma tensed as Hendricks walked to the front of the courtroom. He was, in her opinion, an arrogant prick. As if to prove her thoughts, Hendricks paused at the table where she was sitting, stared at her for a moment, smiled, then walked with a swagger to the witness stand.

Gregory didn't waste any time after Hendricks was sworn in. "Good afternoon, Officer Hendricks."

"Good afternoon."

"You are a police officer for the Brantford Police Department; is that correct?"

"Yes."

"For how many years?'

Davies jumped to his feet: "Objection, Your Honour! What merit does the number of years this witness has been with the police force have to do with the trial? Such menial questions are a waste of court time."

Gregory was quick to reply: "I am just establishing the credibility of my witness, Your Honour."

"Objection overruled," Judge McKinnon said. "However, Mr. Gregory, move along with the issues pertinent to the case. The witness will answer the question."

"Twenty years," Hendricks replied to the Crown's question. He glanced over to the jurors and smiled.

"Moving on to the day our victim, Mr. Sanderson was brought into the hospital, you, along with Officer MacDonald, were called to the hospital to investigate his situation ... could you explain why the medical staff saw fit to call in the police?"

"The victim, Mr. Sanderson, had been brought into the ER unconscious, and it was noted by the medical staff that he had been severely beaten. It is the protocol for the police to be called in under such circumstances."

"Let's move ahead to the second visit you paid to Mr. Sanderson when he'd been moved up to the ward. What, or should I say who did you see coming out of the victim's room as you approached?" Gregory turned slightly and let his eyes fall on Emma.

Jeremy made a note to question why Gregory failed to even bring up how Hendricks and MacDonald had first interrogated Janine, assuming she might be the guilty party.

Hendricks coughed, cleared his throat, and looked from the jurors to Emma, and back to Gregory. "We saw Emma Gale leaving Mr. Sanderson's room."

"What did you do then? Did you attempt to stop her?"

"Officer MacDonald followed Miss Gale. She left the ward, entered a room, and when she exited that room, she was dressed in street clothes. Previously, she'd had on a hospital gown, obviously over her clothing. My partner took several photos before and after the change."

"And you are sure the woman your partner took pictures of is Miss Gale?"

"Let's put it this way ... if it isn't, the person in the pictures is an identical twin."

Gregory changed directions for a moment: "Why did your partner not stop Miss Gale?"

"Objection!" Jeremy was on his feet again. "It has not been concretely established that the individual in the blurry

221

pictures taken on Officer MacDonald's phone is in fact of Miss Gale."

"Sustained. Mr. Gregory, please stick to the facts," the judge ordered.

"Okay, let me ask you, Officer Hendricks, why did your partner not stop the woman she was following?"

"MacDonald told me the woman moved quickly to the elevator, and before she had a chance to get to her, the elevator came and the woman was gone before my partner could reach her."

"I see." A pause by the Crown Attorney. "When was the first time you personally met Miss Gale?"

"My partner and I paid a visit to Miss Larson, the victim's girlfriend, to fill her in on what was going on with her boyfriend. As we drove away from the house where Miss Larson is staying, MacDonald noticed Miss Gale in her backyard, which is next door to where Miss Larson resides at the moment. My partner asked me to stop, and she took out her phone and pulled up the pictures she'd taken at the hospital, saying the woman in the backyard looked like the same person as in the pictures."

"What did you do then?"

"We got out of our vehicle and approached Miss Gale. We asked her if she'd been at the hospital the previous morning, which she denied. We showed her the pictures, and she became agitated and told us to leave, then ran into her house and locked the door."

"Did you attempt to pursue her at that time?" Gregory asked.

"No, but when we got back in our car, we decided we were going to keep an eye on her house. There was something about the way she acted that didn't sit right with us."

"Did you have some kind of proof, other than your pictures and your gut feelings, that Miss Gale had something to do with what happened to Mr. Sanderson?"

"That was enough for us, and it proved to be right on. That evening, Miss Gale was caught leaving her home, with a suitcase, on the pretence she was going to visit her brother."

"What did you do then?"

"We drove up and tried to bring her in for questioning. Apparently, she was going to ask her neighbour, Jack Nelson, to look after her dog for a few days. That's the excuse she gave, anyway. Nelson is a retired cop, and he said he wanted to talk to Miss Gale, and he would bring her to the station within two hours. Being who he is—a former officer of the law—we agreed."

"And did Mr. Nelson bring her in?"

"Yes."

"And you questioned Miss Gale that night?"

Hendricks leaned back in his chair and grinned charmingly at the jurors. "Well, it was late, and my partner and I had had a long day. Miss Gale was falling asleep as we attempted to question her, so we thought to call it a day and start fresh in the morning. We locked her up in holding for the night, not trusting that she wouldn't try and make another run for it."

Emma's lawyer jumped to his feet. "Objection, Your Honour! The prosecution is implying that my client is guilty and would try and leave town. He has no way of knowing that!"

The judge scowled at Gregory. "Mr. Gregory, have your client stick to the actual details of the case." Turning to the jurors, "Please disregard the witness' last statement."

Gregory grimaced. He had a gut feeling the judge was sorry he'd even allowed this case to go to trial and that he was trying to sabotage the prosecution. Glancing over at Emma, he figured why—how could a fragile, sweet-looking young woman be capable of such deeds. Gregory cleared his throat and continued. "When you interviewed Miss Gale in the morning, did she reveal anything of any significance that made you decide to continue questioning her?" Gregory asked.

"Actually, I was just beginning my questioning when a phone call came through from the hospital. Doctor Carmichael called to tell us that they had found Rohypnol in Sanderson's urine sample."

"What did you do with this knowledge?"

"I called my captain right away and asked him to send a team over to Sanderson's house to go through it with a fine-tooth comb to see if there was any evidence of the drug at his house."

"Was there?"

"No. Just a lot of alcohol bottles—mostly empty ones. There was also a glass in a baggie under the couch. I assume the paramedics bagged it for evidence, but probably forgot it in their haste to get Mr. Sanderson to the hospital."

"All this has led you to believe what?" Gregory pursued.

"That someone else gave him the drug."

"Do you know what happened to the glass?"

"It was sent for testing of prints and traces of drugs; protocol would suggest that."

"You received another phone call while you had Miss Gale in the interrogation room, didn't you?" Without waiting for him to answer his first question, Gregory asked his next one: "Who was that from, and what information did you glean from it that was pertinent to the case you were building against Miss Gale?"

"The call came from Jack Nelson. He told me that while he was over at Miss Gale's house to feed her dog, Toby, his cat, found a ring under the stairs in the basement. It turned out to be Mike Sanderson's ring, which was identified at the time by Janine Larson, Sanderson's girlfriend. It was a ring she'd given him." Hendricks paused and threw another knowing look at Emma. "Jack also brought me a bottle of Rohypnol, which had been found in Miss Gale's bathroom by Miss Larson."

"So, this new evidence led you to believe that Miss Gale had something to do with Mr. Sanderson's condition—that at the very least, she had met him?"

"You bet it did!"

"Did you question Miss Gale about these items?"

"We certainly did, but she had a reason for both items— more like a story, if you ask me," Hendricks smirked.

"Objection!" Jeremy shouted out. "The witness cannot say for sure if Miss Gale was telling a story or telling the truth. That is for the jury to decide."

"Sustained." Judge McKinnon glanced at his watch again, his stomach rumbling from lack of his afternoon snack. "Keep your comments to the facts, Officer Hendricks," he added.

"Yes, Your Honour." Hendricks peeked over to the jurors. He knew he'd made his point, and that was all he cared about. Emma Gale was guilty of something, and he was going to make sure she paid for whatever it was!

Gregory walked over to his table and sat down on the edge of it. He tarried a moment, looking around the courtroom, especially at the jurors, before continuing. "What reasons did Miss Gale give you for having the drug Rohypnol and Mr. Sanderson's ring in her possession?"

"She claimed the drug was for her own use … something about erasing nightmares she had … and she claimed she found Sanderson's ring at a park when she was out jogging."

"You didn't believe her?"

"Well, as an experienced law enforcement officer, I've interrogated a lot of people over the years. With that evidence, and with the pictures we had from the hospital, I seriously doubted Miss Gale was telling me the truth. So, we arrested her."

Gregory turned to Jeremy Davies. "Your witness."

Before Jeremy could come forward to question Hendricks, Judge McKinnon intervened. "I am calling a twenty-minute recess before Mr. Davies questions this witness." He banged his gavel on his desk and left the room quickly, anxious to get to his quarters where he had a sandwich and piece of cake waiting for him in his mini-fridge.

Sixty-eight

Twenty minutes later, everyone was back in their places in the courtroom. Jeremy approached Hendricks. "I need not remind you that you are still under oath?"

"Of course not."

"You've testified that you were called to the hospital when the nurses saw that Mr. Sanderson looked as though he'd been beaten. I also understand, as per Miss Larson's testimony, you first questioned her, believing her to be the perpetrator of this possible crime. Why did you steer your attention to Miss Gale?"

"I won't speak for Officer MacDonald, but I believed, once other evidence presented itself, Miss Larson was telling us the truth. When we saw Miss Gale—I mean, a woman exiting the victim's hospital room, acting strangely, the spitting image of Miss Gale—I discussed this with my partner, and we decided to look in a different direction from Miss Larson."

"But, at the time you were not coming to arrest Miss Gale … you were going to Jack Nelson's house to question Janine Larson again, weren't you?"

"Yeah." Hendricks shuffled uncomfortably in his chair.

"And it wasn't until you left Janine Larson and drove past Miss Gale's house that you even suspected her, and only because of her similarity to some fuzzy pictures taken by Officer Macdonald in the hospital … is this correct?"

Hendricks' eyes shifted to the floor. "Yeah."

"So, other than the pictures from the hospital, you had no reason to even suspect Jack Nelson's neighbour, my client, of anything … is that correct?"

"Yes, but…"

227

Jeremy drove on, not allowing Hendricks to finish: "And hadn't Miss Gale told you, when you confronted her in her yard, she had not been at the hospital on the day in question? That in fact, she never even left her house?"

"Yes, but..."

"And didn't, Miss Gale explain to you during your interrogation, once you had this other evidence that you claim all pointed the finger at her ... to have gone to a man's house that she didn't know, drug him and beat him ... didn't she explain to you why she had the Rohypnol and Mr. Sanderson's ring in her possession?" Still driving forward: "Did she not tell you she suffered from nightmares and was taking Rohypnol to try and get her brain to forget her past torments, and that she found the ring in the park while out for a run—both very plausible explanations?"

"Yes, but..." Hendricks was attempting to get a word in, but once again Jeremy Davies cut him off.

"I suggest that you were just trying to build a case against an innocent woman—anyone would do. And when the first one wasn't looking so good for the deed, you moved on to another possible candidate."

The Crown Attorney objected to Jeremy's line of questions, saying he was badgering the police officer for just doing his job, but Judge McKinnon waved it off.

Jeremy continued. "You said you asked your captain to go through Mr. Sanderson's house looking for traces of Rohypnol, and you also stated that there was none found there. You have mentioned here there was a bagged glass under the couch ... has this been sent for testing?"

"I don't know. I wasn't in on the house search. As I already said before, I assume it has if protocol was followed."

"Heard anything from forensics?"

"No, some tests take time." Hendricks squirmed in his chair.

"Was the glass dusted for prints?" Jeremy asked. "Usually, it doesn't take long to get a result for fingerprints, especially if they are in the system," he added.

"Yes."

"Were Emma Gale's prints on the glass?"

"No."

"Were there prints on the glass, and if so, whose?"

"The only prints on the glass were Mike Sanderson's." Hendricks looked totally uncomfortable having to answer questions about the glass.

"Moving on, then … is it not possible Mr. Sanderson dumped any trace of the drug, or that maybe someone else removed such evidence? Washed the glass? That way, there'd be no trace of Rophypnol residue."

Hendricks knew when he was fighting a losing battle, and Jeremy Davies was not a lawyer to be taken lightly. He thought it best to keep what dignity he had and give Jeremy the answers he was looking for. It would be up to Gregory to tear Emma apart if and when she took the stand.

"Both are possibilities, I guess," Hendricks answered.

"And is it not possible that Mr. Sanderson lost his ring in the park, the same park where just days before he had accosted his girlfriend in a violent confrontation, and that Miss Gale, who runs a regular route, said park being on her way, did find the ring and take it home … and, as she explained, it fell out of her pocket when she went to her basement to work out. She probably never thought of it again, a found ring not being of much importance to her. Is this a possibility, Officer Hendricks?"

"Possible." *But not likely.*

"Thank you, Officer Hendricks. Nothing further."

A look of surprise crossed over the Crown Attorney's face and the judge's, as well. However, Judge McKinnon recovered quickly and dismissed the court for the day, saying they would reconvene at ten o'clock in the morning. As he made his way to his chambers, the judge thought he should have just dismissed the entire affair. Mike Sanderson was a woman beating alcoholic. If he didn't do this to himself, whoever did should receive a medal!

Emma slept well for the first time in a long while. The way Jeremy Davies had torn the cop's testimony apart gave her hope that she was going to walk away from this unscathed. Despite her good feelings, though, Emma knew her ordeal wasn't over.

Janine was confused about what had happened in court. She was distressed at how Emma's lawyer had gone after her, making it look as though she could possibly have done something to Mike. She'd voiced her concerns to Jack, but he'd told her it was just a way to put reasonable doubt in the jurors' minds. His explanation didn't make her feel any better. After her conversation with Jack, Janine had excused herself and gone to her room.

"Who am I fooling," she mumbled to the empty room. "Emma is Jack's first priority. He's known her a lot longer than he has me. And, Toby is close to her too, even though he seems to know something we don't." Janine drew in a nervous breath. "I need to tread carefully here. It might even be wiser for me to just go to a hotel, or if worse comes to worse, stay with Mike. I don't think he'll hurt me now. He seems so vulnerable."

Janine decided to sleep on it and make her decision when she woke up.

Jack filled Toby in on the court proceedings, just for someone to talk to. Toby sat listening with rapt attention, taking in every detail. When Jack finished, he flicked on the television, tuning into some *Law and Order* re-runs.

Toby was going over everything Jack had relayed. *Oh, Emma ... you're so lucky to have Jack and me in your corner. Jack couldn't have picked anyone better to take on your case. Jeremy Davies sounds like he destroyed the prosecution's witnesses, especially that cop, Hendricks. But, as Jack said, tomorrow could be a different day. Mike Sanderson is scheduled to take the stand. If he still can't remember what happened to him, that would be beneficial; however, if he recognizes Emma, that could spell her doom!*

Toby curled up on the back of his couch—his vigil point—to keep an eye on Emma's place. Just in case she decided to pursue what Toby had come to understand might be her mission—dispensing her own sense of justice against abusers.

Sixty-nine

Emma sat beside Jeremy the next morning, dressed in a floral dress that modestly tickled her calves. Her hair was pulled back into a severe bun and her fake glasses were perched on an immaculately made-up face. She smiled when she remembered her answer to Jack when he had questioned her about the glasses. She had told him that when she was stressed, they helped her not get a headache. As far as she could tell, he had bought her explanation.

Looking around, Emma saw Mike Sanderson enter the courtroom. He took his seat, and then his eyes focused on her. Emma could tell he seemed to be trying to think if he had ever met her before. Quickly she turned and faced the front of the room.

The judge made his entrance fashionably late, as usual, and the court proceedings began. Brian Gregory called his first witness of the day: "I call Mike Sanderson to the stand."

Mike made his way down the aisle of the visitors' gallery, and as he passed Emma, he paused and eyeballed her. Shaking his head, he moved forward to the witness stand and was sworn in.

Gregory approached slowly, a look of concern on his face. "Mr. Sanderson ... I understand you've been going through quite a trying time lately."

"It seems so." Mike twisted his hands nervously in his lap.

"Can you fill the jury in on what's been going on ... just to give them an idea of where your life is at the moment ... maybe starting with before your girlfriend left you?"

232

Mike looked over at the jury and searched the gallery for Janine. His heart was heavy because he remembered more and more of what had happened. He saw the look of misery on Janine's face, and although he knew her pain shouldn't give him hope, it did. It gave him hope that there might still be a chance for them to get back together, especially now that he was cleaning up his act.

"I lost my job … well, not actually lost it … got laid off," Mike began. "I felt useless, and when bad things happen to me, I can't help myself … I start drinking … sometimes I even do some drugs … nothing hard, though. Janine started getting on my back about lying around the house all day. Said I should be out looking for some work to do while I was laid off. I guess I began to resent her attitude and got pissed off and started hitting her when she got on my case."

Mike drew in a shuddering breath, as though he were about to cry. In fact, when he looked up at the judge, there were the beginning hints of tears in his eyes. "I know I shouldn't have hit her; I don't blame her for leaving me."

Gregory broke in with another question, changing direction before Mike could say anymore. "It was Janine who found you unconscious in your house … is that correct?"

"That's what I've been told."

"In your opinion, is Janine capable of drugging you and beating you?"

Davies was on his feet again, protesting: "Your Honour, this witness has no idea of what his ex-girlfriend would be capable of doing and is not qualified to answer such a question."

"I heartily disagree," Gregory countered. "Mr. Sanderson lived with Miss Larson for over a year. I would think he would know what she was capable or not capable of."

Davies smirked. "Really? He only knew the nice Miss Larson—the one he hadn't beaten yet. How would he know what she was capable of when backed into a corner as he was beating her? Anyone, no matter how nice they are, might retaliate against such abuse!"

"Your Honour!" Gregory was red-faced. "Mr. Davies is trying to paint Mr. Sanderson as some sort of criminal…"

Before Gregory had a chance to finish his statement, Davies retorted: "Well he is … any man who beats a woman…"

Judge McKinnon banged his gavel on his desk. "Approach!" he roared to the two bickering lawyers. He leaned over and whispered harshly to Gregory and Davies, "I will not have this case turn into a free-for-all. Stick to the points here. A young woman is on trial, not Mr. Sanderson. Your objection, Mr. Davies, is overruled."

Both lawyers returned to their tables—Gregory feeling smug that he'd won this round; Davies smiling because he'd emphasized the point to the jury that Sanderson was a low-life who beat his girlfriend.

Gregory threw Davies a triumphant glance. Davies grinned, unsettling the prosecutor. *What are you up to, Davies?* Turning back to Mike, "So, now you can answer the question I asked … in your opinion, is Janine capable of drugging and beating you?"

"I don't think so," Mike answered, his voice heavy with emotion. "But, like that other lawyer said, who knows what someone might be capable of when pushed too far."

Mike's declaration caught Gregory off-guard, and it was out of Mike's mouth before the lawyer could stop him. Davies tried but failed to hide the smirk that etched his lips.

Gregory knew he was losing ground with his witness. He needed to salvage something before it was too late. He cleared his throat. "Mr. Sanderson, you admit you're an alcoholic?"

"Yes."

"And you have taken drugs?"

Mike nodded. "Yes."

"When you were brought into the hospital, a high level of an extremely potent drug—Rohypnol—was found in your system. Can you explain how it got there?"

"No. Never heard of that drug."

"Are you able to explain how you were beaten, and who might have done that to you?"

Mike shook his head again. "No idea."

"You don't remember being beaten?"

"No, sir."

Gregory turned his attention to the jury now, ready to spiel out to them the side-effects of the drug, Rohypnol. He explained how the drug impaired the memory, thus being used as a date-rape drug. He went on to say that it caused confusion, impaired judgement, dizziness, drowsiness, decreased action time, lack of coordination—all of which, if someone had slipped a pill or two into one of Mike's drinks, could have caused him to be incapable of defending himself, or even of remembering who beat him.

"Mr. Sanderson ..., do you know the defendant?"

Mike studied Emma. He shook his head. "I don't think so. She looks familiar ... maybe ... then again, she might just look like someone from my past. I've known a lot of women."

"The defendant, Emma Gale, uses Rohypnol. She also took Mr. Sanderson's girlfriend under her wing, which means that she probably was aware of his violent actions."

Davies was on his feet again. "Your Honour, the prosecution is testifying now, which he has no right to do!"

"Objection sustained." Turning to Gregory, Judge McKinnon glowered. "I think we've heard enough about this drug, Mr. Gregory. Move on, please, and refrain from making testimonial statements. We are not to closing arguments yet."

Gregory had been hoping that at some point Mike Sanderson would recognize Emma. The cop, Hendricks, had assured Gregory that Emma was the perpetrator, and he also felt that if given enough time, Sanderson would I.D. her. However, it wasn't happening, and this weakened his case. Gregory knew as soon as he sat down, Mike Sanderson was going to be putty in Davies' hands.

"Mr. Gregory," Judge McKinnon was growing impatient. "Do you have anything further to ask this witness?"

Gregory shook his head: "No, Your Honour. Not at this time, but I would like to reserve the right to recall Mr. Sanderson at a later date."

"So be it." The judge looked down at Davies. "You're up, councillor."

Seventy

Emma watched her lawyer as he slowly made his way to Mike Sanderson. She knew—felt—Davies was going to rip Mike apart, and she couldn't wait to see the destruction, something she wished she'd been able to accomplish. But Janine had thwarted that plan when she'd saved the scumbag's life.

Jeremy Davies had learned early in his career that there were times when less was more. This was one of those times. To everyone's surprise, he asked only one question. "Mr. Sanderson, according to your testimony, you have no idea who the defendant is … is this true?"

Mike looked over at Emma again briefly. Jeremy manoeuvred his body into his line of vision; the less time the man had to study Emma, the better. Jeremy was no fool; he had a gut feeling his client was hiding some dark secrets, but it was his job to defend her.

Finally, "No, I don't know her."

"Thank you. No further questions." Turning to the judge, "I would like to reserve the right to recall this witness at a later time if necessary."

Judge McKinnon glanced at his watch. He'd had enough for the day. His refrigerator snacks were calling to him. He hit his gavel on the desk. "Court will reconvene at two o'clock this afternoon."

Everyone in the room rushed to stand as the Honourable Judge McKinnon hurried to the door leading to his private chamber.

Jeremy was smiling when he sat down beside Emma. He leaned over to her, noticing his client's puzzled look. "You're wondering why only one question to Mr. Sanderson?"

Emma nodded.

"The less time he has to study you, the less chance he will put two and two together … don't you agree, Emma?" Jeremy looked intensely into Emma's eyes.

"But I don't know him, and he doesn't know me." Emma felt the butterflies taking flight in the pit of her stomach.

"So you say, Emma." Jeremy began gathering his papers together. "I'll see you back here at 1:30. I have a feeling that the prosecution doesn't really have much more to offer other than a strong closing argument. Get yourself some lunch. Relax. Be ready to take the stand this afternoon."

Emma found herself sitting alone at the table, unsure of where to go. Jack came to her rescue. "Emma, how about we get some lunch?" he suggested, tapping her on the shoulder.

Turning, Emma saw Jack waiting for her. She had no idea how long she'd sat there, but the courtroom was cleared entirely except for Jack and her, and a security guard at the back door. Emma stood and together, she and Jack left.

Jack took Emma to a downtown restaurant, The Works, where they both ordered a burger. Emma wondered where Janine was but didn't bother to pry. Janine was becoming a thorn in her side.

"My lawyer thinks I did it," Emma initiated the conversation, wanting to hear Jack's take on the situation.

"What makes you assume that?"

Emma informed Jack of the short conversation that had passed between Jeremy and her before he'd left the courtroom. Jack knew his friend thought Emma was guilty. That, at the least, she knew Sanderson. How involved she was in Sanderson's problems was still in question. Jack studied the fragile woman in front of him and wondered what game she was playing. Toby knew their friend seemed changed, but he was a cat. Even at the best of times, Toby managed to get his points across, to save the day, but this was different. Toby was agitated about something to do with Emma. If only the old cat could really talk, Jack bet the current state of affairs could be cleared up in no time.

"Jack?" Emma reached out and laid a cold hand on Jack's arm. "You believe me, don't you?"

Looking into Emma's tear-filled eyes, all Jack could do was nod. Emma's heart skipped to an irregular rhythm as she realized Jack didn't have confidence in her story either.

1:30 came all too soon for Emma. She was feeling the weight of having to take the stand and was praying she could continue to keep her version of the events straight and accurate. After lunch, she and Jack had sat in Victoria Park, across from the courthouse, and Emma had rehearsed in her mind everything she'd told the police and Jack.

Jeremy Davies rushed into the lobby of the courthouse a few minutes after 1:30. He didn't think it necessary to apologize to Emma for his tardiness; instead, Jeremy drove straight to the point.

"Are you ready to take the stand?" he asked curtly.

Emma nodded.

Jeremy positioned himself directly in front of Emma and placed a hand on her shoulder. "Just keep your story accurate to what you've already said to the authorities. If you do, we should be able to wrap this up quickly. No jury is going to convict you based on what the prosecution has presented." Jeremy paused long enough to let his last statement sink in. Then, pursing his lips, "However, if you slip up, who knows what will happen." Motioning to the stairway, "Shall we?" As they walked to the steps, Jeremy added, "Let the truth come out, and the innocent go free."

Emma's blood ran cold as she noted the look of disgust on Jeremy's face before he took the stairs up to the courtroom.

Judge McKinnon, for a change, was on time for the two o'clock court session. He pointed to the prosecution: "Call your next witness."

Gregory stood. "I call Mrs. Gladys Small to the stand."

"Your Honour!" Emma's lawyer jumped to his feet. "We have no knowledge of this witness. She is not on the list presented to us."

The judge raised his eyebrows as he glanced over to Gregory, silently demanding an explanation.

Gregory shuffled a few papers before speaking: "This witness just came forward a few hours ago. She was reading about the trial in the newspaper and felt she had pertinent information that would help our case."

Jeremy took his cell phone out of his pocket and sent a message to someone, then sat back with a scowl on his face. He didn't like surprises like this.

Judge McKinnon didn't like it but had no alternative other than to allow Mrs. Small to take the stand. "I'll allow this witness. Mr. Davies, you will have your opportunity to cross-examine her."

Emma watched as Gladys Small made her way to the witness box. She was elderly, barely able to walk, even with her cane. Her face donned an oversized pair of glasses, which she continually pushed back into place as she walked. Her hand shook as she rose it in the air to be sworn in.

Once Gladys was seated, Gregory began: "Mrs. Small ... good of you to come in today. I am sure you'd much rather be home tending to your flowers, or sitting with a cup of tea and your cat. I appreciate your taking the time…"

"Your Honour," Davies jumped to his feet. "Is the prosecution going to ask a question of this witness, or is he just passing the time of day with her? A young woman is on trial here."

"Get to the point, Gregory," Judge McKinnon ordered, a hint of irritability in his tone.

Gregory nodded. He turned and pointed to Emma. "Have you seen this young woman before?"

Gladys squinted as she looked over to where Emma was sitting. Her voice quivered with age when she answered. "I believe I have."

"Where is it that you saw her?"

"At my neighbour's house."

"And who is your neighbour, Mrs. Small?"

"Mike Sanderson … a nice young man … helps me with my snow and rakes my leaves for me in the fall … nice young man."

Jeremy Davies was writing notes. He knew he was going to have to shred this woman's testimony, despite not wanting to have to do that to a fragile senior citizen.

"What was the defendant doing when you saw her?" Gregory pushed.

"She was returning Mike's truck. It was late … in the middle of the night … I'd gotten up to make myself some warm milk because I couldn't sleep … I heard the truck pull into the driveway, which I can see from my kitchen window. Being the curious person I am, I looked out and saw that young woman getting out of the truck."

"What did she do then—after getting out of the truck?"

"She looked around … I believe she made a call to someone on her cell phone, and then started jogging away."

"Did you ever see the defendant any other time at Mike Sanderson's house?"

Gladys shook her head: "No, just that once."

"And you are sure who you saw is the defendant?"

"Yes, that's her."

"No further questions ... Your witness." Gregory returned to his table and sat down.

Jeremy took his time getting up to question the surprise witness. He'd noticed the worried look on Emma's face when the witness mentioned seeing the woman returning Mike's truck.

Jeremy's cell phone buzzed; he checked his messages and grinned. At long last, he stood and approached the witness, knowing that coming down too hard on Gladys would not bode well for his case. No one liked to see a senior get beat up on a witness stand. "Good afternoon, Mrs. Small ... I won't take up much of your time because I know, as Mr. Gregory alluded to, you would rather be anywhere but here today."

Gladys nodded and smiled and relaxed back in her chair.

"Do you read the newspaper?" Jeremy asked.

"Yes, I have the Brantford *Expositor* delivered to my house. I read it every morning while drinking my tea."

"That's good ..., not many people read newspapers today." Jeremy paused. "By any chance, did you read the article about this case?"

"Oh, yes," Mrs. Small beamed proudly.

"I understand there was a picture of the defendant in the paper."

"Oh, yes. A pretty young thing. Hard to believe she could do something like this."

"So, let me get this straight. You woke up in the middle of the night because you couldn't sleep, and you came out to your kitchen to fix yourself a cup of warm milk?"

"That's what I said, young man." Gladys nodded her head toward the jurors.

Jeremy grinned. "Please be patient with me, Gladys. I just want to make sure we are all on the same page—that we get our facts straight." Jeremy took his cell phone from his pocket and turned the screen to Gladys. "Is this the picture you saw in the newspaper?"

Gladys squinted as she looked at the screen. "I think so." She sat forward to get a better look. "Yes ... yes, that's her."

"You had a difficult time making sure this was the picture you saw in the paper ... are you sure the defendant is the same person you saw in Mr. Sanderson's driveway in the middle of the night ... in the dark?"

Emma refrained from smiling, knowing it would not benefit her case, but inside she was jumping for joy. Mr. Davies was worth every penny Jack might be paying him, despite him not really believing her story.

"How far away is your house from Mr. Sanderson's driveway?" Jeremy asked.

"Not too far."

"Would you say one hundred feet ... two hundred ... three hundred?"

"Maybe between one or two hundred," Gladys replied, looking confused.

"Is there a clear view, or are there trees or shrubs along your property line?"

"A couple of trees..."

"Big ones?" Jeremy cut in.

"Oh, yes. Two big maples and a large blue spruce. My husband and I planted them when we moved to the house fifty years ago." Gladys smiled at the memory of the seedlings she had nurtured those first few years of her marriage. How she wished

George could see the fruits of their labour now, but God had taken him way too young.

Jeremy walked over to the jury, and, glancing at them, resumed. "So, you were able to identify the individual who was driving Mr. Sanderson's truck ... in the middle of the night ... from, let's say one hundred and fifty feet away ... through a barrier of three large trees?"

Gladys squirmed nervously in her chair, but before she had a chance to reply, Jeremy hit her with his next question. "Were you wearing your glasses when you got up to prepare your warm milk?"

Confusion spread across Gladys' face, and she wrung her hands in her lap. She creased her eyes, trying to remember. "I think so," she eventually replied.

"Are you sure? Remember, it was late at night. You were tired. Is it not possible that you might not have put your glasses on when you got out of bed?"

"Your honour, Mr. Davies is badgering this witness!" Gregory called out in frustration, knowing where Jeremy was going with this line of questions.

Jeremy was quick to reply: "Your Honour, I am just trying to establish if Mrs. Small was truly capable of seeing clearly in the middle of a dark night, especially if she wasn't wearing her glasses."

"Objection overruled. The witness will answer the question."

"Shall I repeat the question for you, Gladys?"

Gladys shook her head. For the life of her, she couldn't remember now if she was wearing her glasses or not that night. Sometimes she put them on when she got up in the night; sometimes she didn't. "I don't remember," she answered, her shoulders slumping in defeat.

"Just one more question, Gladys, and then you can go home … can you say for sure that the defendant is the person you saw that night … the person who returned Mike Sanderson's truck to his house? Remember … it was dark … you might not have had your glasses on … you were probably tired … the trees were in the way."

A couple tears dropped to Gladys' cheek as she realized she might have been mistaken. "No, I guess I can't be sure."

Jeremy laid a hand on Gladys' shoulder. "Thank you, Mrs. Small. No more questions."

Time seemed to pause as Gladys made her way across the courtroom floor. After the door closed behind her, Judge McKinnon looked to Gregory and asked him if he had any more witnesses. "The prosecution rests, Your Honour." After the beating his last witness had taken on the stand, Gregory felt his best chance of winning a victory, in this case, would be by having an exceedingly strong closing argument.

"Okay, then. Mr. Davies, call your first witness." Judge McKinnon looked at his watch, checking the time and the date. He hoped the defence would be quick and the jury would come to a speedy verdict. He was eager to leave early for his trailer on Friday.

Jeremy was hoping for the same, but for other reasons. He'd agreed to take on Emma's case as a favour for an old friend, but he hadn't expected it to go on for so long. He'd been under the impression, at first, that it was a slam-dunk case. His workload at the office was piling up, and he had paying customers to look after.

"I call Emma Gale to the stand."

Seventy-one

Emma stood, ran her hands down the front of her dress, then made her way to the witness box. She walked with a confident but demure step, wanting to ensure that the jurors saw her as a victim, not a perpetrator. She placed her hand on the Bible and was sworn in, feeling no remorse for the lies she was about to tell. God had forsaken her a long time ago!

Jeremy wasted no time: "Emma, you are being tried for the brutal beating and drugging of Mike Sanderson ... did you do this?"

"No."

"Do you even know Mike Sanderson?"

"No."

"You've never met him?"

"Never ... this is the first time I've seen him, here in this courtroom."

Jeremy made sure to keep his body in front of Emma as he questioned her, blocking a direct view from the people in the seating gallery. "Okay, let's briefly go over the assumed evidence the prosecution has on you ... first, let's talk about the drug found in Mr. Sanderson's bloodstream—Rohypnol. The prosecution would have us believe that you somehow drugged a man you've never met. Did you drug Mr. Sanderson?"

"No. Like I said, I've never met the man before this trial."

"But this drug was found in your house, wasn't it?"

"Yes."

"Why would you have such a drug?"

"As I've been trying to explain to everyone, I suffer from nightmares," Emma said, tearing up. "I was raped..."

Gregory was on his feet. "Objection, Your Honour. The defendant's past has nothing to do with this trial or the charges against her!"

"It has everything to do with this trial, Your Honour," Jeremy retorted quickly. "It is the explanation for why she chose to use Rohypnol."

"Objection overruled," Judge McKinnon stated testily. "But keep it short and to the point," he ordered Jeremy.

Jeremy nodded for Emma to continue. "You were saying that you were raped…"

Emma squeezed a few tears from her eyes. "I was raped––the first time—when I was ten years old. And many times afterward … until my brother discovered what was happening and took me away. However, despite being away from all those men who raped me … took advantage of a young foster child…" Emma wiped away the tears that were now flowing more freely. "There are so many ghosts in my past … demons that keep haunting my sleep … mocking me … telling me, in my dreams, they are coming for me. After my brother was sent away, the dreams started happening more often. I was alone. Everywhere I looked in my house, the ghosts were there.

"I researched if there was any drug I could take that would help me to forget what had happened to me, and when I read about Rohypnol, I decided to give it a try. I know it's illegal here in Canada, but I was able to mail-order it from Mexico. I was desperate."

"Did it help you?"

"Yes, a bit. But I haven't been taking it all that long, and I didn't take much of it, not wanting to get addicted."

Jeremy glanced over to the jurors. "A perfectly plausible explanation of why Miss Larson had the drug Rohypnol in her possession … to chase away—eliminate—the ghosts of her past." Returning his attention to Emma, "Mike Sanderson's ring was

247

found in your house ... in your basement, under the stairs. Please tell us how it got there."

Emma straightened up in the chair and swallowed hard, pushing back further tears that were threatening to let loose on her. "After my brother left, I took up jogging. I always go with my dog, Duke. You know, to be safe. I normally take the same route and pass by several parks. It was in one of these parks I found the ring."

"Was that also the park where you came across Mr. Sanderson's girlfriend in distress?" Jeremy intervened. "And you called an ambulance for her—a stranger. Not something a felonious individual would even think of doing, I am sure," he added quickly.

"Yes, to both statements," Emma replied, looking at the jurors.

"So it is possible, as was established earlier by Mr. Sanderson, this was the park where he and his girlfriend had a disagreement, and that during their altercation, he could very well have lost his ring?"

The prosecution jumped to his feet. "Your Honour ... the defence is drawing conclusions now ... he has no way of knowing for a fact that Mr. Sanderson lost his ring in the park ... we only have Miss Gale's word that is where she found it," Gregory fumed.

Jeremy was about to defend his line of questioning, but Judge McKinnon raised his hand and waved him off. "I see no problem with this ... objection overruled. Continue, Mr. Davies."

"Would you like me to repeat the question?" Jeremy asked Emma.

"No ... I guess it is possible he lost his ring there ... from what his girlfriend told me, he was quite rough with her, and the condition in which I found her lays testament to that fact.

Actually, I have wondered how no one else saw what was going on and stepped in to help her. She was badly be…"

"Your Honour!" Gregory's face was beet-red with frustration.

The judge cleared his throat. "Please keep your answers confined to the matter at hand, Miss Gale."

Emma nodded shyly and blushed. Jeremy quickly pushed on with his questioning. "So, you found a ring in a park when you went jogging?"

"Yes."

"What did you do with the ring?"

"I put it in my pocket, intending to hand it in to the police, but I guess when I got home and went down to my basement to finish my workout, it must have fallen out of my pocket. I never gave it another thought."

"So now, we've established the reason you have the same drug as was found in Mr. Sanderson's system, and how his ring came to be in your possession—we only have this photo left, taken in the hospital, which the police claim is you." Jeremy walked to his table, then back to Emma. He handed her a picture. "Is this you, Miss Gale?"

Emma pretended to study the photo. She didn't want to answer too quickly, as though she'd rehearsed what she'd say. After a long pause, "No, that isn't me. And, like I told the officers, over and over again, I was not at the hospital that day. Why would I go and visit a man I don't even know?" Emma managed to get in.

Jeremy couldn't have wished for a better ending.

Gregory felt his case slipping away. He pondered if it was even worth questioning Emma; her answers would only reinforce what the jury had already heard, leading to reasonable doubt in their minds. He decided his best bet was to beat her testimony to a pulp during his closing argument so that the ridiculousness of her story was fresh in their minds when they entered deliberations.

Jeremy was about to end his questioning when he remembered the incident of the cops coming to arrest his client. He raised a finger in the air: "One more thing, Miss Gale ... you were leaving the night the police came to arrest you, right?"

"Yes."

"Where were you going?"

"To see my brother. He's in jail and I hadn't seen him for a long time. Despite what he did, he's all I've got in this world."

"The police didn't believe you?"

"No."

"Why do you think they didn't believe you?"

"They had it in their heads that I was the person in the hospital, I guess. Especially the guy. He was relentless. Kept trying to make me say I had something to do with the condition Mr. Sanderson was in." Emma started to cry. "I had nothing to do with it ... honestly." Emma looked at the jurors. "I don't even know Mr. Sanderson ... at least not until now ... here in this courtroom."

Jeremy looked up at the judge. "No further questions, Your Honour. Prosecution's witness."

Gregory stood. "No questions."

"Okay then," the judge said. "Call your next witness, Mr. Davies."

"Defense rests, Your Honour."

Judge McKinnon looked at his watch. "All right, we'll hear closing arguments in the morning ... ten o'clock sharp. Court adjourned."

Jeremy returned to the table where Emma was sitting and gathered his papers together, shoving them into his briefcase. "I'll see you in the morning."

Emma watched her lawyer walk quickly from the room. Her eyes scanned the audience for Jack. He was waiting by the door for her. As she approached him, Jack smiled and put an arm around her shoulders, ushering her out. Once outside, he spoke: "Hopefully, your nightmare will be over tomorrow. I cannot see any jury convicting you on the scant evidence the Crown has put forth."

Emma sighed. She watched enough court television shows that she knew closing arguments could be more lethal than the actual witness testimony paraded in front of a jury. Closing arguments were the final words stuck in a juror's mind. Emma had confidence that despite what Jeremy Davis seemed to think of her, he would present an unflappable closing argument that would set her free from this mess. Then, she could lay low for a while before going on with her plans.

And next time, she'd be a lot more careful.

Seventy-two

Emma decided to go for a run after Jack dropped her off at the house. It had been a couple days and she knew Duke would appreciate the exercise, as well.

Not wanting to jog past the park where the altercation had taken place between Janine and Mike, Emma proceeded in the direction of her downtown route—the one where she would pick up the river trail. It always afforded her some noteworthy subjects to follow up on.

And tonight wasn't any different.

Jack filled Toby in on what happened in court, telling the old cat that he was glad the entire mess would be over soon. "If the jury votes the way I think they will, we should be out of there early tomorrow," Jack surmised. "Jeremy is doing a great job, as I expected he would," Jack continued. "But I don't think he believes Emma is innocent," he added.

She isn't. Our sweet Emma is as guilty as they come, Jack. But she needs help. We need to help her before she goes down the same road Camden did.

"To be truthful," Jack continued, "There are moments I am unconvinced of Emma's innocence."

Janine had mixed feelings about what was going to happen in court in the morning. She had even more mixed feelings about Emma. On the one hand, Janine appreciated what the woman had done for her—saved her life. On the other hand, there was something hidden in Emma's eyes—something disturbing. Janine had taken note of how Emma made herself up for court, a totally different look from the woman she'd first met—from the woman who lived next door to Jack and Toby.

"It's as though Emma is trying to disguise who she is," Janine mumbled to the empty room. "If only I could prove, somehow, Emma actually met Mike … knew him. That old lady was pretty sure it was Emma at Mike's house, but the lawyer destroyed her testimony."

Janine paced back and forth by the window in her room. She caught a glimpse of Emma leaving her house with the dog. The Emma she recognized. The Emma who was not made up to look different for court.

"I wonder where she's going … what should it matter if she's going for a jog … we've all been locked up in a courtroom these past few days … it probably wouldn't hurt for me to go for a walk and get some fresh air..."

Despite knowing getting out for some exercise might clear her mind, Janine was tired. She lay down on the bed: "I'll just close my eyes for a few minutes." Sleep fell quickly and along with sleep came a dream.

Janine dreamt of a happy time with Mike, when they first met. She dreamed of all the days that followed, days filled with discussions of their future together … the type of home they wanted … the places they wanted to visit … the number of children they would have. The dream shifted, not to the abuses she'd suffered after he was laid off, but to the courtroom where Mike looked so confused, so child-like. In Janine's dream, she embraced him and told him everything was going to be okay. She was there for him.

Tears were streaming down Janine's face when she woke from her nap. "Oh, Mike," she sobbed. Slowly, Janine got off the bed and fetched her suitcase from the closet. "I'm coming home, Mike … we'll work this out together. As long as you keep on the path you're on now … attending your AA meetings … going to counselling … we'll make it. As soon as this trial is over, I'll come home."

Janine started packing her suitcase.

Jeremy Davies was in turmoil. His gut feeling was still leaning toward his client being guilty. This was the one thing he didn't like about being a criminal defence lawyer—it was his sworn duty to defend a client, despite their possible guilt. In his mind, Emma was guilty, in spite of the explanations she'd come up with that contradicted the evidence the police had gathered.

Pouring a glass of scotch, Jeremy perused his closing argument notes. Tossing back his drink, he set both glass and notes on the coffee table. "No way a jury cannot see reasonable doubt and let my client go. I just hope this whole affair doesn't backfire on Jack!"

Brian Gregory wasn't pleased with the way things had gone in court. After leaving the building, Officer Hendricks approached him.

"She's guilty, you know," Hendricks stated, a dark look in his eyes.

Gregory snorted. "The guilty don't always go down for their crimes when they have a lawyer like Jeremy Davies. There's no better defence lawyer in Brantford, and he did his job. I can't wait to hear his closing argument."

"I think yours should be stronger. The jurors need to hear how ridiculous Miss Gale's explanations are—really hear! You need to make sure you tear apart Jeremy's closing argument." Hendricks' face was red. His blood pressure elevated as he thought of how a criminal was possibly going to walk.

"The biggest problem we face is we don't have a significant witness that can place Emma and Mike together at any point. The victim doesn't even recognize her! Jeremy ripped apart the one witness we had, which had promised us a glimmer of hope. I can only do what I can with the little we have left. Emma presents quite a convincing picture of a weak, innocent young woman who is being victimized. And, don't forget," Gregory took his glasses off and looked out over Victoria Park, "Emma saved Miss Larson's life. That, in itself, has made her more of a hero—especially with the female jurors—than someone who would drug and beat someone, and leave them for dead."

"Well, I just hope, if she gets off, we aren't back in court down the road, charging her with another offence. One that might be even worse than this one … one where her victim didn't make it … didn't have someone to save him before it was too late. That's what I hope." Hendricks turned and walked away, heading to his cruiser.

Gregory's shoulders slumped as he made his way to his car, as though he'd already accepted defeat.

Mike Sanderson looked around his empty house. He'd managed to clean up most of the mess he'd made after the incident with Janine. His goal was to prove to her that he could be again the man he used to be.

Picking up his phone, Mike called his AA sponsor. He needed to talk to someone. He didn't want to close his eyes and sleep because he kept having weird dreams. Dreams where he was tied up and being beaten. And the one punching him appeared to be a woman, but he could never see her face.

Half an hour later, Mike was sitting in Coffee Culture with his sponsor, having a cup of coffee and a muffin. Just as he was about to take a bite of his muffin, Mike caught sight of a woman and a large dog jogging past the window. There was something really familiar about both of them. He tried to get a better look, but the pair passed by too quickly.

"Everything okay?" Mike's sponsor asked.

"Yeah … yeah … thought it was someone I knew," Mike replied.

Later that night, after falling asleep, the dream returned. More vivid. A misty face began to show. Mike shot up in his bed as he realized who it might be!

Judge McKinnon sat down to his supper, a frozen dinner his wife had prepared for him for those days when she wasn't around. There'd been a lot of days, lately, he'd been eating alone. He should have retired a couple years ago but kept procrastinating. His wife had decided she wasn't going to wait any longer to enjoy life and began taking trips with a senior group she'd joined.

"This case is a total waste of court time," the judge said, looking down at the dog sitting beside him. "I should have dismissed it from the beginning." He leaned back in his chair and sighed. "Well, hopefully, Davies will do a good enough job with his closing argument that the jury will reach a quick verdict and we can all go home early."

The judge pushed away from the table and made his way to his living room. The old dog clipped along behind his master and curled up on the carpet beside the couch. The judge grinned: "Can't make it up on the couch anymore, eh, old boy. Age creeping fast on us, isn't it?" The judge turned the television on, wanting to catch the national news before he retired for the night. "Going to give my notice on Monday morning," he told his furry companion, then leaned back on the pillows to watch his news.

Within minutes, the living room was filled with a chorus of snoring.

Seventy-three

Morning dawned dismally with rain falling in thick sheets, flowing off the sidewalks and into the sewers in torrents. Emma grabbed her umbrella and rushed over to Jack's. He was waiting for her in his truck.

"Where's Janine?" Emma asked as she climbed into the front seat.

"Said she would meet us there," Jack replied.

The courtroom was slowly filling up by the time Emma and Jack arrived. She thought about how humans liked to congregate around someone else's misery—especially news reporters—hoping to be the first ones to pounce on the verdict. Emma sat with Jack until she saw Jeremy Davies, then joined her lawyer at his table. She watched as he glanced over some notes before shoving the papers back into his briefcase.

As the door opened and closed at the back of the room, Emma kept her focus on the door the jury would come through. She didn't care about anything else right now. They were the ones who could convict her or set her free.

Finally, everyone was in place, including Judge McKinnon. He called on Brian Gregory to begin with his closing argument.

Gregory stood slowly. He looked from the jury to Emma and back again. "Ladies and gentlemen of the jury … we are here today to decide the fate of the young woman sitting here, accused of drugging and beating Mike Sanderson. Some of you might find it difficult to believe such a fragile young woman would be capable of such a crime. But, as history has shown us, we cannot always see the wolf inside the sheep's skin.

"Is the defendant, Miss Gale, a wolf? I think so. The defence is going to try and paint her as the victim here, but let's look at the facts in this case. Mr. Sanderson was drugged and brutally beaten by someone. He was drugged with a highly effective drug—Rohypnol—which erases much of a person's memory of what might have happened to them. It is commonly referred to as the date rape drug just for this reason. While drugged—and let me point out here, he was overdosed on Rohypnol—Mr. Sanderson's body was beaten terribly. Pictures taken in the hospital can confirm this. Anyone could be capable of doing that, even someone as petite and fragile-looking as the defendant. Remember, our victim was unconscious from the drug overdose he'd been given—helpless in anyone's hands.

"And here's the thing, ladies and gentlemen, Miss Gale was in possession of the drug, Rohypnol. She also was in contact with Mr. Sanderson's girlfriend, finding her in a park in the throes of a miscarriage. Miss Gale was aware of how Mike Sanderson had beaten his girlfriend and caused the loss of their baby. I suggest to you that Miss Larson's story set off sirens in Miss Gale's mind. I suggest to you that Miss Gale's past abuses reared up and caused her to search out Mike Sanderson and make sure he received a vigilante justice. It would have been easy enough to find out where he lived.

"Miss Gale's explanation as to why she had the Rohypnol is flimsy—one of many flimsy reasons she claims. I ask you to consider that just because she says she needed the Rohypnol for her own use, to erase her supposed nightmares, that doesn't stop her from applying the same drug to someone she despised. Don't take me wrong … Mike Sanderson might not have been someone she initially knew, but he was the picture of numerous men who had abused her in the past. He needed to be punished.

"Let's move on to the picture Officer MacDonald took in the hospital after she and Officer Hendricks noticed a woman exiting Mike Sanderson's room. The defence will have you believe it is not a picture of Emma Gale, but if you look closely at the picture when you go into deliberations, you will see differently." Gregory stepped to the side to allow the jurors a good view of Emma. "Look at Miss Gale ... look hard. I am sure she has done her best to look different for this court than from what she looks on regular days. Maybe changed her hairstyle ... her makeup ... her clothing style?

"When confronted by the police officers with the picture and when questioned about her whereabouts the previous morning, Miss Gale was combative with the officers. She told them she was not at the hospital that morning, and then she ran into her house and locked the door. Later that evening, the police, who were keeping a watch on Miss Gale because they didn't believe her story about not being at the hospital, caught her trying to leave town.

"What was her excuse? She was supposedly going to see her brother, who is in prison for murder. A brother who she hadn't been to visit since his incarceration. How convenient. Another flimsy excuse. Think about it, ladies and gentlemen. I believe Miss Gale was fleeing town because she was about to get caught for a heinous crime, and she had no intention of returning any time soon—if ever.

"Moving on to the ring that was found by Miss Gale's neighbour in the basement of her house. Miss Gale's flimsy explanation for this is that she found it in a park, indicating it was the same park where Mr. Sanderson had accosted his girlfriend. She claims she put it in her pocket intending to turn it into the police. But did she? No. She claims it must have fallen from her pant's pocket and that she never thought of it again.

"Let me ask you, ladies and gentlemen, if you found a ring in the park, would you have forgotten about it? Would you not have called the police immediately upon discovering such an item? Yes, you would have. You have nothing to hide. You haven't drugged and beaten someone and left them for dead. You haven't taken the ring from their finger, thinking you might eventually get a few dollars for it. I am suggesting to you, ladies and gentlemen of the jury, that is precisely what Miss Gale did before she left Mr. Sanderson for dead. She removed the ring from his finger and then when it was found in her basement, she concocted the story of having found it in the park and that it must have dropped, unnoticed, from her pocket when she went downstairs to work out. Flimsy.

"The defence had a hay day with our witness who saw Miss Gale at Mike Sanderson's house, ripping apart her testimony. But, Mrs. Small saw a young woman, who looked precisely like Emma Gale, and she had the courage to come forward and tell the court that, putting Miss Gale in the presence of Mr. Sanderson at least once. This confirms Miss Gale is lying when she tries to tell this court that the first time she met our victim was here in this courtroom.

"In closing, ladies and gentlemen, I would ask you to take a good look at the actual evidence presented to you—not the flimsy comebacks Emma Gale gave us. Mrs. Small saw her at our victim's house ... Emma Gale was in possession of our victim's ring ... she was also in possession of Rohypnol, which was found in massive doses in our victim's blood. It was witnessed by two officers of the law, after one of them caught Miss Gale on camera, that Emma Gale was the woman seen leaving our victims room at the hospital. Miss Gale was fleeing Brantford the night the police confronted her with the picture from the hospital, with a flimsy excuse of going to see a brother in prison, whom she hadn't visited yet. Why then? Ask yourselves that.

"And remember ... Miss Emma Gale may look like an innocent young lamb, even a fragile lamb, but I need to point out to you, there is a wolf under that wool ... a vicious creature that set out to punish Mike Sanderson for what he'd done to his girlfriend. Emma Gale was wreaking her own sense of vengeance on a stranger against all the men who'd abused her. See the wolf in her, ladies and gentlemen. Peel back the wool and see the wolf, and I am sure you will come to the right conclusion. Emma Gale is guilty of drugging and brutally beating Mr. Sanderson and leaving him for dead! That is the only just conclusion you can arrive at. Thank you."

Emma watched the jurors closely as Gregory spoke. He sounded convincing with all his theories, but she knew her lawyer was going to rip each one of those theories apart with his closing. She was thankful the defence got to give their summation last.

Some of the jurors had been difficult to read, especially the men. But the women, it seemed to Emma, when asked to take a good look at her, appeared to be showing sympathy. A good sign.

Judge McKinnon checked his watch. His stomach had started to grumble toward the end of Gregory's closing, and the judge decided a half-hour recess was in order. He banged his gavel on his desk, and so ordered it.

Seventy-four

Half an hour later, everyone was back in court. Emma noticed, as she made her way to the front, Mike Sanderson staring at her as though he recognized her now. She looked away quickly.

"Mr. Davies … your closing arguments," Judge McKinnon nodded to Jeremy.

Jeremy stood and sauntered across the floor to the jury box. He walked from one end of it to the other, smiling charmingly at each juror as he passed them. Finally, he began: "Ladies and gentlemen of the jury … first, I would like to thank you for your time. It must be difficult to leave your families and serve on a jury. I commend you for your patience." Jeremy paused. After the momentary lull, he dove straight into his summary statements.

"I also want you to take a good look at the defendant, Emma Gale. The prosecution is asking you to believe she is a wolf in sheep's clothing. The prosecution is trying to ask you to accept as true that everything—everything!—Miss Gale says is a lie—is nothing more than flimsy counters for the meagre bits of evidence the prosecution has against her. I don't see a wolf sitting at that table; do you? I see a young woman who did nothing more than assist a stranger in a park … saving her life, I am inclined to remind you. Not the actions of someone who would drug and beat a fellow human being.

"Unfortunately, the woman Emma Gale saved that day was Mike Sanderson's girlfriend, which is the link and the noose the prosecution is attempting to secure around Miss Gale's neck. Assuming, because she helped Miss Larson, she also was privy to knowledge about Mr. Sanderson and used that knowledge to hunt down and drug and torture him.

"Ladies and gentlemen ... I ask you to take a look out into the audience and fix your eyes on Mike Sanderson, a man of medium height ... well-muscled ... sturdy looking. Then, I ask you to take a look at Emma Gale, a young woman of petite stature, frail-looking—innocent. Not a wolf. Not even a sheep. A slip of a young woman, who takes her dog with her when she ventures out for jogs to ensure she is safe.

"I am not going to bore you with a lengthy rehashing of all the evidence here. Nevertheless, it is my duty to remind you of Miss Gale's testimony to refute the evidence the police and the prosecution presented. Did Miss Gale have the drug Rohypnol in her possession? Yes. Did she acquire this drug so she could drug Mr. Sanderson and then beat him for what he'd done to his girlfriend? No. She'd only just met Janine Larson. Hardly enough time to research and then order, via mail, such a drug. No, it is as Miss Gale has told this court. She searched the internet for a drug that could help her with the nightmares she suffered from due to traumas she'd endured in her childhood. She's been taking this drug briefly, as she openly admitted to us.

"Moving on to this blurry picture that the police took at the hospital. Haven't we all joked about having a twin out there somewhere? How many times has someone come up to you or someone you know and said you have a twin somewhere? My own father mistook a gentleman for his brother one day in a grocery store, the resemblance was so close. Miss Gale swore to the officers when they accosted her in the privacy of her backyard, she was not the person in the picture and that she'd not been to the hospital. But they chose not to believe her, and they pursued their quest to find someone—anyone—to pin the crime on. Miss Gale was not combative that afternoon; the police were. She was suffering from a bad headache; she told them it wasn't her in the picture and left them standing in her yard while she went inside her house.

"The prosecution would have you believe that Miss Gale changed her appearance to throw off Mr. Sanderson when he was asked to identify his attacker. Flimsy. In Mr. Gregory's own words—flimsy! Was Miss Gale supposed to attend court in an unkempt manner, wearing her pyjamas maybe, or a sweat suit, or maybe some ripped jeans and an old t-shirt? Is she not allowed to shower, do her hair neatly, put on some nice clothes to come to court, as any one of you would do? As you all seem to have done?"

Jeremy paused, allowing time for the jurors to look around at each other, confirming what he'd just pointed out to them.

Continuing, Jeremy made his way to Emma and sat on the edge of the table for a moment. "The prosecution assumes, because our over-zealous police officers told them, wanting to close their case, Emma was not going to see her brother that night, but was fleeing Brantford and the crime she allegedly committed. Flimsy. Where was she going? She has no one else but her brother and the good neighbour who lives next door to her. And her faithful dog, that she was in the process of asking her neighbour to look after while she was gone for a few days. Her brother is in prison. Her neighbour is here with her today, helping her, believing in her." Jeremy returned to the jury box.

"Next we have the ring that mysteriously appeared in Emma Gale's basement, discovered by the neighbour's cat under the stairway. The prosecution would have you believe Miss Gale ripped the ring off Mr. Sanderson's finger after she drugged and beat him, wanting to pawn it at some time for money. Flimsy! Miss Gale says she found the ring in the park—the same park where Mr. Sanderson beat his girlfriend—and shoved it into her pocket, intending to turn it into the police. Unfortunately, it fell out of her pocket on her way down to her basement and she never thought anything more about it. The ring was not of any importance to her.

"Just a few more moments of your time, ladies and gentlemen … The witness, Mrs. Small … a sweet, elderly lady thinking she was doing her civic duty, especially after she saw a picture of Miss Gale in the newspaper. It was late at night. She was tired. She wasn't wearing her glasses. There are big trees between her property and Mr. Sanderson's. She finally admitted, on the witness stand, under oath, she really couldn't be sure the person she saw that night in Mr. Sanderson's driveway was Emma Gale.

"So, there we have it, ladies and gentlemen. All of this circumstantial evidence against Miss Gale has been explained away by her and by the facts. In her own words, Miss Gale never met Mike Sanderson before his appearance in court here. She did not visit him in the hospital. She was not trying to flee Brantford because she'd committed some heinous crime. She admitted to taking a drug to help her with nightmare memories from her past. She admitted to finding a ring, and to not thinking anything further about it. The one thing Miss Gale has not admitted to is the drugging and beating of Mike Sanderson.

"Take another look, ladies and gentlemen. At Emma Gale. At Mike Sanderson. At the facts presented in this case. Everything the prosecution has told you is circumstantial. Everything Emma Gale has told you are facts. She was there. She's been living this nightmare of harassment. The only choice you have here is to find her not guilty of this crime. Don't see a wolf sitting there, as Mr. Gregory wants you to see. See the real victim in this whole charade and let this innocent woman go home."

Emma breathed a sigh of relief as her lawyer made his way back to their table. As she'd hoped, Jeremy had blown a hole in every argument the prosecution had presented. Emma's mind wandered to what she would do once she got out of the courtroom. She didn't hear one word of the judge's summation to the jury. Only when the jurors stood and filed out of the room for deliberations did Emma look up.

Seventy-five

Two hours later, the sun shining down on the wet grass, Emma walked out of the courtroom a free woman. Janine motioned to Jack that she wished to talk to him. Emma saw Jack shake his head, then nod and shrug his shoulders. Janine walked away, to her ex-boyfriend, Mike. They embraced, which sent cold shivers down Emma's spine.

"What's up with Janine?" Emma asked as Jack fell into step beside her.

"She's going to give it another go with Mike. Says she feels he's changed, and he's trying."

"Sad."

"Yep. Said she would come around tomorrow and gather her things." Jack hooked his arm in Emma's. "Let's go home and give Toby the good news. It's been killing him that he wasn't allowed to come to the trial."

"I need to say goodbye to Mr. Davies first," Emma said, looking around for her lawyer.

Jack blushed nervously. "He had some pressing matters to tend to," he stated, not looking Emma in the eyes. "Told me to say goodbye to you and that he'd be in touch."

Emma nodded. *Not likely, Jeremy. You only did what you did to get me off as a favour for your friend. I bet you're drowning yourself in remorse right now, still wondering if you did the right thing by getting me off—especially when you believe I'm guilty.*

Toby was ecstatic when he heard the news. Now he and Jack would be able to help Emma. He rubbed around Emma's legs, purring loudly. *Even though I know you are guilty, Emma, I believe you're worth saving. Hopefully, having almost gotten caught, you will back off whatever your plans are to bring justice to abused women. Because that's what I think you were trying to do. But it isn't yours to bear. You need to leave the job to professionals like me ... and Jack.* Toby stopped and bumped Emma's leg, then looked up at her imploringly.

Emma laughed and bent down and bundled Toby up in her arms. It felt comfortable there, and Toby was positive life was going to go back to normal, to the way it used to be with his Emma. He would go for daily visits. She would lock up the mutt and give him treats. Toby buried his head under Emma's chin and accepted the closeness of her arms.

"Well, Toby, I'd love to stay longer, but I need to get home and let Duke out." Emma set Toby down on the couch. "Poor guy hasn't seen much of me lately." She turned to Jack: "Once again, Jack, I can't tell you how much I appreciate all your help and you sticking by me. I've never had such good friends as what you and Toby are. I don't know how I'll ever be able to repay you."

Jack blushed. "No problem, Emma. But there is one thing you can do ... keep seeing the counsellor. I think she can really help you with all those past ghosts you've been dealing with. It's time to send them on their way. Promise me, you'll do this."

Emma paused, not wanting to make such a promise, especially with the plans she still meant to implement. But she knew she had to be more careful. She couldn't take any chances and get caught up in another scenario like she'd just been through. "I promise," Emma finally answered. "I have to admit, the counsellor has really been helping me," she lied. *The woman is an idiot ... so easy to manipulate. She believes everything I'm feeding her. Actually thinks she's breaking down my barriers, getting through to me, eradicating my pain. I know how to do that myself ... and, it isn't through talking with a stranger. It's by taking charge and eliminating problems ... any way I can!*

Jeremy Davies left the courthouse in a hurry after the verdict was read. He knew there could be no other possible outcome; the prosecution hadn't proven their case beyond a reasonable doubt.

So why is it I feel uncomfortable with having gotten Emma Gale off? She looks innocent enough, but there's something in her eyes. She's hard to read, and when I can't read someone...

Jeremy decided to call Jack in the morning and relay his concerns. He had the feeling his good friend was going to have to be cautious, and, if possible, keep his eye on his young neighbour.

Brian Gregory returned to his office, his tail between his legs. He was pissed at how things had gone. He knew from the beginning that his case was weak. The one police officer, Hendricks, had been adamant, though, that Emma had committed a crime and needed to be punished. Nevertheless, when reading through all the details, Brian didn't like the victim. He didn't cotton to anyone who abused their spouse.

"Maybe, my heart wasn't in it," he mumbled. "Maybe, if I'd dug deeper, I might have found something or someone else who could have witnessed Miss Gale knowing Sanderson. On the other hand, he's an abuser. He got away with what he did to Miss Larson. Maybe, if Miss Gale did do this, she taught him a lesson. One that will turn his life around. Perhaps justice has been served—all around the table.

Judge McKinnon put his feet up on the coffee table. He leaned his head back on a pillow lodged between his neck and the back of the couch and closed his eyes, and reflected about the conversation in the jury room after the verdict was given.

Some of the jurors, mostly men, didn't believe Emma's story. They felt Emma's explanations against the evidence the police had gathered were weak. However, in the end, the men had finally agreed there wasn't enough concrete proof to convict Miss Gale, and they conceded to the majority vote. The judge, to make everyone feel better about their verdict, had told them there really was no other ruling they could have come to.

The judge sighed, got up from the couch and moved slowly down the hall to his office. His wife was due home soon. He wanted to surprise her with a letter of resignation, and if he had time, maybe a pair of two-way tickets to Scotland, a place she had a yearning to visit.

Mike and Janine sat in the living room of the home they had shared. For the first few minutes, neither of them spoke. Finally, Mike broke the silence.

"I won't let you down ever again, Janine," Mike stated humbly.

Janine reached across the end table and took hold of Mike's hand: "I said I would give our relationship another try, Mike, but I'm not going to do that under the same roof. I can't move back in yet until I'm positive you've changed. But I'm here for you, Mike. I'll see you through this if you let me. I am going to warn you from now—if you ever touch another drop of alcohol or do any drug, including marijuana, there will be no third chance. I'll leave and won't look back. Do you understand that?"

Tears streamed down Mike's face and he nodded. "I won't ever touch the stuff again. I have a great AA sponsor who is helping me work through some of my issues, and the hospital set me up in a good group program, as well."

"I'm pleased to hear that. And, like I said, I'm here for you." Janine took a deep breath. "Tomorrow morning we can go and pick up my things from Jack's place. I'd like you to meet him, and his companion, Toby…"

For the first time in a while, Mike snickered. "Is Jack gay?"

Janine laughed. "Oh no, Mike; Toby is an oversized orange tabby cat who, according to Jack, thinks he's a detective. Long story. We'll talk about it later."

The rest of the evening was spent quietly watching a movie, and then Mike drove Janine to a nearby hotel. He saw her to her room.

"Are you sure you'll be okay?" Mike asked, not wanting to leave Janine.

Janine reached out and touched Mike on the cheek. "It's going to be okay, Mike, as long as you keep up your part of the bargain. You just need to give me time."

Mike kissed the back of Janine's hand, turned it over and whispered into her palm, "I'm so sorry."

Janine closed the hotel room door when Mike disappeared into the elevator. Walking over to her bed, she flopped down on the quilt and fell instantly to sleep.

Mike went straight to bed when he got home. Something was bothering him. He kept picturing Emma in his mind. He kept thinking he knew her. Finally, his mind succumbed to sleep. But, it was not as peaceful as he'd hoped.

Visions of being tied in a chair in a dark room flashed through his dreams again. There was someone in the room with him. Someone brutalizing him. Beating him. Calling him names. The torture finally stopped, and the person turned around. As they left the room, the face that appeared in the doorway was one he recognized.

Emma Gale!

Seventy-six

The first thing Emma did when she arrived home was get out of her court clothes, put on a jogging outfit, then head out the door with Duke. He pulled anxiously on the leash.

"Okay, boy, let's do it," Emma said, taking off down the sidewalk at a fast run.

From Jack's house, Toby watched his friend leave her home. *I would have thought you might want to rest, Emma. Where are you going at this time of the day? So fast?* Toby stood and stretched. He glanced over at Jack, sleeping in his easy chair. Supper was most likely going to have to wait. Jack looked exhausted. Age was creeping on his friend, as it skulked on him. *Time for us to take a break, Jack. Maybe go fishing. You love fishing. I love sleeping around under trees.*

Toby returned his attention to the street, attempting to catch another glimpse of Emma, but she was nothing more than a speck in the distance, and soon enough, even the speck disappeared.

Emma made her way through downtown Brantford, past the Royal Bank, down Icomm Drive toward the Casino. Turning off the sidewalk, Emma took the river trail, keeping the same fast pace she'd started out with. Emma was so focused on where she was going, she failed to notice a police car was following her since shortly after she'd left her house.

Hendricks was furious at the outcome of the trial. He was an old cop. An old dog that had sniffed out a lot of criminals over the years, and he was seldom wrong about his hunches. He knew Emma Gale had something to do with what had happened to

273

Mike Sanderson. However, even he had to admit the evidence was meagre. He'd voiced his concerns to his partner, MacDonald, but she told him the trial was over and it was time to move on to their next case. They couldn't win them all.

"I'm going to keep my eye on you, little lady. Eventually, I'll find out what you're up to." Hendricks moved on when Emma disappeared onto the trail. "And when I do, next time, I'll make sure I have enough evidence to bury you!"

Morning dawned with heavy clouds hanging over the Grand River, waiting to release another torrent of moisture into its water. Emma decided to do some gardening before the rain came.

Toby had an early breakfast, then jumped up to the kitchen windowsill overlooking Emma's backyard.

Good, Emma's in her yard. Time for an early morning visit to get some treats. I don't see the mutt anywhere close by.

As Jack entered the kitchen, he caught sight of Toby's tail disappearing out the cat door. He chuckled. "Well, I can see things are going back to normal."

Jack plugged his kettle in. He felt like having a tea this morning instead of coffee. Before his tea was steeped, the doorbell rang. Opening the door, he was greeted by Janine and Mike.

"Good morning, Jack," Janine said. "We've come for my things. And I would like to formally introduce you to Mike. He's truly sorry for what he did, and he's getting the help he needs."

Mike extended his hand to Jack. "I want to thank you, man, for looking after Janine. You have no idea how sorry I am for what I did."

Jack hesitated. When he finally grasped Mike's hand, "Time will tell, won't it?" Jack stepped aside to allow the couple into the house. "I shall leave you to it," he said. "I was just about to have my breakfast. You know where everything is, Janine."

Janine nodded, unhappy that Jack's reception wasn't more congenial. Deep down, though, she knew she couldn't blame him for being cautious. Quickly, she fetched her suitcases from the room where she'd stayed and set them by the front door. Then she led Mike down to the basement where her other items were.

As Janine and Mike loaded her belongings into Mike's truck, Mike glanced over to the next-door house. His heart caught in his throat when he saw Emma, triggered by a memory, or by the dream he'd had the previous night. The individuals in both were the same.

Shoving the last piece of luggage into the back of the truck, Mike jumped in the cab. "Let's get out of here," he said to Janine.

She hopped up beside him, noticing the strange look on his face. "Okay. Is there something wrong?"

Mike shoved the keys into the ignition and started the truck. "Later, Janine. I just want to go home and start our life over."

As the truck backed out of Jack's driveway, Emma looked up from her gardening. Her heart skipped a beat as she locked eyes with Mike, seeing the recognition on his face.

Epilogue

A week after the Emma Gale trial, Officer Hendricks received a phone call from an anxious young woman. Her boyfriend had gone missing a few days ago.

"Why didn't you call sooner?" Hendricks asked.

"Well, you see, it's complicated. Sometimes he disappears for a couple days, but this time, for some reason, I'm worried. It's been three days now, and I haven't heard from him."

"I see. Where did you last see him?"

"Well, it was in our apartment. We had a big fight out on our balcony—I thought he was going to push me off it at one point—and he took off to take a walk on the trails. That's usually where he goes after a fight."

"I see."

Emma sat across from her brother, Camden, in the prison visiting room. They weren't allowed to touch hands, but their eyes greeted each other with love. Tears flowed on both sides of the table.

"I'm sorry I haven't been to see you," Emma opened with. "It's been difficult for me. I had a lot of thinking to do about my life—about our lives."

"No problem, Emma. But I have missed you. It's horrible in here, but better than the first place I was." Camden looked down at the floor, averting eye contact with his sister.

"I need to move closer to you, Camden. I need to see you more often." Emma opened the door for her telling her brother what she needed to say to him.

Camden looked puzzled. "Are you not happy in Brantford. Jack is a good friend, isn't he?"

"Yes. And Toby." Emma looked away for a moment. Then, looking back at her brother, she leaned as far over the table as she dared. "I've continued our work, Camden."

Camden cocked his head to the side, puzzled.

"The work you started. The justice we needed for all that was done to us when we were young." Emma hesitated. "I was almost caught, Camden. But Jack hired a good lawyer, and I had a reason for everything the police threw at me."

Emma lowered her voice to a soft whisper and briefly told Camden what she had done. When she finished, she leaned back in her chair. Camden's face had gone pale. He'd never wanted his sister to suffer, yet here she was, bearing the brunt of all that he'd done. As though she read his thoughts, Emma told Camden it was not his fault.

The guard called out a five-minute warning. Quickly, Camden gave his blessing for Emma to move, and they said their goodbyes.

Three months later, Jack and Toby stood in the driveway and watched Emma drive away in a U-Haul truck. She'd hired someone to drive the truck for her. Tears streamed down Emma's face as she hugged Jack goodbye. Her tears dampened Toby's fur as she'd buried her face in his neck and mumbled farewell.

Toby was heart-sick that his friend was leaving him. However, he knew she had to go. He assumed she was hunting— and not four-legged animals. Men. Abusers. As of yet, though, Toby didn't think she'd stepped over any lines, but he knew it might only be a matter of time.

Jack and Toby stood in the driveway until the truck disappeared around a corner, then turned and headed back into their house.

Hendricks hit his steering wheel with his fist. He'd spent the last three months following Emma around town, whenever he could during his off-work time. But she was smart. It was as though she knew she was being followed and was determined not to give Hendricks any ammunition against her. He'd watched from a distance as her possessions were loaded into the U-Haul, and as it drove away.

"You're not out of the woods, little lady," Hendricks grumbled to himself. "I know where you're going, and all it will take is one little slip. Then, it will be game over!"

A month later, a body washed up on the shore of the Grand River, close to Hagersville. Hendricks received a call from the O.P.P. about the victim—an individual who had been missing for almost four months.

"Bingo!" Hendricks exclaimed as he pulled out and read the name in the file he'd done up when the young woman had called him about her missing boyfriend.

When Emma Gale had still been in town.

Author Page

Mary M. Cushnie-Mansour is a freelance creative writer who resides in Brantford, Ontario, with her husband, Ed.

In March 2006, Mary completed a freelance journalism course at Waterloo University, Waterloo, Ontario, after which she wrote freelance articles and a fictional short story column for *The Brantford Expositor*. Mary has published several poetry anthologies, collections of short stories, biographies, youth novels, and children's picture books, some of which are bilingual (English/French). Mary is most infamously known for her *Night's Vampire Series* and the *Detective Toby Series*. She also writes a blog, *Writer on the Run*.

Mary believes in encouraging people's imaginations and spent several years running the "Just Imagine" program for the local school board. She has also been involved in the local writing community, inspiring adults to follow their dreams. Mary is available for select readings and workshops. To inquire about a possible appearance, contact Mary through her website—

http://www.writerontherun.ca

or via email

mary@writerontherun.ca

Mary's Moto—To live without a dream would be like living in a house without windows ... how many of us will fulfill our dreams before the cobwebs of time cover the caverns of our minds?

Past Ghosts